THE JEALOUS HEART

A HUNDRED HUES OF GREEN IN THE TIME OF THE BUDDHA

THE SATI TRILOGY
BOOK 2

BY
SUSAN CAROL STONE

THIS
BREATH
PRESS

THIS
BREATH
PRESS

Charlottesville, Virginia, U.S.A.

susancarolstone.com

Cover and interior design by Denise Gibson, Design Den

ISBN 9781523897278

> "Always exercise your heart's knowing.
> You might as well attempt something real
> Along the path."
>   Hafiz

CONTENTS

Preface...5

1. Cancellation, Questions...7
2. The Tipping Point...15
3. Monastic Understandings and Discord...21
4. Despicable Acts...31
5. A Royal Demon...51
6. A Confession, Long Postponed...65
7. End of Shilly-Shallying...75
8. The Snake and the Arrow...89
9. The Ultimate Strategy...101
10. The Taste of Ashes...115
11. A Splendid Illusion...135
12. The Buddha's Arrival...147
13. Asoka's Spring...163
14. Execution...177
15. Sati's Panic...193
16. The New Abbot...201
17. The Return...211

Background Notes...215
A Partial List of Resources...221
Glossary...223
Acknowledgments...237
About the Author...239

PREFACE

The *Jealous Heart*, the second volume of *The Sati Trilogy*, is based on a Buddhist legend that is virtually unknown in the West. Regarded as history by countless Asians over the millennia, the legend tells of a jealous queen in the north Indian capital of Kosambi in the Buddha's time who murders a rival queen, a devout follower of the Buddha, and in turn is executed for her evil deed, along with her extended family. Amidst the legendary triumph of small-mindedness and violence unfolds the on-going story of Sati and his fellow monks at the Buddhist monastery known as Ghosita's Park.

Sati and his monastic brothers train, not always successfully, to embody the Buddha's teachings of wisdom and compassion. In *The Jealous Heart*, they try to salve their own wounds and weaknesses as well as those borne by the people of Kosambi, who are traumatized by the grisly royal tragedy. Sati has grown from the teen-age orphan of the first novel, *The Kosambi Intrigue*, to a monk in his thirties who assumes, with great trepidation, a leadership role in the monastery.

For those in our time who despair over the havoc we are creating by our senseless treatment of our planet and each other, *The Jealous Heart* shines a light across the ages. Whether we are Buddhists or not, like the monks in Kosambi, we can strive to uncover and act upon the love that is at the heart of despair. *The Jealous Heart* reminds us that, although we may stumble, this intention is a golden thread shot through all the actions of our life.

CHAPTER 1

CANCELLATION, QUESTIONS

September 25, 432 B.C. There it is again! His insides slam shut like a door blown by a monsoon blast. For weeks—or is it months?— Venerable Candana has been aware that something new has been happening in his body, but he has dismissed it. Imagination, maybe, or exhaustion. He has been too busy to notice. Now, however, after lunch and a nap, now as he meditates in his small monastic hut, there is no excuse. His hand is shaking. Not so much that anybody else would notice, but it's clear to him: His left hand has a will of its own. The terrain of Candana's life shifts, and he knows there is no way back to normal. He wants to jump up, run, scream, do something! At least open his eyes. But he is frozen by this new awareness.

Meanwhile, outside, life carries on as though nothing special has happened. Turtles are motionless on rocks and logs dotting the banks of the Yamuna, which in these days since the monsoon's end has resumed its long, lazy, blue flow beyond the walls of the Buddhist monastic center known as Ghosita's Park. Birds drowse, readying themselves for their swoopings and gorgings on a pick of insects later on, and the sun drenches all with brilliance but no scorch.

It is perfect weather along the lower reaches of the river where Kosambi dozes with a self-satisfied air. The palace, government buildings, multi-storied houses adorned with gardens, small thatched-roofed dwellings, markets selling an enticing variety of goods—all are encircled by protective ramparts, and all are quiet. Even the bustle of the suburbs outside the walls bows to the lethargy of midday.

Only Candana's immobility fails to signify relaxed contentment. The inner snowfield that buries him as he sits in his hut in Ghosita's Park at the city's eastern edge is so deep that at first he doesn't hear the knock on the doorframe.

It repeats, accentuated by a quiet cough. The door is already open to admit the delicious afternoon, and Venerable Sati stands on the portico, his back to the entrance, politely gazing around the grounds. Wooden huts like this one are nestled amid trees and ornamental shrubs. The grey, sandy soil, punctuated by a few stubbly weeds, is empty of monastic traffic. Sati alone is in the sunlit compound, and he's sorry to interrupt Candana at his meditation.

"Yes, Sati?" With effort, Candana emerges from the snowpack and looks toward to the door.

Turning and stepping inside, Sati apologizes. "I'm sorry to bother you, sir, but I think you'll want to know."

With hands respectfully joined to palm in *anjali*, he quickly sits cross-legged on the other mat so his head won't be higher than Candana's—that would be disrespectful. While Sati, at thirty-two, is a *thera* or elder, Candana is senior to him, as indeed he is to all other monks at this monastic center, having been ordained longer than they. Candana serves as *de facto* abbot in these early days of the Buddha's order when titles haven't been assigned to monastic functions.

"Venerable Asoka has just arrived," Sati says. "He'll be staying a few weeks. He sprained his ankle on a rut in the road from Prayaga. It's badly swollen and discolored." Sati gestures with his hands to emphasize the size of the swelling. "He needs to rest and give it a chance to heal."

"I'm sorry to hear it. Of course he's welcome."

Sorry, yes, but delighted, too. Asoka is an old friend. In the early days of their monastic careers, they trained together under the Buddha, and as far as Candana is concerned, his arrival is good news.

"Yes, sir," says Sati, who is functioning as guest master. He has already seen to Asoka's lodging. It was an easy task. Many of the huts are empty because their residents are off traveling and begging, as is customary during the dry months. From mid-September to mid-June, when the annual monsoon doesn't dominate the weather system and the behavior of everyone subject to it, during this three-quarters of the year, not only Buddhist monks, but all religious wanderers range over the Ganges plain in search of enlightenment. They almost form their own social class. Monks in the Buddha's order are the first among the seekers to gather in settlements. The settlements will later be called "monasteries" and have full-time residents, but in these early days, they are known as "monastic parks" because wealthy lay followers of the Buddha have donated parklands and constructed living facilities there. They are places where monks may reside full-time, or if they prefer, as most do, from which they may depart for nine months and to which they may return during the monsoon season and rejoin their community. Ghosita's Park is one of the first. Currently, sixteen of the usual monastic residents are traveling, so there are many housing options for Venerable Asoka.

"Venerable Dhammika came with him," Sati adds. "They met on the road, and it's a good thing they did because the venerable was just hobbling along. I don't know how long it would have taken him to get here on his own or what his ankle would have looked like when he made it. Dhammika was his crutch."

Candana nods sympathetically and adds, "Have Sirivaddha look at the ankle tomorrow," referring to the physician who attends to monks at Ghosita's Park.

Sati bobbles his head in a sideways figure eight of agreement, and continues with another bit of monastic news. Candana stops listening.

He envisions the small, wiry man, whom he hasn't seen for years. Quick on his feet as with his words. In his late fifties now, like me, Candana muses, and he wonders how the years have changed his friend. This accident will cramp his style, he smiles slightly, recalling Asoka's love for the wandering life. But he'll handle it with good humor as usual, that's for sure.

Another knock on the doorframe. What now? This might as well be the assembly hall, Candana grumbles silently. At this time of day, monks are either meditating or sleeping, and they usually honor each other's prerogative to do the same.

Sati looks over his shoulder to the door, and Candana lifts his gaze and asks, "Yes, venerable?"

Pindola Bharadvaja steps ponderously into the room. His girth makes the place crowded. In his mid-twenties, Pindola is not only taller than Sati and almost as tall as Candana, but wider than both by a long shot. No one is sure where he got his height because his father is a small man. "The gods bestowed it upon him," the senior Bharadvaja is fond of saying. He doesn't comment on his son's width, which has been expanding alarmingly since he was a young teen.

Pindola is irritated to see Sati. He carefully chose this time to deliver his message, assuming he'd be alone with Candana. Now, there isn't even a mat to sit on. Though Candana is the senior-most monk at the monastic park, he lives simply—two mats are enough.

Having been ordained for five years, Pindola is junior to both, and this rankles. He anjalis quickly, and, making the best of the awkwardness, selects a spot between the two but fractionally closer to Candana. He lowers himself into a squat, balancing remarkably gracefully on the balls of his feet, despite his bulk. Naturally he doesn't crouch flat-footed on his haunches, which is a lowly posture— Pindola has never in his life done so. Nor does he sit cross-legged on the bare wooden floor, for that doesn't suit his dignity either. His head is higher than Candana's, but never mind. It's the best he can do under the circumstances.

Ignoring Sati, Pindola looks at the abbot and declares, "Excuse me for interrupting, sir, but the royal chaplain asked me to deliver a message."

Candana's right eyebrow twitches. Pindola carrying a message from the chaplain?

"He wants me to inform you that you are not to come to the palace again to teach the ladies." He corrects himself. "Actually, he said that King Udena *commands* you to cease your teaching sessions with Queen Samavati and her women."

His right eyebrow soars, but he is otherwise still. Years of monastic restraint have shaped this response—a small gesture, but one that belies a sharp reaction. He waits silently for Pindola to continue, which he is clearly about to do.

"He wants you to know that the king is not pleased with your visits. They are to stop immediately." A shade of smugness appears on Pindola's lips, the left side turning up slightly. His satisfaction isn't rooted in the content of the message but in the fact that he, Pindola, is its bearer.

"Is there anything else?" Candana would like an explanation.

"No, venerable, that's all."

Candana nods slightly, his face impassive. They sit.

Am I being dismissed? Pindola wonders after several silent moments. Deciding that he is, he presses fingertips against the floor and pushes himself up with a low grunt. Performing anjali again, he backs out of the hut. Pindola knows his protocol.

On his way out, he discharges a sidelong glance at Sati. *It's not so bad that he's here after all. He's sees how important I am.*

Sati feels his skin crawl.

Candana is astounded by the message. He has been offering the Buddha's *Dhamma*, or teachings, to women of the palace regularly since Prince Bodhi was born. That was thirteen years ago. At the time, the king had been trying mightily to please Queen Samavati, mother of the infant prince. Taking advantage of his momentary favor, she, a devout follower of the Buddha, had asked that a monk from the Buddha's order be allowed to teach her and her women.

Udena lacked any shred of spiritual inclination. This Samavati knew. And too, she knew that her husband suspected the Buddha and other ascetic wanderers of donning a religious guise to shirk honest work. "Slackers, that's what they are, slackers!" he had declared many times. And he still does. He denounces the Buddha most strongly of all—"the recluse" he calls him dismissively or, worse, "charlatan." That the Buddha has gained a multitude of followers, notably the two most powerful monarchs in northern part of the subcontinent, festers, for Udena's own kingdom of Vamsa is one of the weaker of the four in the Ganges region. To the king's idiosyncratic way of thinking, the Buddha and his monks in Kosambi are orange-robed spies who pass on all manner of intelligence to his rivals via their ever-wandering cohort of monastic beggars. What chance does a poor king have with only a handful of his own spies?

So when Samavati asked to be allowed to receive the Buddha's teachings, he weighed his rancor against his desire to please her and concluded, Hell, they're just women. What do they know? An occasional meeting can't do any harm.

"If it would make you happy, my treasure, then yes, it can be arranged."

But Samavati pressed her victory. Holding her breath, she asked for fortnightly meetings at the palace.

Fortnightly sessions? At the palace? Udena was startled. He was envisioning granting meetings now and then, when he happened to be in a benevolent mood, and, of course, they would be held at the royal pleasure park outside of town, where the women would be accompanied by a contingent of guards. The palace was out of bounds, she knew that. What a bold one!

Samavati continued sensibly and very sweetly, "The time has come, my lord, when we wish to hear the Buddha's teachings about peace more often. Such sessions would fill us with happiness and with endless gratitude to you, our great lord, for allowing us to attend them." She had rehearsed well. "We wouldn't need to meet in the women's building. It could be in one of the offices in the main building. It would be simple to arrange. Meetings at the pleasure park are so difficult. It's far away, and trips there are uncertain. The horses might be needed at any time for state business, not for transporting women." She added smilingly, "And we'd be very tired in the evenings when we returned."

Ah! Good point. Udena wants his women fresh when he chooses to visit. He paused, then declared, "All right, all right, my precious, I'll make an exception, just for you and our son." Candana has been teaching at the palace ever since.

Candana is baffled by the cancellation. He knows the king has been pleased with the sessions. He has publically declared it, approving of the serenity the teachings have promoted. With a multitude of state problems to deal with, a king doesn't want a contentious harem, though, in fact, a contentious harem is what Udena has got, the Buddha's *Dhamma* (teachings) notwithstanding. Three queens and several lesser women, their numbers always shifting, living in quarters so close they can practically hear each other's thoughts—these don't make for a peaceful setting.

Candana ponders the king's new command. Granted he's an erratic man. No one ever counted on Udena for consistency, but why did he change his mind now? Is there a connection between his decision and Samavati's request at the last teaching session?

At the beginning of that session, Samavati approached Candana and asked for a private word afterwards. She looked frightened—like a hunted animal, he thought. So unlike her usual sweet, calm demeanor. But before the session ended, she was called home because one of her children had had a bad fall, and they had no time to speak. He assumed they'd talk next time.

Samavati's obvious anguish and now this cancellation are all the harder to understand because rumors, which circle royal goings-on like vultures, told of the king's eagerness to please her. Prince Bodhi, has recently been elevated to the position of crown prince, and the king has been as solicitous of his mother as when the boy was born.

That last teaching session, which was just three days ago, was the first since the rains had stopped. So what happened to change things since then? he wonders. With a little jolt he realizes that he won't be returning to the palace to find out.

Pulling out of his thoughts, Candana turns to Sati, who is gazing at him questioningly. "This cancellation is strange business," is all he offers, sighing. "All right, Sati, I'll see Asoka this evening before meditation. I know you'll look after him well."

That's what you get for interrupting someone in the middle of the afternoon, Sati smiles to himself, rising. As he presses palm to palm and backs out of the hut, he too wonders about the cancellation. And about Pindola. Arrogant bastard! Then he chides himself, *Where's your wise speech, Sati? Your lovingkindness?* Remembering that the Buddha says the tongue is an axe in the mouth, he observes, It's the same for thoughts, isn't it? An axe. But Sati's inner censor has the last word. Well, axe or not, it's true. He *is* an arrogant bastard!

Candana, still seated, is likewise thinking about Pindola, who genealogically isn't a bastard at all. Far from it: He is the son of the royal chaplain, Unnabha Bharadvaja, a brahmin and the most powerful man in the king's government. But his power notwithstanding, the chaplain has no proper role in state dealings with Ghosita's Park, even if his son is a *bhikkhu*, a monk, in the Buddha's order.

Religious affairs aren't subject to civil authority, and the bhikkhus are careful to guard their autonomy. Furthermore, the royal chaplain's religious domain is the ancient Vedic teachings, not the Buddha's. So what point is being made here? Why did Pindola deliver the message?

Neither he nor Sati will learn the answers to these questions, but they and everyone else in Kosambi will, soon enough, know the effects.

CHAPTER 2

THE TIPPING POINT

September 25. "Talk to Mommy. Let's hear you say it: 'Owwww, keep doing that, darling."

"Owwww, keep doing that, darling.'"

While Candana is conferring with Sati and Pindola, Queen Magandiya is in her lavishly furnished parlor instructing her pet mynah. King Udena's second consort is restless. She abandoned her attempt at an afternoon nap, as she has frequently lately. Nights aren't much better. She fears her beauty is being ruined. The mynah, however, is getting much attention. Magandiya has kept a mynah, sometimes two, ever since she arrived at the palace as a bride. To please her husband, she teaches them a large vocabulary, one that consists mainly of amorous phrases. The king obligingly makes a show of enjoying the little game when he visits on an evening. Though she avoids instruction in curses, with which she has intimate acquaintance, lately she has been adding a stray word or two to the creature's linguistic store, like "hairpin." She is indifferent as to whether it displays these to her husband or not.

Right now, the bird, peering from his golden cage, is paying more attention to the training session than is his mommy. Her thoughts are running along their tired path, the central tragedy in her life: her childlessness. Her main function as queen is to bear children. Everyone expects it of her, she expects it of herself, but she has failed utterly. In her thirties, she has been wed for nineteen years and not even one measly girl!

Magandiya has tried everything she knows. She has doggedly seduced her husband, hoping that a more amorous union would produce the desired result. She has consulted priests, several, in fact, because, who knows, some might have more influence in these matters than others.

A queen can't freely leave the palace to visit a priest, nor can she confer with them in her own residence—none of the king's women are permitted to be alone with a man other than the king himself. Feeling desperately in need of divine favor, Magandiya found the restriction intolerable, and she persuaded her husband to make an exception. He now allows her to meet with holy ones in a public room in the main building. A dismal little place devoid of all cheer, it is the conference room the king uses when briefed by his spies. During her meetings there, a guard stands outside the door, bantering with a maid, who waits for her in the hallway. She has never liked the place, and in recent years she trudges there with a heavy heart—another useless meeting in a room as barren as she is.

The priests, however, covet the opportunity. "This time it's a special prayer," they assure her, "bound to be efficacious." They've long since given up on her, convinced that no prayers can help this queen, poor woman. Her barrenness, however, has made her a steady customer, and their visits provide them with a goodly portion of their monthly income, so they are assiduously pious. Sometimes their chanting soars to great amplitude, and the guard and maid exchange awed glances outside the door. At other times it sinks to a whisper, the words being so sacred no mortal ears should hear them, not even a queen's.

Servants view the priestly traffic benignly, and they approve of the queen's piety. Only a few suspect her desperation.

To cover her bases, Magandiya also visits supernatural beings—*yakkas*, formless beings known to live in certain ancient trees, and *nagas*, sacred serpents that frequent the *ghats*, the landing areas on the banks of the Yamuna, the holy river that generates flourishing commerce in this capital city. Yakkas and nagas are known to have the power to make women fertile if they so choose and are properly propitiated. The queen contrives to visit them when she receives her husband's occasional permission to call on relatives in town. Then, she makes a secret side trip to a sacred tree on the town's outskirts or to a ghat and offers flowers, milk blessed by a priest, everything she can think of. All has been futile.

Why, she has agonized, why do the gods hate me? What have I done wrong? When she was young, Magandiya never thought herself evil, but clearly the gods do now. Is this some evil karma from a past life? That would be the conclusion of most people in the subcontinent, who regard rebirth as a fact of existence. They understand that karma, the law of cause and effect, operates impersonally over lifetimes as a result of one's actions, and they've been taught to accept its consequences, no matter how onerous. Magandiya, however, has her own ideas about how this curse happened, and her response is anything but accepting.

"Well!" she challenges other-worldly beings who might be in the vicinity, "Maybe you're right! Evil? Maybe I am! You sent her to steal his affections and humiliate me. You've made her disgustingly fertile, and not me. I can't do anything about you" (though in fact she intends to continue propitiating) "but I can sure as hell do something about that bitch. I can make her life as miserable as she's making mine!"

Samavati, her nemesis. Udena's third queen has already produced four royal offspring, two of them, boys. Who knows how many more are coming after this! Magandiya is convinced that her distress over Samavati's success has made her barren. Otherwise, she herself would have produced an abundance of heirs—not just two boys, but at least three—so that when the sickly crown prince died, as everyone knew he would, one of her own sons would be next in the line of succession.

The only surprise about Prince Kumara's death was that it took so long to happen. The son of the chief consort, Queen Vasuladatta, had been plagued with a circulatory ailment since birth. Always lacking in energy, as a child, he was petulant and, as a teen, moody. From the start, cynical courtiers took bets as to when he would die, but nobody guessed right. He lived to the age of twenty and passed in April.

After Kumara's death, a special ceremony was needed to proclaim the new crown prince. This was Prince Bodhi, Samavati's son. Although his birth had been joyously celebrated throughout the city, it had not been honored with the pomp that accompanies the birth of a crown prince. So astrologers set the date for the consecration, as they do for all important occasions, and the royal chaplain officiated. Held in late May, before the rains, it was a splendid ceremony, stifling heat notwithstanding. Magandiya will never forget it. The crown prince was seated, sweating, on a platform in the center of a pavilion specially built on the palace grounds. The platform was surrounded by vases containing lustral water, flowers, a small throne symbolic of the real one he would someday inherit, other ceremonial accouterments and a spectacular pile of gifts.

Behind him, on the royal platform, sat the proud parents, Udena leaning over to Samavati, whispering, beaming proudly, even laughing and regally ignoring the itchy heat rash on his chest. And, oh yes, she, Magandiya, was there all right—in the second row! So was Vasuladatta, but in such deep grief for Kumara that she didn't seem to know where she was or care. Chief consort or not, she could be counted out. It was only herself, Magandiya, who bore the humiliation of that day.

It should have been *my* son! *I* should have been at the king's side, she raged silently. The gods permitted this atrocity—a wretched merchant girl, mother of the crown prince! The gods permitted it, but *I* don't accept it! *I* was born for better than this!

"Keep doing that darling keep doing that darling," the bird shrieks. She turns her attention back to him. Such a drab, homely creature. She doesn't approve of brown. Or those thick yellow legs. Or the bald spot behind it eyes—indecent. Her precious should have the grace of a swan, the plumage of a peacock. Even here, I'm thwarted! she fumes.

But since the consecration, Samavati, not the bird, has been the target of her thoughts. Samavati and destruction. If she were to divulge her thoughts, people would say she had gone mad. And indeed, the prop that upheld her mind, always fragile, has given way. Her world has closed in, and she has lost all sense of balance.

Immediately after the ceremony, ideas about how to avenge herself came helter-skelter. She nearly panicked under the onslaught because time was against her. The monsoon was about to arrive, the season when all but the most essential activities come to a halt, when she herself is lethargic and her thoughts grow fuzzy, or, to be accurate, fuzzier. About a week after the ceremony, came a stunning insight: There's no hurry. Ahhhh—yes! Her plans could just as well be implemented after the rains. Even better. She'd have more time to think.

But as she sat day after day watching the rain fall, fall, fall, she could only think, This is what being pregnant must be like. Nothing to do but wait, fuck it!

To relieve the tedium, she directed her thoughts away from rain and toward Samavati. Daily she devised new forms of ill will. It was her entertainment, a malignant game at which she grew quite creative. This she counted as progress, intangible as it was. She prided herself on the single-pointed focus of her attention.

Now at last, the monsoon is done, and Magandiya's mental efforts have been fruitful. She has developed and acted upon two plans, both geared toward intimidating her enemy. They are mere tactics, but, like a commander on the battlefield, she intends to gradually escalate the pressure. She will move past mere intimidation and stop only when total victory is achieved, whatever "total victory" means.

"Owwww keep doing that darling."

She smiles upon the ugly one as she contemplates her cunning.

CHAPTER 3.

MONASTIC
UNDERSTANDINGS
AND DISCORD

September 26. This evening, before the monastic gathering in the assembly hall, Candana and Asoka are sitting side by side on the portico of Asoka's hut, their backs against the wall. This is their first chance to exchange more than brief greetings because yesterday Asoka was tired and hurting badly.

Bare-chested, Candana sits in mountain posture with knees bent and feet flat on the floor. His orange under-robe covers his legs, and his forearms rest on his knees. His usually agile body had trouble folding into the position. Asoka, who is similarly garbed, has been attended to by Sirivaddha. He sits on a cushion with his right leg bent and the left stretched in front. His ankle, newly splinted, is resting on additional cushions. A crutch lies at his side.

"How many years has it been, eh? Fifteen? Sixteen?" muses Asoka, his head turned toward his friend. "Ah, no, I came by for a day or two six or seven years ago, didn't I? Well, it's my fault—I admit it. Ever since the troubles here, I haven't wanted to stay for any length of time."

Asoka is referring to the schism, which, fourteen years ago split the monastic community at Ghosita's Park and reverberated throughout the Buddha's order. "I was quietly tucked away at Bamboo Wood during that rains retreat," referring to a large monastic park outside of the city of Rajagaha, far east of Kosambi.

The rains retreat or *vassa* is held during the three-month monsoon season when travel is nearly impossible; roads become quagmires and much of the countryside is inundated. Turning adversity to advantage, the Buddha instituted an annual retreat, a time for his peripatetic monks to gather, hear the teachings and renew their sense of community.

Candana nods ruefully. It's true. The schism is over, but memory of the fractiousness lingers even today. Partly in an effort to offset the notoriety, the following year Candana sent Sati and Arittha, another resident, on their first travels as bhikkhus, entrusting them with the task of re-assuring their monastic brothers that harmony had been restored. The assurance was nearly true, for nothing is perfect, not even among monastics. Every year since the schism, he has asked all residents when they are about to set out on their annual travels to remember that their conduct reflects not only on themselves and the Buddha's order as a whole, but also on Ghosita's Park.

Asoka continues, "Ghosita's Park still has a reputation, you know, and, well, if I can be somewhere that doesn't carry such unhappy baggage, I'll do it." He confesses with a shamefaced grin, "I've come through Kosambi several time in recent years, and have stayed at Kukkuta's Park," referring to a monastic center outside of town.

Candana nods. He's heard. He thinks, The baggage is in your mind, friend. You're lugging it around. You could let go if you wanted to. He remains silent, however.

Then anxious that Candana not misunderstand, Asoka raises his hand, "It wasn't about you, Candana. In fact, I've felt for you. I've been sending you blessings ever since I learned about the troubles. Did you get them?" His features soften. "I've never stopped sending them."

Candana smiles. "And I reciprocate every one of them." How he likes this sweet, talkative brother so long absent from his life! He likes him even though his comments are a bit thoughtless at times.

Candana has always considered himself on temporary assignment at Ghosita's Park. He came at the Buddha's request, and he has been pleased to tell himself that he was ready to leave any time, but it's not so. The little pang in his chest that is evoked by the criticism of his monastery reminds him that he is attached to this place, bad karma or not.

Bhikkhus strive to travel freely in life with as few encumbrances as possible, whether material or mental, for these block the road to liberation. This is the Buddha's Third Noble Truth: Suffering, which has its source in attachment, is only truly alleviated by letting go. Asoka and I both have some unloading to do, he reflects as he notices the knot near his heart.

He sighs. They can't be willed away, attachments. He's learned that! Many bhikkhus try to evict them by denial and avoidance, but he knows such struggle only leads to failure. This he gently points out to his disciples, but finally, everyone must learn for themselves: Attachments diminish naturally with compassionate practice. When one understands that everything is fleeting and thus unreliable, enchantment with phenomena erodes. He bows inwardly to the immensity of the process.

Asoka goes on, "Actually I was planning to stop by this time. Really. At least for a few days. I wanted to see you—it's been so long. Dhammika was on his way here, too. So, here I am. But with more than I bargained for." He looks at his ankle wryly.

One of the problems with being talkative is that you can easily slip into unskillful speech, and Asoka, fearing that he may have done it again, leans toward Candana and says hastily, "I, I don't mean to sound unappreciative, friend. I'm grateful that you're taking in this old bhikkhu. Very grateful. I want you to know that."

Candana's hand brushes the air, dismissing any notion of offense.

The monologue continues. "In all these years of walking, aside from my back—you remember my back, don't you? old story—aside from that, I've never had much more than a scratch or bruise. Well, sooner or later the body catches up with you, the aging body." And he smiles again, "*Bhagava* is so right," using the reverential title by which followers commonly address the Buddha.

Don't I know it! thinks Candana. A pulse of envy grips his heart. I wish my problem were just a sprained ankle!

"But I'll be up and gone in a week or so. Don't worry. I don't want to overstay my welcome."

"No, Asoka, there's no way you can overstay. Your welcome is unlimited. Stay as long as you like—if you can bear it! Besides, you can't leave until Sirivaddha says the ankle is healed, and from the looks of it, it's going to take longer than a week. You don't want to sprain it again by walking on it too soon. I'm sorry to tell you this." He looks anything but sorry.

They reminisce and exchange news about monastic brothers until it's time for the evening's gathering. Candana rises. "Got to go back to the hut to get my mat and robe," referring to his outer robe. "Rest now, and keep that leg elevated. After meditation, someone will check in on you."

Asoka joins his palms gratefully.

While Candana and Asoka are talking, Harika approaches Pindola, who is seated in the assembly hall where monks are beginning to gather for the nightly meditation and discussion. Pindola's eyes are shut, but Harika doesn't hesitate to interrupt. He assumes that in these early minutes of the meditation session Pindola's concentration is as scattered as his usually is.

Harika is one of the senior monks at the monastic park and the most notorious, though notoriety is hardly a quality that bhikkhus cultivate. Harika didn't mean to, either, but years ago, his rigid adherence to the disciplinary rules put him at odds with Candana and the Buddha and caused the first schism in the Buddha's order, the one that Asoka is referring to in his conversation with Candana.

Over the years, Harika changed. The old caustic edge has been dulled. This is partly because he never fully regained his health after a bout of pneumonia during the schism. He simply doesn't have the energy to be fiercely combative. More importantly, since the schism, he has spent two three-month retreats with the Buddha. The purpose as Harika saw it was to work on monastic legal issues, an area for which he has a genius. The effect, however, was the onset of wisdom. The Buddha's presence has a way of opening one's heart and mind, even when he isn't teaching. So you'd hardly recognize Harika now. He's become receptive to the content of the Buddha's teachings, rather than focusing exclusively on disciplinary rules.

He hasn't changed completely, though. He is still dominated by his mind and is largely blind to heart qualities of kindness and compassion, which are part of the Buddha's teachings.

Harika is attracted to others like himself and is especially interested in Pindola. Ever since the young man with his powerful connections and illustrious lineage arrived at Ghosita's Park, Harika has tried to impress him with his legal brilliance. He envisioned a relationship patterned after his with Migajala, who has long departed Ghosita's Park and isn't missed, except by Harika.

Pindola, however, is unappreciative, being so enamored with his own sense of superiority that he barely notices others unless they are useful to him. Harika responds like a warrior to battle: The more Pindola snubs him, the harder he tries.

"Greetings, friend," Harika begins amiably. Bhikkhus customarily address each other as "friend."

Pindola opens one eye and fixes him with a fishy glance. Can't he see I'm meditating?

Harika's assumption is right, though. He was rehashing his delivery of the king's message yesterday.

"Greetings," he grunts.

Harika unfolds his mat and spreads it companionably next to him. The bhikkhus' sitting positions in the hall are broadly based on seniority, but there is much inconsistency. Harika is conscious of conferring the honor of his senior presence upon this junior monk—maybe it balances out some of the disparity between their brahminic lineages, for his own isn't noteworthy. He ignores Pindola's annoyance.

"How are you? "

"Well enough." Then, because there's not much else to say and it is on his mind, he adds, "You've heard that Candana's teaching sessions at the palace have been cancelled, haven't you?"

Harika hasn't. Nor has anyone else. Neither Candana nor Sati has mentioned it. Harika shakes his head.

"They have," Pindola affirms and highlights his role in the event. Monks around them, who are trying to meditate, cast irritated glances in their direction.

"Let me get this straight." Harika says, his voice rising. "You just said you delivered the king's message to the venerable, right?"

Pindola nods smugly. A nearby monk coughs.

"That's a legal breach! How could you have done it?" Harika's copper-colored eyes flash; his tone is sharp. Nothing rouses him so much as a violation of the law, even a small one. "Religious and civil jurisdictions are separate—you know that! If we're not careful, we could hand our independence over to the state."

These are perhaps his first spontaneous words to the younger monk, and he surprises himself with his vehemence. He never meant to talk to Pindola like this. Nor did he expect his legal exactitude to put him on the same side as Candana. This is a first. Even as he speaks, Harika is aware that Candana, too, knows that the king's messenger, not Pindola, should have delivered the message. What irony!

"This may be an offense. Be careful, friend. You're walking a fine line." With this warning, he ends the conversation and closes his eyes. *What have I just done?* Other monks, who have been passive parties to the interchange, have a new topic to distract them from their meditation.

Pindola has no wish to continue the discussion, either. He doesn't know why the king cancelled the teaching sessions, though he has idly wondered. He is unaware of Magandiya's schemes, unaware that on one of those monotonous rainy days, she saw the plan as clearly as if the sun had parted the piles of clouds and had shone specially on her: Accuse Candana of plotting to persuade Samavati to become a nun. Of course! Little arouses their husband like jealousy, however flimsy its foundation.

It worked, though Udena was more cautious than usual. Magandiya had made so many false claims about her rival, the king decided to verify this one before he acted. He consulted his chaplain, assuming that because his son was a bhikkhu, he would be privy to schemes hatched behind monastic walls.

"Is it true? Did that bald-pated bastard try to lure Samavati into monastic life?"

Bharadvaja didn't know, but considering any lessening of the Buddha's influence a solemn religious duty, he stored away this piece of intelligence for possible later use and declared with a sideways head bobble, "It could be so." His comment was verification enough for Udena to cancel the teaching sessions.

Bharadvaja is also a father, a long-suffering father of an ungrateful son. Ever since he was a child, Pindola has infuriated him. Becoming a bhikkhu was only the most egregious outrage. It was a humiliation. That he, the foremost brahmin in the land, the guardian of ancient Vedic wisdom, should have a son who was a follower of that shaveling heretic of a recluse was scandalous. Stupid, stubborn boy!

He's banking that Pindola will sooner or later see his folly and re-join his family and sanity. Meanwhile, he hopes the boy is learning discipline—maybe he'll lose some of that girth—and, ever with an eye to self-interest, he appreciates the advantages of having a spy in the Buddha's midst. So, when he recently saw a small opportunity to advance his son's status, he naturally suggested to his royal lord, "Let Pindola deliver the message. I'll be seeing him today anyway." That this was a lie was inconsequential. An instruction was issued to come home immediately, and so it happened.

Pindola accepts his father's tidbits of support as the very least he is due. He is smarter than his older brother—twice as smart, in fact—but he didn't have the advantages his brother did. He didn't go to Takkasila, the premier learning center in the subcontinent. His father didn't listen to his every word with approval. And when being introduced to people who matter, he was always, "And this is my second son, Pindola." He won't become royal chaplain.

Vedic ceremonies are stupid, anyway, he decided when he was nine and realized the limits to his future. All that slaughter makes me want to vomit. But, determined show his father that he could succeed without him, his youthful mind weighed possibilities for years. Eventually, a way, *his* way, grew clear: He would become abbot of Ghosita's Park. Not as good as royal chaplain, true, but it's attainable.

With my family connections, I'd be the obvious choice. How it would anger him! How satisfying!

Pindola's attention returns now to the comment from the insolent pipsqueak next to him. In view of his bright prospects, the occasional conflation of civic and religious authority is a triviality. Pindola closes his eye, engulfed in angry thoughts.

September 27. "May I have a word with you, friend?" Pindola calls after Harika who is ahead of him on the path.

It is morning, and the orange-robed ones are exiting the monastic park, alms bowl in hand, for their daily walk into town. Because they neither store food nor prepare their own meals, the bhikkhus are dependent on the goodwill of the laity. Morning is when they beg, because the Buddha doesn't want them taking advantage of townspeople's generosity by going from door to door all day long.

Harika turns. Ordinarily he would be gratified that Pindola wanted to talk with him, but something in his tone makes him hesitate. "Uh...let's do it later—uh...after the meal."

"No, friend," Pindola counters, "now is better," and he beckons Harika off the path to let other bhikkhus go by.

Why do I have a bad feeling about this? Harika wonders as he follows Pindola to the side of the path.

"Last night you warned me that delivering a message from the king violates the integrity of monastic authority."

He nods warily.

"Well, I haven't mentioned it before, venerable, but I believe now would be an appropriate occasion to do so. My father told me about your connection with him and those secret meetings you had to promote cooperation between the order and the government. Wouldn't you say that breached monastic integrity a bit?"

Harika is unprepared for this. He looks dumbly at the younger monk, who takes his speechlessness for an admission. Which it is.

That again! With a twist in his gut, Harika remembers the most degrading period of his life: his secret negotiations with the royal chaplain. Together they schemed. The point, Bharadvaja maintained, was to ensure harmony between secular and religious spheres by promoting strict law enforcement, and Harika believed him. The improbability of the chaplain's vision didn't occur to him, blinded as he was by the central role it promised for himself. From Ghosita's Park, he would be empowered to enforce disciplinary rules—which, in Harika's view at the time, were the most important part of the Buddha's teachings. To do it, however, undesirable elements like Candana had to be eliminated.

The two conspirators met for several months, and the meetings instilled in Harika a solid sense of mission, a sense that resulted in the schism at Ghosita's Park. Then, just when their goal seemed in sight, Bharadvaja ended the project.

He didn't even explain! Harika's thoughts have long and bitterly lingered on this shameful fact. *He didn't think me worthy of an explanation, after all those meetings!* To this day he wonders what happened, though he understands that Bharadvaja was using him, as—he's faced it—he was using Bharadvaja.

Pindola smiles and shrugs, "Just to keep things in perspective, friend. Just to keep them in perspective." He anjalis—a more sarcastic anjali has never been performed—and walks off.

Harika begins his almsround in shock. *So he's known all along! Of course Bharadvaja would have told him. I'm a fool not to have realized it! He probably described all the foul details.*

Nor has Harika realized that part of his reason for courting Pindola has been to compensate in his relations with the son for his miserable failure with the father. But he does recognize another dashed hope when he sees it. The possibility of gaining Pindola's esteem is last year's fodder.

Will this never go away? Harika laments. *Bhagava has forgiven me. Candana has forgiven me. And others too—they're willing to move on. But here's this spoiled brat throwing it in my face all these* years later! And, yes, he's right, it *was* a breach of monastic integrity, a big breach.

He walks alone into town, his gaze fixed sightlessly on the road. He stands at the door of the first house begging silently. He's only barely aware when the master and his young son come out and put food into his bowl, for at this moment he is stunned by an insight: In a way, Pindola's nastiness isn't about me. It's the law of karma. So this is what Bhagava means when he talks about suffering the consequences of one's actions!

Harika understands laws. They're not personal—that's their beauty. They apply impartially to all. One can't violate a law with impunity.

Though he has long understood the theory, he has seldom recognized its application to his own life. Except after the schism, of course, when the consequences were too onerous to miss. But even then his sickness allowed him to not dwell in too much reality. Since then he has tried to forget his humiliation.

Now the pain of Pindola's comment has reminded him: Karmic consequences apply to him personally, yet they aren't personal. There's life after disaster. Harika doesn't have the wisdom to accept the younger monk's comment with equanimity, but, standing in front of this house with his bowl in his arm, his heart expands a bit. Looking up, he sees the father and son staring at him, clearly wondering why he doesn't leave now that they've made their offering. Harika smiles. With a sense of lightness, he turns away to continue on his almsround and on his spiritual path.

CHAPTER 4

DESPICABLE ACTS

September 28. Candana and Asoka are sitting on the portico of Asoka's hut, silently eating the noonday meal. Candana shared his alms food with Asoka, as did several other bhikkhus, and they'll continue to do so until he is mobile again and can beg for himself.

A small calico cat pads around the corner and stands at a distance, her tail upright, hopeful. One meow. Candana reaches into his bowl and puts a morsel of food on the ground. "Pssst, pssst," calling her softly, then waiting. Tentatively she advances, grabs the food and backs off. Candana and Asoka are still.

More please.

"I see you're sharing with someone else besides me," Asoka laughs as Candana places another morsel on the ground. And another.

"Me and probably every other bhikkhu." He wonders how she found him since he's not on his own portico.

"From the looks of her, she hasn't been overindulged."

"She's been coming around in the last few weeks, since the rains. I think she climbs the *simsapa* outside, the one with the branch that hangs low over the wall."

"Or through the drain pipes," referring to the pipes at the rear of the monastery that carry away waste and rain water."

"Possibly. Or both."

"Well, it looks like you've got a friend."

Candana nods.

Monastic rules don't strictly prohibit talking while eating, but silence is customary. The meal is a good time to practice mindfulness, to give careful attention to lifting the hand, putting food in the mouth, chewing, experiencing flavors, swallowing. In this way bhikkhus learn that life is lived truly when one is present, undistracted by casual conversation and errant thoughts.

The calico, now satisfied, moves apart and engages in a meticulous toilette.

Candana decides he'll set out water for her so she won't have to climb back over the wall to go to the river. This thought, which he doesn't consider errant, is interrupted by a small tremor in his left hand.

He contemplates it as it rests helplessly on his knee. A memory of old Sangarava flashes: Sitting cross-legged, eating at a family gathering. So long ago. I haven't thought about him in decades, Candana muses. The old man's hands shook badly, and the child Candana was fascinated. He stared. Did Sangarava notice? Of course he did! After all these years, Candana is embarrassed.

Sangarava was his what? Oh, yes, his older brother's wife's—no, Nala's *second* wife's cousin on her father's side. Candana remembers the web of family connections that governed his life, as it does the life of all householders, a web of obligations so extensive that attending to it crowds one's mind-space and narrows perspective. He breathes deeply. Even the air of monastic life is different.

Gratitude for the path he has chosen surges through his body. Of course, he thinks realistically, I only went forth after Dhira died and the girls were married. For a moment his thoughts rest sweetly on his wife—he still misses her—and on his two daughters, both now happily and well married. Those were the conditions that enabled him to leave behind family obligations and his brahminic heritage and move into the homeless life of a bhikkhu—and, he observes wryly, into a whole new set of relationships. Smiling as he looks at Asoka and thinks of Sati, he experiences, almost palpably, the different kind of obligation involved in these, one based on caring for each other's higher good.

Sangarava died a few years later, unable to remember his own name. Candana recalls asking his mother about the man's absence from family gatherings. Her response, though gentle, was without emotion. They hadn't been close relatives. Is that how they'll talk about me afterwards, relatives who haven't seen me for years? And what about the bhikkhus—how will they remember me? Shuddering, he turns back to his food, which is almost gone, and back to the present moment. Whatever they'll say, it's not my business. But now, now he realizes that he wants to tell Asoka about his tremors.

September 28. A golden cloud of midges vibrates in the lowering light, zigzagging sparks, maintaining, somehow, a balance between collision and dispersal. It is late afternoon and, as he often does at this time of day, Sati is walking in the simsapa grove at the back of the monastic park. A carpet of brittle leaves rustles under foot. He pauses in a clearing to observe the little airborne mystery, and his thoughts drift to another bright cloud, in another forest many years ago...

He and Arittha were traveling. He was a young monk then, a year after the schism at Ghosita's Park, and this was the first time he traveled. Both he and Arittha had been training under Candana, who had thought it time to release them, to let the birds fly. He requested that they stay together, for Sati hadn't traveled outside of Kosambi, and Arittha's familiarity with life in the forest would be helpful. Candana also asked that they show by example and, where appropriate, by explanation that the schism at Ghosita's Park was done; harmony had returned.

They were in territory far east of Kosambi, in the lush forests along the Ganges in the great kingdom of Magadha. They stopped on the outskirts of a village where the people were generous, and they begged in the mornings and meditated in the afternoons.

It was late that afternoon. Done with meditation and needing to move, Sati left Arittha, who was still meditating under the banyan tree where they had made their home. He walked into a clearing in the forest. A swarm of midges backlit by the angled light entranced him.

Then he saw her. Coming through the trees toward him, moving past the golden cloud, was a girl whose skin was as gold as the light itself. Sati had seen many beautiful women, and as a young adolescent he and a girl had made a game, which was almost innocent, of exploring each other's body. Once he had become a monk, however, he had held to monastic principles, with, granted, one little slip a couple of years earlier, a slip more of the imagination than of the body. But as he stood in the forest on that long-ago day, he knew that this girl, this exquisite girl, would be part of his life.

Drawn by the magnetism of one beautiful young person for another, they moved together until they stood face to face, close enough to touch, he in a golden robe, she in a red sari that highlighted her shining skin. He stared down at her. She lowered her eyes, then ran back into the trees, her long hair streaming behind.

Sati returned to Arittha. The older monk, who had finished meditating, glanced at him and asked, "What's wrong?"

He shook his head. He couldn't speak.

The village was small, and within a day, Sati knew where she lived. They met again a night later, when she stole out of her house and came to him. And the night after that. On the fourth day, Sati told Arittha he was disrobing; he was leaving the Buddha's order and would stay with the girl. Her name was Siha.

Arittha, who at twenty-eight had had his experiences with women, nodded as he listened. He wasn't surprised. It had to happen. Sati was too young when he ordained.

He didn't ask whether Sati and the woman had already had relations, though he was pretty sure. All he said was, "Think about this carefully, Sati. Think about the consequences."

Sati had made a feeble attempt to think, but the power of his passion overwhelmed thought. So he nodded and said, "I have thought." Already wearing the farmers' clothes she had brought, he handed his robes and bowl to Arittha and bowed deeply. Both had tears in their eyes.

He arrived in the village, greeted by her parents' fury and the anguish of the boy to whom she'd been promised. They married within a week. What choice was there? Thus Sati became a farmer and joined the others in the fields.

Arittha remained in the area for two weeks after Sati had disrobed, begging in the village, meditating under the banyan—just in case. The villagers were still generous with food offerings, but resentment simmered, for this bhikkhu was connected with the intruder in their midst.

Though Sati went to the banyan tree in the evenings for meditation, the situation was uncomfortable. Arittha accepted him without comment, neither angry nor welcoming. Other village men also came to meditate and listen to Arittha teach, but there were fewer than before.

Having been a hunter in lay life with little formal education, Arittha taught the Buddha's Dhamma in a simple manner that village folk could easily understand. Sati listened now, as he always did, respectfully, indeed with love, for this man was his friend even though they weren't on speaking terms. His mind, however, was more sophisticated than Arittha's, and he always had to remind himself to be tolerant of his friend's naiveté. Now, though, he recognized arrogance in his judgment.

Who am I to feel superior? I've forfeited the right to teach. He's still doing it.

He felt, too, a painful sense of displacement. Before, when Arittha had taught, Sati sat beside him; in a way he was part of the teaching. Now, he sat in front his friend, an object of it.

Sati hadn't anticipated this. He had had only one consequence in mind when he had made his choice, and he was hurling his life toward it with all the vigor of his youth. As he struggled with his unsettled feelings, it became clear that the evenings under the tree, in fact, Arittha himself, were unwelcome reminders of the past, when he needed to focus on his new life.

Arittha solved the dilemma for him: He left and Sati was relieved. But he was also angry. Arittha hadn't even said good-bye. Not a word! It's the least he could have done after all the time we've spent together, Sati seethed. Then he realized that he himself had barely said good-bye when he had disrobed. After that, whenever he passed "Arittha's tree," he felt dirty.

Together Sati and Siha learned how to make love, how to please each other. Because Sati was imaginative and Siha was eager and no one had told them what could or couldn't be done, they explored pleasures for themselves. The adventures of each night so occupied Sati's thoughts during the day that he was barely present to work or the villagers or even to Siha herself. Lost in an addiction to lovemaking, he felt he could never have enough of her.

His preoccupation blunted the impact of the villagers' hostility. He hardly noticed at first. As far as they were concerned, however, everything was against him. Even his speech. Sati's Magadhi was a different dialect than theirs and, worse, his diction marked him as educated, a man obviously from a different class. "What class?" was one of the first questions put to him. When Sati identified himself as warrior, they were intimidated. He might as well have said he came from the moon.

They were rice farmers, and their fields along the Sona River were among the richest in the Middle Land, as the region of the Ganges plain is known. Extra hands were always needed, but they weren't so sure about Sati's. He had never farmed, and while he willingly did whatever task was assigned him, he had no interest. To these men for whom farming was the whole of life, his attitude was offensive. Some, especially Sati's rival, made fun of his ignorance.

Moreover, he baffled them. How was it that a recluse who hadn't carried more than a begging bowl had such a powerful body? What had he done before that? Fought in wars? Having no intention of mentioning his life as a fisherman, Sati merely smiled enigmatically, a response that triggered speculation and distrust.

In time, he became a father, and a new wonder entered his life. Sati adored his baby daughter. Although, like most people in the Middle Land, he would have preferred a son, when he held his daughter in his arms, her little fingers curled around his big one, a tenderness arose he hadn't known he possessed. He loved watching her nurse and would stand behind and embrace both mother and daughter, his new world. The boy who had been an orphan at sixteen was now a happy man of twenty with a family of his own.

In his joy, he was able to dismiss the fact that the villagers didn't accept their marriage. They continued to call Siha "Ratthapala's daughter," referring to her connection with her father as they had when she was a girl, rather than "Sati's wife," as was customary when referring to a married woman. Once married, a woman left her parents' home to live with her husband and his family, but for Siha and Sati, it was the other way around: They lived in a house provided, very reluctantly, by her parents. He could shrug off the anomaly, but Siha couldn't. She had become an outsider in her own village, a woman denied the dignity of her married status. She suffered grievously, though she said nothing to Sati, for there was no point. She hoped in time her people would come around.

The child was ten months old when she died. Her mother had left her in the charge of older children who were playing by the river while their mothers, a short distance away, washed family clothing. Siha was vigilant, continually glancing over her shoulder, but it wasn't enough. There was a moment when the children were caught up in play, and Siha, standing ankle deep in the water alongside other women, was intent on beating the clothes against a rock. In that moment, the child crawled to a small outcrop at the river's edge, tumbled in and hit her head on the stony riverbed. She died immediately.

Twelve weeks later came a second catastrophe: Siha aborted the fetus she had been carrying, a tiny bloody mass that would never grow to be their son. They were certain that grief over their daughter's death had caused the abortion. Siha felt responsible for both, and, though Sati reassured her that no one was to blame, that it was just karma, in a small corner of his heart, he did blame her. Locked into guilt and resentment, they found no means to communicate, no end to grief. Sati began to understand the Dhamma of suffering in an entirely new way.

They left off lovemaking for weeks. Neither had the heart for it. When eventually the demands of their young bodies drew them together, the delight wasn't the same. Sati lay night after night with his wife in his arms, but despite physical completion, he was dissatisfied. Something was missing, something he felt as a visceral ache. Was this all life was to be? Sex, working in the fields and touchy relations, to which he had now become sensitive, with his new kin and other villagers? They had little in common. Spending a lifetime in their midst began to feel intolerable, even if he were to become a father again. That child might die, too.

He began to doubt his abilities as a lover. Somebody else would probably be better at it than I. Someone else would make her happier. Does she love me at all? What is love anyway?

He grew jealous of the young man to whom she'd been promised. He watched the man's eyes follow her when the women walked to the river to fetch water in the early evenings. He noticed how, as Siha gracefully balanced the tall water jar on her head, she laughed gaily. People stigmatized her marriage, but she knew men still coveted her body, and the knowledge brought some consolation. She laughed especially gaily when passing Sati's rival, and she subtly swung her hips. Sati concluded that they were still in love. Or at least there was attraction.

And it wasn't only that one man. Many of the young men in the village, older ones, too, looked at her longingly. Could he blame them? Her beauty attracted attention, and she seemed to revel in it, discreetly. Am I any different from them? Sati wondered. I saw her and took her—just what they want to do.

He also began to wonder, Beyond being gorgeous and a joy in bed, beyond being a good mother and a flirt, who is she? What are her aspirations? Maybe she doesn't know what an aspiration is. Maybe she has none beyond the boundaries of this village. Because she evaded his questions when asked, he wasn't aware of her deep aspiration for simple acceptance by her village.

He knew all too well, though, that she was disinterested in his former life as a bhikkhu. "Let's start from now," she would object when he talked about his past. Sometimes, he tried to be indirect by casually introducing the principles of the Dhamma in the context of their daily experiences, hoping to catch her interest, for he was convinced that the Dhamma was the medicine that would salve their wounds and enrich their relations in ways he yearned for. But such talk frightened her, and her fear made him feel clumsy.

If only I could find the right words, he lamented. There's got to be a way to reach her. But he found none, and continued efforts only produced greater distance between them. Eventually, he stopped trying.

Three years after he had left, Arittha returned. Word shot around the village like an arrow from its bow. That afternoon after work, Sati ran to greet him. There he was, sitting under the banyan, just like before.

He's come back for me! Sati's joy was conclusive, and in that moment, he knew.

Now, almost ten years later, standing in the simsapa grove in Ghosita's Park, Sati remembers his friend and the similarity of their backgrounds—outcastes both, depending on one's point of view. Arittha inherited his family's trade and social status, as was customary. In a society that professed to abhor violence, hunters were considered beyond the pale of the social structure, which was already stratified into classes. Arittha thus was classless, a fact that scarcely bothered him as a young man living freely in the forest and associating mainly with other hunters and outcastes. After he became a bhikkhu, however, he was made painfully aware of his despicable status, for despite the Buddha's teaching that class status was irrelevant, some of his monastic brothers taunted him.

Sati's background is more complex. He was born a warrior, which ranks high in the social hierarchy, but early on, his father had been involved in a political intrigue and had made a drastic choice: He had moved his family from the capital to a fishing village in the suburbs, where they lived anonymously. Thereafter, they were accepted neither by most members of their family nor by the fisherfolk with whom they lived. In recent years as a bhikkhu, however, he has largely grown beyond the burden of his past. He hardly thinks about it now.

At this moment, Sati misses Arittha but is glad for him, because, when he isn't wandering, Arittha is living with the Bhaggu clan in the forest west of Kosambi, a bhikkhu still. He has found a home among people who honor rather than despise him for his origins.

The midges are gone now. Sati resumes walking among the trees, and his thoughts return to Siha. He left her. He flat out left her. He had said nothing during their last night together—he'd wanted to enjoy her up to the very last moment—so selfish! In the morning he told her he wasn't coming back. She wasn't to wait or hope. Point blank. When she collapsed on the floor in tears, he reached down to comfort her, but decided against it and withdrew his hand. He straightened and, with a heart as torn as hers and only the farmer's clothes he was wearing, he re-joined Arittha, and together they walked away from the village.

Sati rationalized his actions later—for the rest of his life, actually—arguing that Bhagava had done the same. As a young nobleman, he had abandoned his wife and young son to search for enlightenment. Men were leaving their families for the religious life all over the Middle Land. Siha was, he knew, better off than most abandoned wives. Women were reviled by society if they chose to leave their husband and family for the religious life, but they faced a stark choice when their husband did the same: Becoming a status-less widow or following him and becoming a nun. Divorce wasn't an option. It is hardly surprising then that, while the Buddha's followers, from royalty to the casteless, call him "Blessed One," many women curse him as a "widow-maker."

There was no chance Siha would choose a monastic life. Sati knew this and, too, he knew she couldn't remarry. Still, she was beautiful, young and childless, and the village had a way of taking care of its own. At least she's among her own kind, he rationalized. This thought has never allayed his conscience, but neither has he doubted the rightness of his decision.

He took robes again. He and Arittha walked to Rajagaha, the capital of Magadha, and in an ordination ceremony at the Bamboo Wood, Sati once again became a bhikkhu, along with another young man and in the presence of fifteen monks, including Arittha. The Buddha was absent at the time.

Before his ordination, Sati was closely questioned by senior monks. Arittha was, too. The key issue was whether Sati had engaged in sexual activity before disrobing or after. Violating the precept of celibacy was one of the most serious offenses in the order. The punishment for the offense was expulsion.

Arittha had counseled that, when questioned, they should say Sati had disrobed first. It was, after all, only a matter of hours, and Sati, being young, had been carried away by passion; he hadn't been trying to be devious. Once he knew his mind (or rather his body), he had disrobed. Sati agreed. That lie was the other despicable act in his life.

September 29. Candana is sitting on the mat in his hut listening to Sirivaddha. He has decided to consult with the physician about his condition. Sirivaddha visits Ghosita's Park whenever monks are sick. Although he is generously reimbursed by Ghosita, the park's patron, Sirivaddha gladly offers his services.

He usually comes in the late afternoon after he has finished seeing his own patients. Today, when he came to check Asoka's ankle and visit another ailing monk, Candana asked him to stop by his hut afterwards.

Sitting cross-legged on the mats, Candana answers as Sirivaddha asks questions. What are his symptoms? Has he noticed any change in his thinking patterns? In his eating? Has he had an accident recently? What are his feelings about what he's noticing? It's a long list. Distressed, Candana responds the best he can, though he hasn't thought about some of the questions.

When Sirivaddha finally finishes, he says solemnly, "Venerable, I may be wrong. I'd need to follow this over time to be sure, but..." he pauses.

"Go ahead, " Candana says gruffly. His body is braced.

"Well, I think it may be the palsy. I don't understand what causes it. I've only seen two other people with the condition, both of them were older people like you. Neither were my patients." Another pause. "And neither recovered. I'm very sorry." Sirivaddha opens both hands, palms up, desperately wishing he could offer more than empty hands.

Candana sits numbly.

He coughs and continues in a low voice, uttering each word slowly, mindfully, "A few years ago, when I visited Rajagaha, I met with Jivaka, the king's physician."

Candana nods. Physician to the powerful King Bimbisara of Magadha, Jivaka is a lay follower of the Buddha and is considered the finest physician in the Middle Land.

"We spoke about the shaking palsy—only briefly, mind you. He had treated people with the condition. He told me about one who, like you, had been healthy and hadn't suffered any accident. Tremors began. I think it was her right hand. They became more severe and over months spread to other parts of her body." He stops.

"Go on, tell me the whole thing," Candana whispers. Sirivaddha is confirming what he already knew, but the slight hope, which he has been guarding like a little flame, is extinguished. There's no point fooling himself.

"Eventually—it took years—her body grew so bent that a walking stick couldn't keep her upright; someone had to hold her shoulders when she walked to prevent her from falling over."

"Yes? And?"

He concludes quickly. "Then she couldn't walk. Jivaka tried many things but he couldn't find cure or a remedy to check the disease's progress. Eventually, the woman lost control of her bodily functions, including her thinking, and she died." He hates this part of his job.

They sit silently.

"I may be wrong. There are many reasons tremors develop. This may not be the palsy at all." And because he wants to say something medically useful, he adds, "Whatever it is, you can't go wrong by drinking rice milk. It promotes readiness of mind. I suggest you start right away."

Candana nods.

"But if it is the palsy," he continues, "if it is, then please know, venerable, that I'll care for you as best I can, for as long as I am able. I promise you that. You can rely on me."

Candana looks at this man who has treated monastics unstintingly over the years and who is now offering to support him to the end of his life. Tears flow. Monks don't ordinarily express gratitude to laypeople because that would diminish the spiritual merit they receive for their acts of generosity. That's the understanding: Monks provide the gift of the teaching; lay people offer food and other necessities, thereby gaining merit for this and future lives. Nonetheless, at this moment, through his tears, Candana says, "I'm more grateful to you than I can say. Thank you." And he bows, palms joined.

Sirivaddha is stunned. Far from feeling a lessening of merit, he, who as a physician is used to being on the up-side of hierarchy with his lay patients, experiences an immense opening of heart. The invisible barrier that has always separated him from the bhikkhus dissolves. In this moment there is a precious affirmation of the common humanity between himself and this bhikkhu whom he so admires. Unaccustomed tears fill his own eyes. He breathes deeply, lowers his gaze and anjalis in return.

October 1. "Mommy, when's Daddy coming?"

Queen Samavati and her three children are playing with small balls on the parlor floor amid a scatter of colorful cushions. For the past half hour, Jinadatta, her younger daughter, has been asking the question. Samavati's response hasn't changed. "I don't know, sweetheart. Soon I think."

"But *when*? He *said* he'd come! He said he'd take me with him."

"Yes, darling, I know, but your father is a busy man, and sometimes he doesn't have time to visit us or the horses either." This is getting tedious.

The king visits in the afternoon two or three times a week to see the children. He comes just before his daily pilgrimage to the state horse. Samavati's residence, in the northeast corner of the palace grounds, is located close to the stables. The state horse, a white stallion of the noble Sindhi breed, and its counterpart, the state elephant, have the honor of being the only animals privileged to carry the royal personage. Only the horse, however, is lodged on the palace grounds.

The king is fond of horses and even fonder of the status they signify in this land where few people own them. His father, King Parantapa, initiated the daily stable visit, and Udena, in whom imagination isn't a significant trait, hasn't varied it a jot. He meets with the state equerry, who dresses in a formal tunic as befits the occasion, and proceeds to the stable, offering a word to his several horses as he passes their stalls on his way to the extra large stall at the end of the row. There, the king and his equerry step inside, and Udena speaks to the big stallion, displaying more genuine affection for him than he shows some of his women. He proudly offers a handful of grain and a pat or two, all the while earnestly discussing the animal's welfare with the equerry.

Samavati knows that the timing of her husband's visits is a convenient way of fulfilling his parental obligation, and she suspects him of enjoying seeing the horse more than his children. Sometimes though, he takes one or more with him to the stables, just as he had accompanied his own father. More than a week ago, he promised Jinadatta that he would take her next time. The seven-year-old loves horses, and she regularly makes a pest of herself, begging to go along on the stable visits.

Samavati doesn't personally miss him, but she aches for her little daughter. She wonders what's keeping him away, and she worries. It is a new worry.

In addition to his daytime visits, Udena usually comes to her every couple of weeks for a few nights at a time. It's part of his regular rotation among the queens and other women of the harem. Udena is diligent in performing this royal duty. It's been more than two weeks, however, and again so far today, there's been no message instructing her to ready herself for a nocturnal visit.

Life as Udena's wife has schooled Samavati in vigilance. She is always on the lookout for indications of the way the wind of his moods are blowing. Ever fitful, they form the dominant weather system in her life. She hasn't yet managed to achieve inner independence from them.

Where is he? This she has been wondering more often than Jinadatta. Sleeping has been hard these past few nights, for she has something she urgently needs to discuss. It's not easy, however, for a queen to speak with her husband when she wishes, especially if he doesn't want to be spoken to. Samavati's residence provides cherished privacy, it's true, but it offers no way to casually encounter him. She could send a servant with a message, but she has been hoping he'd stop by. In the early days it was easier.

When Samavati lived in the palace, she spent much time outdoors in the lovely garden courtyard adjacent to the women's building. There, women of the harem relaxed and were occasionally honored with the presence their king. Samavati also saw him in the evenings at the gatherings in the harem at which Udena was the centerpiece. How she hated those long, unhappy evenings with all the women vying for their lord's attention! Samavati doesn't appreciate much about Udena, but she is profoundly grateful for his decision, shortly after Bodhi was born, to acquire separate residences for his three queens.

The king hadn't wanted the infant prince to be carried up and down all those stairs. Initially, Samavati had occupied a specially built rooftop apartment in the women's building. Its only entrance was an external stairway from the third floor. That wasn't a problem for Samavati as a young bride; however, once the prince was born, Udena ordered the construction of an indoor stairway. Even that was risky, though: One careless step on the part of the wet nurse climbing any of the four flights of stairs with the babe in her arms—it was too appalling to think about. No, new living quarters were necessary. Besides, he was a maharaja, a great king who controlled ancillary territories, and his urban palace grounds needed to adequately display his status.

Udena remembers his grand title "maharaja" only in moments when he feels especially expansive, for it reminds him unpleasantly that his father did all the fighting; that, through personal bravery and astuteness, his father quelled the outlying territories that are so much a part of the kingdom today as to hardly warrant thought. To claim the title as his truly own, Udena would need to expand his frontiers. But he doesn't like war. War is uncomfortable. Thus, while dangling the possibility of territorial expansion is a useful strategy to keep people on their toes, he has never had the least intention of implementing it.

Expanding the boundary of his palace grounds was another matter. When the prince was an infant, the owner of one of the three villas on the northern perimeter of the royal property had died without leaving a rightful heir; therefore, the property legally fell to the king's possession. Technically, it was his possession to begin with. All land was; others occupied it on his sufferance. It was no problem, therefore, to obtain the other two villas. He provided the families with attractive alternatives, for he was a benevolent monarch.

And so it was. Samavati came down from her rooftop and the other two queens, from their second floor apartments in the women's building, and they happily moved into residences of their own. The king had the palace walls extended to include his acquisitions.

The advantages of the new arrangement included, as far as Udena was concerned, the opening up of three apartments in the women's building—luxurious ones at that. His three wives were young enough then—Vasuladatta and Magandiya were still in their twenties and Samavati, only nineteen. But still, two of them were mothers and he was no longer the sole focus of their attention, and all of them would be aging soon enough. He relished the opportunity of offering the queens' former apartments to favorites in his harem and conferring the blessing of palace residency on three new beauties.

Now, in the parlor of her mother's residence, Jinadatta, whines, "But he didn't come yesterday. Or the day before or before that either." She pauses a moment, then adds, "And he *did* go to the stables yesterday."

"How do you know that?" Samavati's brow knits in sudden consternation.

"I saw him there, and he didn't take me. He promised!"

Samavati's stern look draws forth the explanation. "I hid from Mutta," she confesses, a bit shamefaced, referring to the maid who looks after the girls. "I went to the stables, just to see if he'd come. And he did! He didn't see me," she adds with a note of pride. "I hid behind the grain jars."

At this revelation, Samavati smiles inadvertently. This was just what her beloved servant Khujjuttara did when she was a girl, a slave, growing up in the palace—she hid behind the grain jars to watch while the king, then Parantapa, visited the state horse. Samavati asks sharply, "You didn't go into the stall, did you?"

"Oh no, Mommy, I didn't."

"You must never, never go into that stall or any other stall alone without your father or another adult," she says sharply. "Do you understand? Never! Promise me that."

"Yes, Mommy, I promise," the child responds contritely, nodding her head.

Samavati softens. She thinks of the young Khujjuttara's accident, the one that left her crippled. Being an inquisitive child, just like Jinadatta, the servant quietly crept into the state horse's stall after Parantapa had left. The surprised stallion—then a powerful chestnut—kicked her and broke her leg. The bone didn't heal properly and her leg is crooked and shorter than the other; walking is painful.

"I'll tell you what, children." Samavati says brightly. "You go out in the garden and play, and, Jinadatta, when your father comes, I'll call you, and you can go with him to the stables."

Rajadatta, the prince, who is two and a half, chooses this moment to squeal and point in the direction of the stables, "See horsies! See horsies!"

"No, darling, not today," she replies, smiling at him, then turns to the maidservant and wet nurse, who are sitting on the floor with them, "Take them outside," Samavati directs.

As they rise, Uppalavanna, her older daughter, objects, "But I want to see him, too!"

"Yes, yes, of course, sweetheart," Samavati soothes the nine-year old. "That's what I meant. You'll all see him. Then Jina will go with him to the stables."

The nurse picks up the toddler, who immediately reaches for her breast, all thought of horses vanquished. The prince will be allowed to nurse for a few more months yet, for it is common belief that the longer a child nurses, the stronger it will be. And this baby is going to be very strong!

Watching them walk toward the door, Samavati worries about Jina's stable adventure. Why didn't Mutta keep a better eye on her? And why didn't she tell me the child was missing? Good gods! For a moment, Samavati considers dismissing the maid, but the girl has a good heart and so does Samavati. I'll have a word with her. I'll give her another chance. But only one.

As they near the door, Uppalavanna, turns and asks, "Is Daddy mad at us?" Ever thoughtful, she has been brooding about this all morning.

Samavati raises her eyebrows. "No, he's not. Why do you ask?"

"Because Citta says when Daddy's mad at them, he stops coming to their house." Uppalavanna is referring to her half-sister, Queen Vasuladatta's thirteen-year-old daughter. Children in the palace, like servants, have an unofficial communications network, the efficiency of which would appall their parents if they knew.

Samavati, sighs audibly, "No, Daddy is not mad. He's busy. Like I told you. Now go out and play, all of you."

She is relieved to be alone. She places her elbow on the low table next to her, rests her cheek in her palm and closes her eyes. The jeweled bangles on her wrist slide toward her elbow with a silvery click that is so much a part of her life that she doesn't notice. An onlooker would see a beautiful woman in repose, clothed in yellow like the morning light.

That's just what I want to know. Is he mad at me? What now? One day it's one thing, the next day another—I can't keep up! A large, familiar knot tightens in the middle of her torso.

As she falters, Samavati thinks about her lovingkindness practice. Silently repeating the Buddha's words, she offers it first to herself. 'May I be happy and secure. May I have a happy mind. Whatever living beings there may be, without exception, may all beings have a happy mind.'

But she feels neither love nor peace for herself and all beings. There's only the knot in her stomach. "I'm sorry, Bhagava," she whispers. "I tried."

A thought arises from nowhere, a new thought: Maybe I don't have to *feel* love. Maybe trying, just saying the words with sincerity is enough. Maybe...

CHAPTER 5.

A ROYAL DEMON

October 3. Samavati's legs feel like any moment they'll refuse to carry her another step. In all these years of marriage she's never had to face her husband in a formal audience, but yesterday, she was officially summoned to one, in the throne room in the palace. There was no explanation.

"At least I'll find out what's going on," she comments to Khujjuttara who limps painfully at her side as they walk to the palace. "I suppose that's something."

Udena's change in attitude is stunning. After Kumara died, he was excessively attentive. His clumsy efforts to please her were actually touching, though Samavati wished they'd been inspired by an appreciation for herself rather by the death of another woman's son and the elevation of her own. She sighs. So it goes with palace life—it has nothing to do with who you are or what you want.

Such speculations aren't on her mind now, however. Because not only is she worried about her husband's absence and, now, this command, but there's the terrifying issue. She needs to talk about it and doesn't want to do it under these circumstances. A formal audience is the wrong setting.

Samavati and Khujjuttara have exhausted these subjects. There's nothing left to say. Samavati's comment curls like a wisp of smoke in still air and dissolves into their silence, a silence broken only by the tinkle of pebbles in the hollow silver beads of her anklets as they walk on the brick pathway. Her turquoise sari, one of her husband's favorites, flashes in the sun.

While in recent years Samavati has eased up on the elaborate toilette expected of a queen, today it has been deployed in full force. Her maids spent two-and-a-half hours this morning tweezing, bathing, oiling and perfuming her body. They arranged her long, dark hair in a perfect bun at the nape of her neck. Her eyes are bewitch-ingly lined with aromatic *kol*; her lips, hands and feet, rubbed with red *lac*; aromatic flowers are tucked into her hair; and a battery of jeweled bangles adorn her arms.

Such is Samavati's poor political arsenal—cosmetics, jewelry and a sari. She hopes it will please her husband and soften whatever is coming at her.

They walk through the public entrance of the main building and down the hallway to the throne room. Khujjuttara stops outside the wooden double doors, while two servants open to admit Samavati. She has been in this splendid room only once before. Making an ef-fort to hide her overwhelm, she walks, with head high and with what she hopes is royal composure, up the long carpeted central aisle, up toward her husband at the other end. He is seated there in regal dig-nity on a glittering throne that is elevated on a dais. In this silent chamber, the tinkle of her anklets is embarrassingly loud.

Uncharacteristically, Udena is alone. In deference to his wife, he has dispensed with the presence of advisors. And, too, with the scantily clad female servants with fans and flywhisks whose job it is to make the royal body comfortable. Their presence would only dis-comfit his wife. Besides, it's October. The weather is delightfully cool, and flies are largely absent.

As she approaches, she lowers her gaze appropriately, then bows before him. She doesn't see him gazing appreciatively at her, and by the time she looks up, the royal face is contorted into a belligerent expression. A wall of fire and ice.

Gesturing for her to take the chair at floor level but not waiting until she's seated, he booms, "Wife, what's been going on at those meetings with the recluse? I demand the truth!"

"Truth?"

"Yes. It's a simple word—"truth." Tell me, in your own words, what does he want?"

Too impatient to wait for her response, he supplies, "I know what that scoundrel wants. He wants to steal my wife, to lure you into joining the nuns, that's what he wants. Go ahead, admit it!"

When Magandiya informed their husband that Candana was trying to entice Samavati into becoming a nun, she confided that one of her servants had attended the recluse's last teaching session and with her very own ears heard him talking to Samavati in private. They hadn't noticed her standing by.

The two weeks between Magandiya's accusation and this audience has done nothing to instill a balanced perspective in Udena. He decided to wait to inform Samavati about the cancellation and tell her in a way that would make his point, that would remind her who is in control. He is pretty sure she wouldn't abandon the children, but you never know how persuasive the damned recluses can be. To increase her agitation, he has stopped visiting her and the children.

She'll worry about that. Let her worry! Let her think about all she'd lose if she leaves me. And if the accusation is false, he concluded, well, there's no harm, just a bit of worry. *I'll make that right the first night I visit her. She'll be all honey afterwards.*

Udena is unaware of his arrogance. He is merely being a king: All power is his; others, especially women, have none.

Now husband and wife are at their worst, he glaring down on her uncomprehending face, and she, looking helplessly up at him.

"Don't play coy with me, Samavati," he bellows. "I know what you two are scheming. At the beginning of the last meeting—remember? All those teaching sessions were a charade. He thought he could put one over on me! I'll tell you now, wife: I've cancelled them. There will be no more teaching sessions. The venerable has already been informed, and now you know it, too."

This is too much to take in. Tears spring into her eyes and start to spill over. An important part of her life has been ripped away, just like that. The precious opportunity to hear the Buddha's Dhamma from Venerable Candana, from someone who knows, who himself embodies it, who is close to the Blessed One—it is gone. And, importantly, out of her reach now is someone she desperately needs to consult.

"Don't try that woman's stuff on me! Tears won't do you any good. I never want to see the bastard again! " He can't see her tears from his lofty perch, but he knows his wife.

In all her speculations about the purpose of this audience, this never occurred to her! As Udena continues his tirade, Samavati grabs for the words that have become her life raft: "May all beings be happy and secure. May all beings have a happy mind. As a mother would risk her own life to protect her only child, even so, towards all living beings one should cultivate a boundless heart. A boundless heart, a boundless heart." Her lips move as she silently repeats phrases on lovingkindness.

He rants. She begins to rally. When he pauses, she takes a deep breath, looks up at him and declares, "My husband, this is completely untrue! He did not say that. And I'd never leave you, not for all the nuns in the world!" More truthfully, she adds quietly, "And I'd never leave the children."

Samavati has become good at this. She has been responding to Magandiya's accusations for years. Of course, she knows Magandiya is at the heart of this. Resilience isn't a concept Samavati would invoke, but an ample stock of it has developed within her.

At this point she launches her most potent weapon: her sweet, engaging, and at the moment, quite damp smile. It's her standard tactic; she no longer hates herself for insincerity. It's pure self-defense.

Predictably, Udena is caught. Even at thirty-one, she is gorgeous. His belligerence begins to fade. He never seriously believed that Samavati—or that any of his wives—could leave him. To leave a maharaja would be insanity. For what? To become a nun? Ludicrous! But because he can't fathom why anybody would become a recluse under any circumstances, though people are doing it left and right these days, Udena permitted himself to entertain Magandiya's accusation. And because he's never been fully reconciled to allowing another man, even an old monk, in the company of his women, he was happy for the excuse to end the sessions.

"Then what were you and the recluse talking about at the beginning of the meeting?" he asks in a softened tone.

Ah! Here it is: the subject that has claimed her attention for days, the subject that paralyzes her.

"I'll show you." Picking up the plain, woven bag that she set on the floor at her feet, she withdraws a small bundle wrapped in white cloth. White, the color of death.

"Venerable Candana and I had only a few moments; I didn't have a chance to explain. It's what I've been wanting to talk to you about, my husband, but you haven't been available." She emphasizes the last part, for Samavati isn't so naive that she'd miss a chance to point out his lapse.

He ignores the innuendo but watches closely as she unwinds the cloth and reveals a doll. It is a rude wax figure, clothed sari-fashion in an expensive bit of red muslin. She holds the nub of wax that are the legs and raises the doll, rotating her wrist so he can get a full view: Five metal hairpins pierce the body though—at the head, breast and pubic areas and two at the belly. Though from his high seat, he probably can't see them clearly, the pins are intricately ornamented. A quick intake of breath and a small exclamation escape him.

"This was in my bed chamber, on my bed! She's put a curse on me!" There's no need to mention names. Neither of them questions who is responsible. Nor do they try to reconstruct who delivered the doll. Most servants are bribable.

"You have to tell her to stop! She's got to lift the curse!" Samavati loses her carefully fortified composure, and her voice rises to a higher pitch, "I can't live like this! I can't, I can't!"

As he looks down on his wife, it occurs to Udena that if anything were to drive her into nunhood, this might be it, children or no children. Maybe this is why people become recluses.

"I'll talk to her, Samavati. Today. As soon as we finish our meeting. You mustn't get overexcited," he says soothingly. To himself he observes, Men are such fools to get mixed up in women's craziness. He sighs. Affairs of state are easier to manage.

Udena stands up, descends the dais to floor level and, drawing Samavati up from her chair, kisses her forehead. His attention, however, is on the doll in her right hand. He doesn't want it to touch him. "Shhh, now, shhh. It's all right, Samavati. It's all right."

Then holding her at arm's length, one hand on her waist and the other around her right wrist to keep the doll at bay, he looks into her face and smiles. "Go now, my dear, my treasure, and rest easy." Udena can be endearing when he tries.

He releases her gingerly and steps back. Samavati slowly re-wraps the abomination and drops it into her bag. Then she looks solemnly at Udena. He has just made a promise, and she chooses to believe him and be reassured. She's safe, at least for now. With a meaningful nod but omitting the standard bow, she turns and leaves her husband's presence.

She meets Khujjuttara in the hallway with a nod, and together they silently exit the palace. As soon as they're alone outside, Samavati delivers the crucial piece of information, "He'll talk to her!"

Khujjuttara knows who "her" is.

"He's cancelled the teachings, Khujj! The bastard has cancelled the teaching sessions!"

Khujjuttara looks at her mistress, startled, as surprised by her tone and language as by the news she bears. Anger and foul language are so unlike her mistress. But she understands.

"I can just hear her now," Samavati mimics, nodding her head left to right. 'I'm so sorry to tell you, my lord, but one of my servants was at the session, and she heard it with her own ears.' I think I convinced him that none of it is true, but he's not going to let the venerable come back. Sometimes I wish I *were* a nun!"

For a second time today, Udena puts on his angry-king look and readies himself to deal with a wife. "Wife," he says sternly after Magandiya enters the audience chamber and calmly seats herself on the chair at the foot of the dais, "what's this Queen Samavati tells me about a fetish in her bedchamber?"

He is unprepared for her response. She doesn't say a word. She stares at him, a look of cold, blank hatred. Those eyes. Where has he seen them before? He remembers. On a hunt—he hates hunts. For two days beforehand, men had beaten the jungle for tigers and had gotten one cornered so that the royal personage could move in for the kill. It had glared at him like this. He had missed the shot, but fortunately the bowman standing next to him in case of such a contingency, hit the mark.

Now Udena wonders about his wife. Are these the eyes of a human or a demon? Even from his royal distance on the dais above her, he feels chilled.

"This...this...uh...must be stopped." His voice falters under the intensity of her glare. Magandiya senses victory. From the lawless place she occupies, she knows he won't be an obstacle.

She doesn't deny the accusation. There is a lengthy pause. Then she shifts into the honeyed voice that Udena is familiar with. She croons, "Great king, my dearest husband, I am only trying to safeguard the honor of your revered name."

Udena's shoulders relax perceptibly. This is the Magandiya he knows—manipulative, insincere Magandiya. He can manage this. From his relief, he's prepared to listen sympathetically.

She continues soothingly, "My lord, you've done the right thing by cancelling the recluse's visits, exactly the right thing."

Magandiya thought long before accusing Candana. Initially, she had considered repeating her standard allegation of sexual infidelity, shifting the culprit to Candana. But that was implausible. Candana is an old man, attractive in his youth no doubt, but now he's in his fifties. And, anyway, Udena has grown wary of such allegations, even when more appealing candidates were involved, because the charges have always proven groundless. But a different kind of seduction maybe? Yes—it might work!

The maid line was the clincher, though it wasn't her own maid, but one of Samavati's, a new girl in the queen's household, whom Magandiya had bribed. The girl reported that Samavati spoke with the venerable for a few moments before the last session, though she didn't know about what. It was enough for Magandiya.

Now she looks at her husband with wide-eyed alarm and a head waggle, "Imagine the scandal if your queen became a nun! I'm so sorry to say this about another wife, but I've warned you about her before and you don't listen, you don't act. So," she concludes, "it was up to me to save the honor of your great name. Your third wife now has a curse on her. It's what she deserves for betraying you!"

Udena opens his mouth. Her logic confounds him, but the implication that he's a coward is what's most astounding. Magandiya almost laughs. He looks like a fish out of water.

Then, seeing rage gathering on his face, she hastily softens her tone before it erupts. She plays him like a musical instrument. "My dearest lord," she says consolingly, "please, please wake up to what that tricky Sakiyan is really about." She means the Buddha, referring to his clan affiliation.

"He's trying to snare people, women as well as men, into his order, and members of royalty are his biggest catches. He does it any way he can. Even uses his recluses to act for him. He's completely ruthless."

Magandiya, who has her own reasons for hating the Buddha, is well aware of her husband's antipathy toward him.

Udena hesitates. Whom to believe, Samavati or Magandiya? The old familiar dilemma.

Even amidst his uncertainty, he recognizes something new in his wife, something profoundly disturbing—the fetish and that wild look. Magandiya is a brahmin of high lineage, and, like the rest of society, Udena knows brahmin priests possess secret knowledge of the spirit world. He suspects other brahmins do, too. The higher their lineage, the more they know. Maybe.

On occasion, Magandiya alludes to the power of ancient sacred places—though she doesn't disclose her clandestine visits to them nor her purpose. Her intimations have heightened Udena's apprehension. His other two consorts may be mothers, but they're not brahmins; they can't know what Magandiya knows. This thought has always scared him, but he has set it aside. Until now. He wonders, Is she a sorceress? What if she extends the curse to me?

Sensing his fear, Magandiya presses the point, casually observing that through the agency of supernatural forces, curses are known to spread to those who align with the cursed one. She smiles sweetly.

Udena decides it's time to acquiesce and change the subject. "Yes, yes, wife. You're right, I'm sure."

October 4. Candana has been making almsround alone. The Buddha prefers that bhikkhus walk at least in pairs so that generous lay people or their servants won't have to make multiple trips to their front door with food offerings. However, because Candana walks more slowly these days, his almsrounds take longer. So he starts earlier and, disregarding monastic custom, he walks alone.

He isn't ready to make a general announcement yet. It will have to come soon, but he wants to tell individuals first. Sirivaddha and Asoka, he's already told. Also Udayi and Ghosita. They can be relied on for confidentiality.

Then there's Sati. He's the hardest. Candana has been postponing this conversation but knows that every day that he doesn't speak Sati's perplexity and distress grow. They used to walk almsround together regularly, but if they were to continue now, Sati would notice— he doesn't miss much—and he would worry.

In fact, Sati has noticed. Watching Candana on his way to the assembly hall recently, Sati remarked that his stride seemed shorter, his step more hesitant. Were his eyes tricking him in the twilight? He was hopeful. But no—no, he confirmed it over the next few days: He wasn't imagining. Candana wasn't walking with his usual ease. Sati experienced the discovery as though it were a turn of the wheel of his own life, a movement in its sure progress toward the end.

He remembers the first time he saw Candana. He and his father were at the fish market selling the morning's catch. Selling fish was part of the radical change in the family's lifestyle. Sati still doesn't know what caused it. Being young, he was satisfied then with his parents' evasive explanations, and he adapted naturally to his new circumstances, as children do. Ostracized as they were, they were nonetheless a happy family. A few years later, his mother died in child-birth, along with the girl-child she was carrying. Then, when Sati was sixteen, his father died in mysterious circumstances. His skiff was found overturned on the riverbank, his body nearby. He had apparently drowned. It had happened on one of the rare occasions when Sati wasn't with him. He has never stopped wondering.

Other memories, tender ones, return now as well. He and his father observed the unknown bhikkhu on almsround one morning, a tall, well-built man moving with quiet dignity. His father called him "a compelling figure." He's still a compelling figure, Sati thinks with an ache for the man to whom he turned for guidance when he was a sixteen-year-old orphan grieving his father's death.

In recent weeks, Sati has dearly wanted to ask Candana about his health, but he has remained silent. He'll tell me when he's ready, he concluded. Their conversations have been limited to monastic business; so it's clear he hasn't been ready.

Candana can't put it off any longer. Deciding he may as well show as tell Sati, he suggested last night that they walk almsround to-gether. This morning, approaching his mentor, who is waiting by the gate, Sati's broad, handsome face is taut. He dreads what's coming.

They are the first bhikkhus to leave. As the gate closes, in tan-dem they automatically look down at the road. Bhikkhus practice custody of the eyes, avoiding haphazardly gazing around in public in order not to get lost, visually or mentally, in worldly tumult.

Inner tumult is something else. They walk silently for a few blocks, then Candana says in a low voice, "Sati, there's something I need to tell you."

Sati nods, keeping his eyes fixed on the road. He listens to Candana's news without comment.

Candana glances at him sideways. "You knew, didn't you?"

Again Sati nods, glad he's looking down because tears have formed in his eyes. These two don't need words to gauge each other's responses.

"All right, son," Candana says gruffly. He hasn't called Sati "son" for a long time.

In the Buddha's order, the mentor-disciple relationship is formally described as one between father and son. The reality of theirs fully embodies the definition. Between them is not only a spiritual connection—Candana is a wise and compassionate master, and Sati, a deeply sincere disciple—but a personal one, grounded in natural affinity and need, Candana's need for a son, and Sati's, for a father. Maintaining a wise balance between acknowledging their personal attachment, but not indulging it, isn't an easy task, even now after fourteen years.

"All right, this is new territory—for both of us," Candana says consolingly, though he himself is far from consoled. "We'll take it as it comes and do our best, one step at a time."

A third unhappy nod. The helpless gesture carries all the heartache that untrained people might express with impassioned comments and emotional display. Sati says, "Let me know what I can do to help. Now. Or later. Always."

October 4. Samavati is agitated again. Udena visited last night, as she had dreaded he might. She hadn't recovered from the emotional assault of the audience in afternoon, and the prospect of lovemaking was nauseating. She had no choice, however, but to submit and pretend to enjoy it. Emotional honesty has little role in this relationship.

Afterwards, as they lay in bed, she asked if Magandiya had agreed to lift the curse, already knowing the answer. He hedged. Too sickened by his evasiveness to comment, she wondered, why did I trust him?

When he finally left, Samavati's only wish was to forget her life. Without leaving the bed to wash and feeling thoroughly dirty, she drew a light sheet over her nakedness and was graced with the sleep of oblivion.

Now, this late afternoon the day after, Samavati is in the garden with the children. The two girls are playing hopscotch, jumping into rectangles marked by river stones placed on the path. Adults who use the path know to either step within the rectangles, adult hopscotch, or go around. The baby clamors for a turn, and the girls help him through, laughing as they go, displacing only a few stones. For a while Samavati plays with them, but her heart isn't in it, and she retires to a bench to watch.

Sensing her mother's distress, Uppalavanna runs to her, gives her an impulsive hug, then returns to the game. Brightness opens, and Samavati smiles. Then the clouds close in again.

Khujjuttara comes from the house and joins her. If they'd been alone, she would have sat next to Samavati on the bench. They've long ago transcended conventions between mistress and maid. Aside from her children, Khujjuttara is the most important person in Samavati's life, her dearest friend, mother and wise teacher. Because another servant is present, however, Khujjuttara takes the low stool next to the bench, which has become known as "Khujjuttara's stool."

"He was evasive," she says tersely in a low voice. "He didn't ask her. I don't know if he even mentioned it. The coward!"

"Why do you harp on this?" Khujjuttara asks. Her voice is quiet, but irritation edges her words. "Did you really think he would? Surely you know by now that he'll avoid whenever he can. It up to you, my dear to calm your fears. No one can do it for you."

In the past weeks, Khujjuttara has been reminding her mistress that the fetish is only wax, cloth and pins—nothing more. It has no meaning except what her thoughts attach to it.

"The Blessed One would say that you're shooting yourself with a second arrow. Finding the doll was painful, but by worrying about it, by rehashing the story and imaging a curse attached to it, you're shooting yourself again. You're adding suffering to the pain. You don't have to do that, you know. You have a choice."

Khujjuttara has repeated this teaching several times, to no avail. Samavati nods. She knows, but her thoughts swarm around fear anyway. Like flies attracted to dung.

For months Samavati has felt physically attacked by Magandiya's malignant energy. It's not just the fetish. It's hard to explain this to others. It sounds foolish even to herself, but nothing can rid her of the feeling that something threatens her. It's all around, even in her own house, lurking in the corners waiting to attack. It erodes her strength, stifles her spirit and covers her with darkness. The fetish only gave a name to the fear. And yes, she *does* believe curses have power. She's close enough to the superstitions of her culture that she's unable to let go of this one, no matter what the Buddha teaches.

"I know you don't believe in curses, Khujj, but I do! I can't help it."

"And so you're shooting yourself with a second arrow—or by this time, it's the fiftieth."

"More like the five-hundredth." She smiles wryly. She still has a sense of humor. Having opened the door to her suffering, Samavati voices another anguish. "What belongs to me anyway?" Her voice rises in lament. "Everything I possess is at his mercy! Every single thing! My body, my clothes, even my children! I might as well be his slave!"

From their game, Uppalavanna looks over at her mother apprehensively and then glances at her sister. She has noticed, too.

"No, Mistress, you are *not* a slave. Believe me, your experience is nothing like a slave's." Khujjuttara retorts quietly but firmly. She speaks from the depths of a lifetime of bondage.

Roused from self-pity, Samavati leans toward Khujjuttara and puts a hand on her shoulder. "Oh, of course, of course, my darling. You're right. I'm so sorry. It's just that I'm so unhappy! He can take anything from me at any time, just on a stupid whim!"

"That's what it means to be a queen," Khujjuttara reminds her, then adds softly, "and a woman. It's what we all have to bear one way or another when we're born into female bodies—no matter what our class." Patriarchy is so deeply ingrained in the culture that no one questions it. Like sunrise or sunset, it's accepted as normal, even venerated.

"But there is something that *is* yours." She pauses.

Samavati looks at her askance. Her eyes ask, There is? What?

"Your mind and heart, my dear. No one, no circumstances can take your mind and heart from you. And no one can violate your equanimity—unless you let them. That's the Blessed One's Dhamma." Her quiet, low voice resonates with the assurance of one who has learned the hard way.

But Samavati isn't interested. "I'm tired, Khujj. I'm tired of everything, including the Blessed One's Dhamma." She sighs, brushing a hand over her eyes. "Please leave me alone now."

Khujjuttara opens her mouth to comment but thinks better of it. She silently rises and limps back toward the house, her heart heavier than her gait. Both girls watch her leave, and they aren't happy.

CHAPTER 6

A CONFESSION,
LONG POSTPONED

October 7. It has been bothering him for years, his lie. Sati is a bhikkhu by fraud. He wouldn't have been allowed to re-ordain if they had known that he had been in robes when he had had a sexual encounter. He has sat through countless bimonthly Uposatha ceremonies, occasions when bhikkhus confess their offenses and recommit to the precepts, the rules that govern their order, and he has pretended his lie didn't exist. Confession is understood as a purification, a clearing away of obstacles that block the path to liberation, because one can't be liberated and be a liar at the same time.

Eventually, silence grew easier. The initial tug at his conscience was gradually undermined by time and by his conviction that a bhikkhu's life, with its prospect of liberation, is more meaningful than a layman's. He was determined to be an exemplary bhikkhu. In this, he has succeeded. Kind, hard working and deeply sincere, Sati is respected and liked by all, with a few exceptions.

Candana's acknowledgement of his palsy, however, was a catalyst. He was honest, and his admission was an effort. Sati knows that. What about me? That question has dogged him ever since. He had always meant to confess to his mentor—not to others maybe, but certainly to Candana. Now, a time factor is involved. Who's to say Candana's condition won't affect his mind? He explained that mental decline is possible. Of course, it might not happen, Sati reasons. Certainly, he's just as sharp now as ever, and even if it did happen, there's lots of time, years maybe. But the appalling possibility has focused his attention. The more he thinks about it, the more unendurable his own lie has become. He must get rid of it, no matter what the consequences, even if it means expulsion. It has come to that.

When Sati said this morning, just before almsround, that he needed to talk, the urgency in his voice made Candana lift his eyebrows. So now, here they are, after the midday meal, at which Sati only nibbled, sitting in Candana's hut, the site of so many teachings. Sati reveals his last deception, knowing that this conversation could change everything.

"Sir, I've lied to you. I've lied to everybody." He doesn't have to tell Candana about Siha. He did that when he returned to Ghosita's Park, and secretly, though he never said so, Candana was glad that he had lived with a woman. He had been so young when he ordained, so lacking in experience. Though those three years wouldn't prevent physical need from arising afterwards, he returned more experienced, with new clarity about his monastic vocation.

His voice quavering, Sati confesses everything, all except the fact that Arittha had counseled him to lie. It wasn't Arittha's fault. "I didn't tell you when I returned because you didn't ask, and I didn't want to spoil the happiness, and since then, my courage, well, it got less as time went on, and eventually confessing didn't feel so important," Sati ends lamely, shrugging his shoulders. He sniffs and wipes his eyes with the knuckle of his forefinger.

Candana listens without moving, without comment. When he has finished, they sit in a lengthening silence. Sati wants to scream. He hates Candana's expressionless mode. Say something! Anything!

At last, Candana blows air between his lips, his cheeks inflated. "Well," he says and clears his throat because his voice has gone raspy, "this *is* a surprise. And a disappointment. I'll tell you that."

Sati nods. No one could be more disappointed than he is in himself.

"You're right to say something, Sati, even at this late date. Because it would never have gone away. Ever. You'd live under the weight of the lie until your last breath."

Again, Candana is silent for a few moments. "I don't have much to say." He sighs. "Except that, as I see it, you have two choices. You can disrobe now and leave. Or else you can confess at Uposatha and leave it up to your brothers to decide. Which way do you want to go?"

Sati pauses, then croaks, "Uposatha."

October 7. This evening, Samavati and Khujjuttara sit on cushions in Samavati's bedchamber. The children are in bed or are in the care of their maids, and Samavati has instructed her staff not to disturb her. It's three days since their conversation in the garden, and Samavati has regained some equilibrium. She's glad Khujjuttara is here with her. It is another evening when they are discussing the Buddha's teachings. At least, that's what she has told everyone.

The two women are together on many evenings when the king is not visiting and when there is no public talk at Ghosita's Park. Years ago, their meetings raised suspicions that they were engaged in something other than religious discussion, but Samavati's servants loved her too well to speculate openly. When Magandiya, however, heard about the meetings—there are few secrets in the palace—she didn't hesitate. She sternly informed their husband that the two had an "unnatural liaison." Udena didn't believe her. He couldn't conceive that any woman would betray him with another man, much less with another woman and an ugly one at that.

Eventually the speculation died down, but the meetings didn't. It was true that initially they discussed the Buddha's teachings. When Samavati was a young queen overwhelmed by the demands of her erratic husband and by the jealousies that dominated harem life, Khujjuttara introduced her to the Dhamma. The desperate young woman took the teachings as her refuge, and ever since she has been practicing and finding growing inner ease. At least, until recently.

Samavati isn't allowed to leave the palace grounds except with Udena's permission, and attendance at public talks at Ghosita's Park are not on his list of permissible reasons for an outing. Khujjuttara, however, being only a slave, isn't restricted. For years, she has been a regular attendee. Gifted with a photographic memory, she is able afterwards to recite word for word the talks she hears, those of the

Buddha and, in his absence, those of other monks. So in the early years, Samavati listened to her servant's recitations, and together they learned. They pondered the meaning of the Dhamma and explored how to assimilate it into their life. Then, wanting other women in the palace to have the same opportunity, the queen arranged for Khujjuttara to hold regular teaching sessions in the women's building.

Magandiya objected, of course. The fact that Khujjuttara was not only a servant, but a slave, made a mockery, she asserted, of the sanctity of class structure. Magandiya expressed her outrage to Udena. It was part of her growing arsenal of accusations against the third queen. Like her earlier accusations, however, Udena dismissed it, having noticed the salubrious effect of the Buddha's teaching on his women. He growled at her, "It would do you good to attend some of those sessions yourself, Magandiya." She had to drop that line of attack.

And so tonight, Samavati and Khujjuttara are meeting again, and they exchange the smiles of co-conspirators. For they are not simply engaging in religious discussion; they are transcribing the Buddha's teachings. It is a brilliant project, especially for women, whose minds are presumed to be devoid of thoughts beyond marriage, children and ornaments. And it's a secret—no one else in the palace must know, for what they are doing is dangerous.

Although writing has long been practiced in the Indian subcontinent, it has been confined mainly to merchants, who use it in business. Lettering has begun to be known among aristocratic members of the warrior class, who play guessing games about letters traced on an opponent's back; however, to transcribe the holy teachings, Vedic or Buddhist, to actually put them into writing is unthinkable.

In fact, literacy is viewed with suspicion. It's a threat that would undermine the exclusive access brahmins have to the sacred Vedas. Brahmin priests hold Vedic wisdom close, transmitting it orally among themselves—which is how it's always been done. If Vedic knowledge were transcribed, any literate person could have access. The whole body of wisdom, not to mention brahminic power, would be thrown topsy-turvy.

Brahmins maintain that the mind is the only fitting receptacle for the sacred wisdom, and, in a culture where tradition is its own justification, everyone else believes them. Bhikkhus in the Buddha's order are explicitly prohibited from playing the lettering game—not for braminic reasons, but because the game is considered a distraction, as are other forms of play. But Samavati and Khujjuttara aren't monastics, and they are far beyond game-playing.

Samavati was the daughter of a wealthy merchant who taught her to read and write as a child so she could assist in the family business. Years later as a young, intelligent queen who was bored in the harem and surrounded by malice, she conceived the extraordinary idea: With her skill and Khujjuttara's memory, they could transcribe the Buddha's teachings and thus preserve them for future generations.

Inspired, they began the audacious project. But cautiously, because they were well aware of the suspicion with which their work would be greeted if discovered. Several times, when Samavati lived with the harem in the women's building, they were almost found out, but they've managed to work on undetected. And this is what they are doing tonight.

For Samavati, who is now staggering under Magandiya's animosity, transcribing the teachings is a refuge. It is an endeavor that takes her beyond her worries and the pettiness of those around her, a time to expand into the clear truth of the Dhamma.

Now as she transcribes the words that her beloved Khujjuttara is reciting, she soars past words into bliss. Her bamboo stylus, ink-dipped, flows across the birch-bark parchment as though guided from beyond, leaving traces for the ages to read. Khujjuttara's and Samavati's document would someday be known as the *Itivuttaka*, one of the scriptures in the Pali canon, which is the compilation of the Buddha's wisdom.

Their work includes transcriptions not only of the Buddha's talks when he visits Kosambi but also, since his visits are infrequent, transcriptions of other monks' talks, primarily those of Venerable Candana. These, she and Khujjuttara often study. The project provides them with an on-going mission to which they have passionately committed themselves. It is a secret source of joy amid the joylessness of palace intrigue.

Samavati as vigilantly protects their project as she does her own children. It *is* her own child. Or is she its child? Does it protect her? She is immensely grateful to be able turn to it in the evenings, a time when most in the harem, when not occupied with the king, are idle and bored. She hides the documents in a trunk in her residence. And she happily makes a second copy. This one, comprised of the Buddha's talks only, she gives to her stepfather, Ghosita, for safekeeping. Does she have a premonition?

October 10. Samavati's son, the crown prince, is visiting today. He arrived at his mother's residence about an hour ago. Like everyone else in the palace, Magandiya is aware of the occasion. Only too aware, to her way of thinking. With all the hullabaloo next door, how could it be otherwise? In fact, she's seated on the balcony of her residence, fanning herself with her peacock fan, watching.

From her second-story balcony, Magandiya has a good view of the family across the way, which is now picnicking in Samavati's shady garden. Udena is relaxing contentedly on a bench, legs outstretched, as the children tumble about, running and shouting. Bodhi, forgetting for a while the dignity of his new station, plays with them like he used to. Samavati lets them play freely, for the weather is beautiful, and this is a special occasion: Bodhi is leaving tomorrow for Takkasila.

Open to sons of the warrior and brahmin classes, Takkasila offers a variety of courses in higher education, both theoretical and practical. Prince Kumara studied there briefly, but his health was too fragile to withstand the rigorous training, and he returned home to be tutored in the palace. Queen Vasuladatta, who opposed his departure from the beginning, is convinced that the journey alone was enough to kill him. Eight-hundred hard miles by ox-drawn caravan over the trade routes, the trip took more than nine months. The prince was so weakened by the time he returned that, despite the best care of physicians and a loving mother, he died within months.

Young men usually enter Takkasila at sixteen. Prince Bodhi is only thirteen, but he is bright and inquisitive and tall for his age. Height is hardly an educational prerequisite, but it gives his father immense satisfaction, and he regards the boy as almost an adult. The new future king—no, the future maharaja—has already completed his lower education, and now Udena is keen that he continue and receive the very best education available, quickly. He has arranged for a suitable tutor at Takkasila, one who wouldn't be too hard on him and who wouldn't put him up against older boys with whom he couldn't compete.

"Don't worry," Udena has declared to Samavati repeatedly, trying to allay her fears about the hardships of the journey. "He's strong and healthy and he's fourteen." He bolsters his argument by counting the months the prince was in his mother's womb, a common practice in the culture. "He's already coming into his manhood," the king asserts.

Udena has arranged for a contingent of armed guards to accompany the prince's caravan. And the servant who has attended him since infancy will travel with him to ensure his comfort, relatively speaking.

"Think of all he'll learn, Samavati. Think of it. The highest knowledge and skills. The company of the very best young men in the land. What better training can there be for our son? Yes, he'll be fine."

Samavati is not reassured. Now, as she watches her son play with his siblings, she prays to the Buddha, "Bhagava, please, please protect my precious boy." But she knows all the prayers in the world won't erase her worry.

Partly hidden by a lattice but not caring if she is seen, Magandiya watches the easy movements of the youth who will someday be king. She snorts, "Good riddance!" At the same time, she wishes—oh, how she wishes!—he were her son. A maid comes out to see if her mistress needs anything, and Magandiya wordlessly shoos her away with her fan.

Though Bodhi has always known that a prince must leave his family sooner or later, this parting is drastic. He has lived with tutors in the palace and sometimes in town, but he has never been far from home. And this is so very far! Kumara told him about Takkasila. The young prince is excited and, though he doesn't want to show it, scared. "I'll have all kinds of adventures," he boasts to his siblings in his deepened voice, which only occasionally cracks and slips back into boy register. They are greatly impressed. Still, the child within wants to stay right here, in this comfortable, known garden at home.

Watching the happy family from the shadow of her balcony, Magandiya remembers the day Samavati announced she was pregnant. They were young then. Magandiya still had hopes for herself. It was during a family outing at the royal pleasure park—the entire harem was there. Magandiya felt stabbed. A knife couldn't have done a better job. She had the premonition then that it would never happen for her.

Samavati glances up at the balcony to check for Magandiya. Sure enough. She's there, with her peacock fan. The woman has been watching her for years from that balcony. Like an evil cloud hanging over my head, Samavati broods.

She has finally stopped trying to dismiss her sense of foreboding, for regardless of her efforts, it keeps getting stronger. She turns to her husband and, gesturing with her eyes, whispers, "She's up there, watching."

Udena is irritated. He growls quietly between his lips so the children can't hear, "Drop it, Samavati. It's her balcony. She can sit there if she wants."

Samavati says nothing more. Turning her attention back to the children, she laughs with Jinadatta who is riding piggyback on Bodhi's shoulders. The dread, however, doesn't go away; her eyes keep stealing glances upward.

Magandiya watches with a closed heart as the family says their good-byes. The children are hanging onto Bodhi, and he, reaching down, plucks his little brother from his knee and swings him up into a bear hug, while the child shrieks with delight. Now Samavati, her hands on Bodhi's shoulders, looks deeply into his eyes—already he's almost as tall as she is. Magandiya doesn't have to hear to know they are words of love.

Magandiya observes aloud, "Ahh! he's leaving—good. I'll be happy if I never see him again!" She doesn't know it, but in fact, she won't.

CHAPTER 7.
END OF SHILLY-SHALLYING

October 13. An unusual visitor sits on a cushion in Samavati's parlor. Vasuladatta is smiling sadly.

"I am happy to see you, Vasuladatta," Samavati says, and she means it.

Though they live only yards apart—their residences are separated by Magandiya's—they seldom see each other. So Samavati was surprised yesterday when a maid brought a query from her asking if she could visit. Of course! Samavati has always liked the quiet woman.

They are alone in the room except for a maid who moves silently on bare feet as she serves sweetmeats and juice. Samavati, seated on a cushion, her legs folded to one side, is alarmed to see how thin the other woman has grown. Always slender, Vasuladatta now looks as though she'd be at serious risk if she ventured out in a monsoon wind, and her eyes are smudged with dark circles. Life hasn't been easy for either of us, Samavati sighs, and she feels a pulse of affection for the older woman.

Accepting the juice with a nod, Vasuladatta says, "I understand Bodhi has left for Takkasila."

Samavati nods and smiles wistfully.

"May he have safe travels, and a safe return." She looks away. Her own son's travels though life were anything but safe.

When the maid leaves, Vasuladatta looks back and says softly, "Samavati, I've come because... because..." her voice trails off, then in a rush, "Since Kumara died, I do nothing but cry." At the mention of her son's name her lips tremble, and she begins to sob. Hunching over, she covers her face with her hands.

To see Vasuladatta, usually so reserved and self-possessed, in undefended despair is profoundly distressing. Samavati leans toward her and rests a hand on her shoulder. It doesn't take much for Samavati to put herself in Vasuladatta's place.

"Why did he have such bad karma?" the older woman wails into her hands. "What did that sweet child do to deserve it? What have I done to deserve it?" Then, looking up, she pleads, "Oh, Samavati, let Khujjuttara start teaching again!" Like other palace residents, Vasuladatta knows that the king cancelled Venerable Candana's teaching sessions.

The abrupt change of subject catches Samavati off guard. It takes her a moment to register its meaning, to segue from sympathy to reply.

"Please," Vasuladatta whispers. "I've never been interested in the Blessed One's teachings. I didn't attend any of the sessions before, either Khujjuttara's or the venerable's—you know that. But now I want to, I need to. I can't bear my life! I can't bear it!"

Samavati hears her own voice in Vasuladatta's. And the voice of countless others, men and women, who are drawn to the Dhamma because of their suffering—all desperate for relief and sensing it can be found in the Buddha's teaching.

Vasuladatta presses her hand, "Will you do it? I'll come, and I'll bring my women."

She kneels before Vasuladatta and strokes her hair. "Yes, yes, of course, my dear. We'll do it. We will."

Just this morning she and Khujjuttara were talking about re-starting the sessions, bringing the Dhamma to the women in the palace, like they had done before. Now, though, they could meet here in Samavati's parlor instead of the women's building.

"We were talking about it this morning. And you and all of your women will be welcome. I'll let you know when we start. Hush now, darling."

October 15. Few of the fifteen bhikkhus who are entering the assembly hall this evening know what is about to transpire. It is the full-moon day of Uposatha and the bhikkhus, having fasted, are gathering to confess their offenses or bear witness to their brothers' confessions, as they do at every new and full moon. Venerable Udayi is, as usual, serving as preceptor, for all the bhikkhus respect his fairness. Candana has briefed him about Sati's forthcoming confession.

Sitting in front of the bhikkhus along with Candana, Udayi intones in a resonant voice the refrain from the *Vinaya*, the disciplinary code, which is recited at every Uposatha observance, wherever it is held. It affirms the supremacy of *Nirvana*, the ultimate goal of every bhikkhu, and it invokes the vows by which bhikkhus strive to live: to do no evil, to cultivate good, to purify one's mind, and to act with restraint according to the precepts.

'Acting with restraint according to the precepts'—that's just what I haven't done, thinks Sati. Not at first with Siha, and certainly not for the years since then. Every one of those days has been a lie!

He is filled with self-blame and dread. Yet within his misery, hardly perceived, is a tiny brightness, a point of light: Whatever today's outcome, whatever his future, he is committing to cleanness. The shroud that has lain almost unnoticed over his heart for all these years is lifting, and he is relieved.

After reciting three times the ninety-seven precepts that now govern the order, precepts that he has memorized, Udayi asks the fateful question: "Are you pure in these matters?"

Sati lets others go first, to get the little stuff out of the way. Three bhikkhus speak, confessing minor offenses. Then Sati clears his throat noisily. Others turn toward him. This is the moment. Staring at the wall over the heads of the assembled monks, he begins. They are the hardest words of his life.

"I confess the offense of lying and..." after pausing a moment, he says just above a whisper "and the offense of sexual misconduct." Everyone is astounded. Sati?

He continues with the explanation, the barest bones. He gives permission to all assembled to speak to his offense, then fixing on a brown bit of leaf that has blown into the hall and is resting on the floor in front of him, he retreats into its study. Simsapa. It is the image by which he will remember these agonizing moments for the rest of his life. He is at the mercy of the *sangha,* the community of bhikkhus.

Pindola is the first to speak. He's outraged. "Venerables! There's only one word for this offense—expulsion! The penalty for sexual misconduct is expulsion. We all know it. No debate is necessary or possible."

Candana replies quietly, "You are right, friend," he nods at Pindola. "Expulsion is the penalty for sexual misconduct. But we would all do well to remember that Venerable Sati was only nineteen when he committed the offense."

These are the only words he intends to say. Everyone can guess where he stands. Speaking would not be helpful.

Udayi picks up on the thought as though rehearsed, which it has been. "As we all know, the Blessed One in his wisdom has stated in recent years that no aspirant may enter the order before the age of twenty. It is for reasons just such as this that he made that rule. Venerable Sati was young when he ordained and young when he committed the offense. And he wasn't wise. He disrobed as soon as he came to his senses." Two young novices, snicker softly at the images these words elicit.

Udayi ignores them, and, using the same reasoning that Arittha had, he points out, "It was only a matter of hours. He had no intention to deceive."

Pindola retorts, "Hours or weeks, a law is a law! When the venerable entered the order, his youth was permitted; so the law applied to him as well as to everyone else."

Venerable Bhaddaji, who at twenty-two, has been ordained for fifteen months and considers himself too junior to speak, nods emphatically in agreement.

Harika, however, is riled, as he is by almost everything Pindola says these days. He finds these comments particularly offensive. Of all people, Harika knows what it is to be generously dealt with by the community for committing a grave offense, several in fact. The penalty for splitting the sangha, which was just one of Harika's offenses, is expulsion. First-class lying is another. And there was the little matter of publicly disagreeing with and mocking the Buddha. But despite these offenses and more, Harika was allowed to remain in robes. He wasn't even punished.

How that happened, or rather didn't, was a combination of fluke and law. Fourteen years ago at *Pavarana*, the monastic ceremony that concludes the three-month rains retreat, the sangha at Ghosita's Park was still split by schism, so the two sanghas each held their own Pavarana ceremony. This involves identifying any offenses that have occurred during the retreat and imposing appropriate penalties. Because Harika, leader of the breakaway faction, was incapacitated by pneumonia and didn't attend the ceremony and the bhikkhus of his faction were weakened and confused by the turmoil, they didn't speak against him or against each other. Thus no penalties were levied. When the factions were finally reconciled, all bhikkhus tacitly agreed to cover the matter with grass, which is to say, to bypass it, feeling that further inquiry would only revive the controversy. In this, they took their lead from the Teacher himself.

The Buddha had been present at Ghosita's Park during most of the retreat and had tried but failed to reconcile the factions. Aside from calling Harika a fool and a loudmouth, the Buddha refrained from any reference to punishment, because Harika hadn't confessed to wrongdoing, and, according to the disciplinary rules, punishment cannot be levied until the perpetrator confesses. The Buddha left Ghosita's Park in disgust before the retreat's end; it fell to the residents, who didn't have the option of leaving, to make their own decisions.

Those events are long past, but as Harika listens to Pindola's comments, he recognizes that this is just how he used to sound. Like hearing myself all over again, he thinks. He's repulsed.

Pindola repeats, "But a law is a law!"

Harika nods. Oh yes, just like me.

Candana catches the nod out of the corner of his eye. Naturally Harika would agree.

Pindola continues, "If we make exceptions here and there, where would we be? Besides, it's not just the original offense, it's the venerable's lie since then. He's lied every day since he re-ordained. Ten years!"

Actually, nine years and ten-and-a-half months. Pindola is, pardonably, rounding numbers. Bhikkhus keep close track of numbers because monastic status depends on length of ordination; monks' formal relations with each other are governed by it.

Sati is a senior monk, an elder. He became a thera, or senior, two years ago. In these early days of the Buddha's order, the title is given when a junior monk demonstrates wisdom in the Dhamma, regardless of his length of time in robes. None of the bhikkhus disagreed when Candana bestowed it on Sati. Yet, there is a feeling among some that length of time in robes, not wisdom, should determine elder status and that that all bhikkhus should attain it after ten years of full ordination. That way, no long-time bhikkhu would be shamed before his brothers or householders by still being a junior while his contemporaries were addressed as "elder."

Pindola continues, "What kind of thera is he? What kind of example? You begin with an offense punishable by expulsion and then add ten years of lying to it, and what have you got? A transgression so monstrous I can't even comprehend it!"

No one can deny this. The penalty levied for an offense increases in relation to the time between commission and confession.

"Besides," he continues, struck by a new argument, "how do we know the venerable disrobed properly? We only have his word for it, and he's lied for ten years, so should we trust him now? We apparently have the word of Venerable Arittha, as well." Pindola has never met Arittha but knows he's an outcaste by birth, and anything an outcaste says can't be credited in Pindola's view, though he wouldn't openly admit it. "But the Venerable Arittha isn't here. Maybe..."

Hostile looks from the other bhikkhus stop him mid-sentence. The undertone of bigotry is clear: He, a high brahmin, is questioning the veracity of Sati and Arittha, both outcastes. Most are appalled. And they all know the legal implication of this line of reasoning: Not disrobing properly but maintaining that one has, and then acting in ways that are counted as a monastic offense, like marrying, disqualifies one from ever ordaining again. It would make a sham of Sati's re-ordination, and he would have to be expelled and not allowed to retake robes, no matter how repentant. It's too low a suggestion for all but the most rigid of them to consider.

With a tight face and barely controlling his anger, Udayi ignores Pindola's suggestion. It's time to bring this discussion to an end.

"Yes, there has been an intention to deceive, but Venerable Sati has been an impeccable bhikkhu all this time. He has become a learned and competent bhikkhu, knowledgeable in the Dhamma and the Vinaya. He is earnest in practice and compassionate in action," Udayi continues. "And we all appreciate the significant contribution he has made to the running of this monastic park. In view of all the circumstances, therefore, I propose that Venerable Sati *not* be expelled for sexual misconduct or lying, but instead that his first sixteen months as a bhikkhu be disallowed so that the date of his ordination will be considered as starting with his ordination at the Bamboo Grove."

This is extraordinary! No one ever heard of demoting a bhikkhu. Can it be done? Just because Udayi—well, Udayi and Candana—say so? It takes some thinking. It would mean that all bhikkhus who ordained in the sixteen-month period after Sati initially did would now be senior to him. In time, every bhikkhu in the order will learn of his offense, and some will need to adjust their status with regard to him. How humiliating! And is Sati still a senior? Or is he demoted there, too?

Pindola weighs the implications of the judgment. Acceptable? Sati, even if demoted, would still be senior to him, whether he's a thera or not. No, on balance, he'll stick with his first position. He starts to object, "But the law says..."

At this point the Venerable Harika interjects, "I agree."

No surprise, thinks Candana caustically.

"I agree with the Venerable Udayi. The Venerable Sati has been a fine bhikkhu. His was an offense of youth. Who of us hasn't committed an offense sometime in their life, whether as a monk or before?"

Everyone knows the context from which Harika speaks, but they're still stunned. Even though he frequently moderates his comments these days, when it has come to the point, they've never known him to favor the Dhamma, the teachings, over the law of the Vinaya.

Udayi smiles inwardly, So the old nut is softening! Even Sati, who has been too numb to follow the conversation, emerges from his botanical investigation and recognizes the extraordinary nature of Harika's comment.

Harika pointedly directs his question to Pindola, looking at him with hard, coppery eyes. Who hasn't committed an offense in his life?

Pindola shakes his head, his gesture proudly asserting that he never has. Not one.

"Well, you should have!" barks Harika.

Bhaddaji and another young monk are aghast. Pindola should have committed an offense? What kind of talk is this? We're bhikkhus, not a gang of thugs! Their respect for Harika crumbles on the spot.

Asoka, who is attending this Uposatha gathering, empathizes with Sati's plight but, being an outsider, refrains from participating in the discussion. He has been doing some active thinking, though. There's entirely too much drama at Ghosita's Park. He longs to be away from messy people problems and back on the road, free again, which is how Bhagava means it to be, isn't it?

Venerable Uttara, who has also been silent, now interjects gently, trying to move the discussion to a more meaningful level. "Friend Pindola, ultimately this is not about a violation of the discipline. It's about compassion. The observance of the Vinaya is crucial to the orderly running of the sangha, we all agree to that. But without compassion, there is no point in having a sangha. The heart of the Dhamma is kindness and compassion. Unless we as bhikkhus live by these qualities ourselves, what right have we to call ourselves disciples of the Blessed One?"

Udayi nods appreciatively and moves on, "I further propose that the Venerable Sati be required to observe ten weeks of penance, one week for each year of his silence. After that, he'll be considered rehabilitated."

Penance is typically observed by daily confession of one's offense. The bhikkhu, covering his left shoulder with his robe, squats in a flat-footed, lowly posture with palms outstretched at front of the assembly hall in the presence of any bhikkhus who care to attend, and he confesses. It is an act geared toward instilling shame in the offender.

Udayi declares, "Let all who agree remain silent. Let those who disagree signal by speaking up." A second time, leaving a lengthy pause between declarations to give everyone a chance to reflect. Then the third time, "Let all who agree remain silent. Let those who disagree signal it by speaking up."

Pindola and two young monks object, but they are a minority. Udayi nods at Sati as he concludes, "The Venerable Sati's penance begins now. Come to the front of the hall, venerable."

Pindola grumbles, There's nothing like having the seniors on your side. To his way of thinking, this has been all about power. He, who knows what real power is, sneers silently. So pathetic! They think they're powerful!

Though the wisdom of the judgment eludes Pindola, and while his entrenched cynicism hinders his awakening, which, after all, is his declared goal, the essence of his observation is correct: Sati does have the support of the seniors. Once he thaws, he will recognize the compassion that underpinned the judgment. He will remember this teaching and will be more deeply moved to offer the same to others in the future.

October 20. Magandiya is exasperated. Everything she does goes wrong! Now she hears that the wretched slave has begun her teaching sessions again, and even Vasuladatta is attending. Magandiya has always considered Vasuladatta a nonentity, a fixture like a piece of furniture you have to walk around. But now the woman is siding with Samavati.

So where's the power of the fetish? she asks herself. Samavati may be terrified, and Udena, the simpleton, doesn't know how to respond, but the fact is, she has no faith in it at all, never has.

It's just a bit of wax, cloth and pins that she put together herself. She didn't have a priest cast the spell. Most priests are sincere and pious, but some would have worked this bit of magic for her— they're not hard to find when you know the right people. However, Magandiya didn't want word to get around that she, a queen, was dabbling in magic. It's fine to intimidate people with obscure, otherworldly references sometimes, but you don't want to go too far—that could get dangerous. So she concocted a spell herself, and now it's clear what that has amounted to: Nothing. Fuck nothing! No, something else is needed, something decisive. She needs guidance. She needs a strategy.

It is midday and Magandiya, under the pretext of visiting a relative, is petitioning her favorite yakka with flowers and milk blessed by a priest. On the outskirts of town, the wooden altar that rings a venerable tree housing the spirit is grimy with *ghee* (clarified butter) and sour milk, sticky with honey, and laden with flowers, fresh and rotting, some in little pots, and everywhere there is a blanket of petals. A mixture of odors assails her nostrils. The squads of flies that are circling the honey drippings make side-trips to her arms and head. Her hands are busy shooing, and she wishes she had her fan. But despite the offense to her sensibilities, Magandiya makes her offering, and, stretching her arms in supplication, she prays as fervently as any peasant woman, the hues of her sari blending with the chaos of color on the altar—reds, oranges, gold and green. She is almost invisible. Then she hears it. For once, her prayers have been answered! The message is unequivocal: Stop shilly-shallying. If you want a real reward, you need to take real action.

Now, in an evening filled with the music of insects, Magandiya sits on her balcony, her active, misused mind oblivious to all except her new determination. It fortifies her more effectively against the cool of the lowering night than does the fine woven shawl around her shoulders.

A scheme comes to her, as though a gift from the yakka: Convince Udena that Samavati is not simply an unfaithful wife, not simply a wife who is contemplating becoming a nun—that's child's play. No, she's a wife who plans to murder him. Tell him about her dream, an ominous dream about a, uh, snake...yes, a snake and death. What else could the dream mean except that Samavati plans to murder him with a poisonous snake? He, her beloved husband, her lord, needs to beware and protect himself. And—here's the beauty of it—she'll set up the prop, a note of reality. To Magandiya the logic of the scheme is inspired.

October 24. He didn't believe her! He was almost bored when she told him about the dream. Udena is tired of her accusations, even though this one is more serious than the others.

Last night was Magandiya's turn, the first of his three nightly visits. He doesn't make love as often as he used. Sometimes he wants to simply sit and talk, though he tends to cut those evenings quite short. And sometimes, he takes time out from the rotation, as he has always done when he's angry or is favoring another woman or when he simply wants a break because occasionally a man needs to be alone.

She was outraged by his indifference last night, but she's too smart to show it. He'll never know whether I'm pleased or not, she thought. I'll humor him for the next couple of nights, lots of passion if he's in the mood. She envisions some of the positions she'll take and the words she'll use. Ah yes. Then, when it's Samavati's turn, he'll see. Then he'll believe me!

She knows that since his audience with Samavati, Udena has resumed his nocturnal visits to her. She tracks them closely. Samavati is next in line to receive their husband's favors, and Magandiya is making plans.

Obtaining the snake is easy enough; it's the timing that's tricky. The snake needs to be dead, freshly dead, because she certainly isn't going to deal with a live one. She'll time it for what should be the second of his visits, just in case someone else catches his fancy the first night. It will happen while they're strolling in Samavati's garden before retiring to her house. Magandiya has spied often enough to know their routine.

Though the thought of having to place the snake makes her queasy, she doesn't trust anyone else to do it. And, she reasons, I'm the only one who knows their path. At dusk, after the children have gone into the house and before he arrives—that'll be the time to place it. And if he doesn't come? Well, there will be other nights and other snakes, though her stomach turns at the possibility of having to retrieve a dead one after dark. But if he doesn't come, it would ruin everything if someone found the corpse the next day. If I'm careful and lucky, she concludes, it will work right the first time and I won't have to go get the damned thing.

October 26. Asoka is ready. Not just ready but impatient. He has been talking about walking almsround for the past week, and yesterday when Sirivaddha visited, he pressed. The physician hesitated, "It's early yet, venerable. You could injure it again. I think you should

wait a while." This wasn't what he wanted to hear, and he decided to ignore the advice.

This morning as he greets Candana at the gate, his begging bowl cradled in his arm, his spirits are high. "You'll have to keep it slow, Candana. Got to be kind to this old ankle."

Then he remembers Candana's condition. "Oh, sorry," he murmurs contritely, blaming himself for thoughtlessness. Idiot. Aloud he says, "I didn't mean..."

Candana smiles and waves away the comment, and they move out of the grounds in companionable silence—good old friends. But Candana's thoughts linger on the comment. I wish I just had a sprained ankle, he thinks again, then sighs.

They haven't walked far into the neighborhoods when Candana says quietly, "Let's slow down." Asoka nods and immediately lessens his pace. He thought they *were* walking slowly. He realizes how much effort almsround is for his companion.

As usual, their eyes are fixed on the ground in front of them, but Asoka's thoughts are focused on Candana. For most of the walk, he sends thoughts of lovingkindness to him, starting with the Buddha's phrases. 'May you be happy and secure, may you have a happy mind.' But other words irresistibly bubble up, and he improvises: May your illness be cured. May your health be completely restored, like to what it was when you were twenty...well, thirty. May all your troubles dissolve and never return. May you live a carefree life, a paragon of bhikkhus. And he acknowledges, You already *are* a paragon, but anyway... May we remain brothers until the end.

On the return journey, their bowls filled with alms food, Asoka's lovingkindness offering is interrupted. He feels a twinge. Uh-oh. Maybe almsround wasn't such a good idea. Maybe Sirivaddha was right. Pain shoots through his left ankle. By the time they pass through the gate, he is grimacing and limping. Candana notices, but says nothing.

When they reach Asoka's hut and set their bowls on the mats, Asoka looks up at him and ruefully admits, "I guess I was too impatient."

They exchange knowing smiles. Two old men bearing the baggage of aging bodies.

CHAPTER 8.

THE SNAKE
AND THE ARROW

October 27. This evening Udena visits Samavati again. It's the second of his three nights. From her balcony, Magandiya sees him approaching accompanied by a servant.

Right on schedule. I'm in luck.

The king enters the residence while the servant stations himself outside the door. Then, as if in one of the plays sometimes enacted at the royal park, the couple exits the back door and strolls leisurely into the garden along their customary path, talking quietly.

Too easy, Magandiya snorts.

Udena and Samavati move slowly into the small mango grove at the farther end of the garden, where they're hidden from view. But she knows they're making their way to their favorite spot, a bench in a secluded corner. Like a cat that has located its prey, she peers into the darkening scene, listening intently, waiting, waiting, and...yes! Shouts from the grove.

Victory!

Samavati screams in terror when she spots a snake lying on their bench—a cobra!

Seeing it an instant later, Udena immediately remembers Magandiya's dream. It's the omen! Looking more closely, he notices the creature is dead, but it's just like Magandiya said. Samavati *is* trying to murder him! Udena's response is no more rational than his wife's.

Samavati reaches reflexively for her husband's hand for comfort, but he flings it away and turns on her. "You vile woman!" he shouts, his face contorted with fury and disgust. "Evil demon! Don't you touch me—not now or ever!"

She staggers backward as though punched. "Wha...what did I do?" *Am I hearing him right?* she questions herself. *Is he really saying that?* The expression on his face assures her that he is. She will remember this expression.

Their voices are Magandiya's signal. She races downstairs and sprints through the garden, charging through the hopscotch crossing, scattering some of the stones, then into the grove.

"I told you so! I told you!" she screams, looking like a demon herself, shaking a fist at her husband. "It's the omen, the evil omen. Now you'll listen to me!"

That none consider her intrusion bizarre is a sign of how high emotions are running. Undone by the sudden horror, Samavati turns her back on her husband and his second wife, who are glaring at each other, and runs, gasping for breath, toward her back door.

What just happened? Why is he yelling at me? Then she wonders, *How did Magandiya get into this?* By the time she reaches the door, she understands: more treachery.

October 28. "The king commands your presence in your garden in half an hour."

Samavati has left the dining area where she and the children were breakfasting and meets the royal messenger, who has been ushered into her parlor. He delivers the message almost apologetically. He knows this isn't good news.

After last evening's nightmare and the one she had in the early hours this morning when sleeping, she knew something was coming. She dreamt that Magandiya's fan was hovering over her, waving of its own will. Its jeweled base glittered, and the peacock-feather eyes stared evilly while the fan swayed and swayed, back and forth, and she was small and caught, in her turquoise sari, and Udena glowered down from his dais with Magandiya next to him, side by side.

She fixes on the messenger's turban, the king's colors—red, yellow and black—not her favorite. She makes an effort to listen but already knows the import. With an automatic nod, she dismisses him and her hand brushes over her forehead. She returns to the children.

"What's wrong, Mama?"

"Nothing, nothing darling. I just have a little headache, that's all."

Uppalavanna isn't fooled. She and her sister exchange glances. They knew something was wrong when they first sat down to breakfast. Adults are always doing this. They never tell you the truth.

"Well, my loves," Samavati says abruptly, her voice unsteady, "I need to go upstairs and get ready. I have a meeting this morning. You stay inside and play. I'll see you afterwards." She pauses. "I love you so much. So very, very much."

She reaches down and hugs each daughter. It seems to them that she holds them longer than usual. Then she catches the prince who, having escaped from his nurse's lap and losing his little loin cloth in the process, is in mid-air flight. He's running about naked, flapping his arms and flying like a falcon, the one in the story his nurse told him, and squawking like a falcon squawks. When Samavati lifts him, the falcon grabs for her nose, and she smiles. She rubs noses with him, plants a kiss on his chubby cheek, then hands him back to the nurse, who may release the fearsome bird to fly again or keep him captive, her choice.

With fast withering composure, she instructs the servant in the dining room to tell Khujjuttara to meet her in her bedchamber. Her daughters' gaze follows her as she walks out. Once out of their sight, her composure dissolves, and she bounds up, gasping. She already told Khujjuttara about last night's events—she did that as soon as she entered the house—and the blessed woman spoke to her soothingly. Now, as Khujjuttara steps into her room, before she even closes the door, Samavati blurts out, "A meeting. Now. In t...the garden. Make sure the children stay inside, far away. And, and...see they're taken care of...please." She ends on a whisper.

Khujjuttara understands the movement of her mistress's heart. She always has. She enfolds her in an embrace and putting Samavati's head on her chest, strokes her hair.

"Oh, Khujj!"

She is alone in the garden, standing on the path as far from the mango grove as possible. A mature growth of rhododendron, its dark leaves shining in the sun, blocks a view of her from the house. In an unconscious effort to forestall this meeting, she has turned her back to the path, the obvious direction from which he will come. She gazes at the shiny leaves, unseeing. Her attention is fixed on sounds.

There. She doesn't turn. When he is within some thirty feet and she still hasn't looked around, he stops, lifts the bow, aims, then calls in a low voice, "Samavati." He wants to give her time to realize just what he is planning to do, no mistake.

She looks over her shoulder, and her eyes widen, her mouth falls open. She turns toward him, her heart thudding against her chest wall like the hooves of a galloping horse. She will face him squarely.

She closes her eyes. Her heart cries, "Bhagava!" and she whispers the Blessed One's words. They flow automatically. "As a mother would risk her own life to protect her only child, even so towards all living beings one should cultivate a boundless heart." They have come to carry more than the meaning of the words themselves. They are emblematic of everything she believes and has tried to live for—her faith, her love, her belief in goodness and dignity.

For a moment, Udena regrets his decision, which was hardly a decision at all. His fury and Magandiya's goading didn't allow much room for thought. He just blindly reacted. Now he hesitates. She's so lovely, even in her terror. Then, remembering his outrage, he draws the bow and the arrow flies...

...and it misses!

The idiot! The fucking idiot, how could he have missed? Magandiya shrieks silently.

Of course she is watching. She'd been on her balcony since early this morning waiting to catch sight of him. She knew he would come, for she knows her man, and nothing in the world would have kept her from watching this consummation of her strategy. Once he arrived, she hurried to Samavati's garden and hid amidst the shrubs in a corner where she would have a good view of the action. She had identified the spot beforehand but had assumed with a smirk that it hardly mattered whether she was hidden or not: Udena would be so preoccupied he wouldn't notice, and Samavati, well, she'd be dead.

Her response now to this fiasco is to let loose a silent stream of foul language. How could the bastard have missed? Is he blind? She is incredulous and enraged.

The truth is that archery is a skill Udena never seriously cultivated. He misses tigers when they're staring him in the face, and he now misses his wife as well. Archery may be the premier sport of aristocrats, but he never cared for it. Too much concentration. When young, he practiced just enough to please his tutor and his father. As a forty-one-year-old monarch, he hasn't needed to please anyone. A warrior king he is not. For his pacifist inclinations Udena has gained the reputation of peacemaker. His hands are shaking badly.

Samavati hears the whizz as the arrow pierces the air, cuts through the rhododendron and, with a thunk, lodges in a tree behind. It takes her a few seconds to realize what has happened. Opening her eyes and shaking uncontrollably, she sees her husband standing before her. He is rigid with disbelief. How could this be?

It dawns on him—there can be only one explanation: Samavati is blessed by the recluse Gotama. He has suspected it for some time. There is a spell over her, a spell of goodness; otherwise, there is no way he could have missed at this close range. And if she is blessed, what does that make him? He tried to kill her. Suddenly bald fear courses through this man who has seldom acknowledged fear. It seizes his body with contractions.

What kind of evil karma have I just created? How am I going to be punished? By all the gods, this is terrifying!

Certainly it's more terrifying than Magandiya's doll—what's a doll compared with this? In fact, he doesn't think about the doll. All thought is washed away by the prospect of the curse he has just brought onto his head.

Udena drops the bow and stumbles toward her. Falling to his knees, tears streaming down his face, he begs, "My precious precious darling my beloved my wife my heart please forgive me I beg you to forgive this foolish man I didn't know what I was doing I..." The words tumble out and are lost in his sobs.

Oblivious to the melodrama he is enacting, he clutches her hand and tugs insistently, the pressure underscoring his earnestness. He is like a child pleading at his mother's skirts, though his own mother was so removed from his life that this gesture is a first. He is holding Samavati's hand too tightly to notice that it is shaking.

He looks up beseechingly. She stares at her moving hand as if it were a stranger's and then at him, and inclines her head slightly, unable to speak.

Ahhh—reprieve! Accepting her gesture as forgiveness, he relaxes and smiles through his tears. "My dearest love," he murmurs, bringing his lips to her much-exercised hand. He throws out a silent "thank the gods" and knows that any lingering bad karma can be thought about later, but what's important now is that she forgives him. The main brunt of the evil has been averted!

Samavati can't extricate herself quickly enough, and it isn't because her circulation has been stopped—she hardly notices that. She pulls her hand away and, for the second time in two days, she flees to her residence. Emotion does not, however, blind her to the figure crouching in the shrubs. Magandiya. So she's seen it all. Samavati moves on without acknowledging her presence.

By the time Samavati has passed, Magandiya, too, is frozen with fear. She is a military commander no longer. Everything has gone wrong! Her initial disbelief and outrage give way to the realization that she'll be the one to suffer his wrath now. She understands her husband's mind perfectly.

She begins to assess her options. Samavati saw her, but the king mustn't. She squats further into the shrubs as he picks up his bow, goes around the rhododendron and grasps the lousy arrow and, with some difficulty and audible curses, yanks it from the tree. Then, he propels himself unsteadily down the bricked path toward the palace. He doesn't notice Magandiya.

Straightening up, she brushes a few leaves from her lovely sari and walks, head high like a queen, back to her own garden. She knows Samavati's women are watching from the house but doesn't glance in their direction. She doesn't give a damn. She needs to think quickly.

There's little time. First, avoid him as long as possible, let his anger mellow. But how long can that be? There aren't many ways to avoid a king if he wants to see you.

A plan begins to form: The next time, she'll tell him she's been sick and has had many strange dreams. Maybe the snake dream was just one of those? She told him about it because she loves him so dearly and wants to make sure he is safe. And she'll say that she's been nauseated in the mornings these past few weeks, which is maybe why the dreams are happening. With hesitancy, she'll venture that she hasn't wanted to speak too soon, she didn't want to get his hopes up, but is it possible, maybe, that she's with child?

Right, that's an old one. Will he believe it? But he doesn't have to. All he needs to do is consider the possibility. The man is desperate enough for male offspring, especially after Kumara's death, that he might overlook the improbable timing. And Brahma willing, maybe it really will happen! She must speak to one of the priests again. Maybe even the royal chaplain. A special ceremony. And, if by chance, I'm not so blessed—face it, what are the chances after all these years?—I'll inform him that, alas, alas, it isn't so, and I'll grieve for failing my lord in this way. That, at least, would be real enough. The strategy might work!

This mental workout hasn't quite exhausted her ingenuity. Her robust sense of self-preservation has revived, and she adds another refinement as she opens the door: Jenti. Jenti, her head maid, washes her underwear and knows the truth about her monthly periods—and a lot of other things. How much does she need to bribe Jenti?

Samavati runs through the back door without regard for queenly bearing. She dashes through the hallway and up the stairs and collapses onto her bed. The children, who are in another part of the house, don't see her, but Khujjuttara does. Along with several other servants, she watched from a window. Although some of the action was hidden, they understood the gist—the king, the arrow, the despicable Magandiya. They looked at each other horrified. None wished to talk about what they had witnessed, nor did they mention the other queen's name. Khujjuttara follows her mistress into her bedchamber.

"He sh... should have done it—he should've ki... killed me!" she hiccups, her hands clenched. "I'll do it for him! I'll give him a boon and do it myself—that's what he wants! I'll do it for him!" she shrieks. "Why go on living in this hell, this prison? I hate it, hate it, hate it!" Her whole body shakes.

Khujjuttara is silent while her mistress sobs out her agony. Then, after time, in a low, quiet voice that has penetrated to the end of all things, she says, "My dear, you are a queen and I am a slave but we, both of us, face the same choice: In the circumstances where we find ourselves, we can either shriek and resist—even kill ourselves—or we can accept what we hate and love anyway. And you, my darling, and I have already chosen love. And we must keep on choosing it, moment by moment—anything else is unacceptable. You know this, don't you?"

Samavati, her face buried in the bed linens, lies still. Then slowly, reluctantly, she nods her head. Yes, it is so. She must choose love.

Khujjuttara gently caresses her shoulder until, under her hand, she feels a shift, the gathering of a new, quiet energy. Samavati turns, sits up and through her tears, she smiles an ancient smile. They gaze at each other—two souls are one. Then, in a universal womanly gesture, they hug and shed tears together.

She enters her residence, shrieking, "The fucking bastard!" Her bare feet pound the carpets. She brushes aside two maidservants, who are in the hallway sweeping the floor and dusting fixtures.

What is it this time? Women serving this queen understand that they risk stomach disorders and other ailments. There is a large store of medicaments in the maids' pantry. As she storms past, the maids look at each other knowingly and, like twins, roll their eyes and waggle their heads. Why must service be so hard?

From his elaborate cage in the adjacent parlor, the mynah ruffles his brown feathers. "Fuckin bastard!" he squawks as Magandiya dashes past.

"Why, why, why?" she shouts, bounding up the stairs two at a time. "Every step I take, the gods are against me! It's that damned recluse! He started it all! May he reincarnate as a worm in dung!" When she isn't blaming Samavati, she's blaming the Buddha.

The beautiful Magandiya had just come of marriageable age, when the Buddha, still in his thirties and newly embarked on his teaching mission, visited Kuru country and its capital city Kammasadhamma (near the site of modern Delhi). There, Magandiya's father had a fateful encounter with him.

A small crowd of listeners had gathered around the holy man as he taught in the early evening under the banyan tree in the town's center. Magandiya's father, who was passing, joined the group. He listened and was so impressed by the tall ascetic's person and presence that, after the talk, as the crowd dispersed, he respectfully approached the Buddha and, without much preamble, offered his daughter in marriage. It was a naïve offer, to say the least, for he knew wandering ascetics aren't in the habit of marrying. But Magandiya was his treasure, and their family lineage was ancient, their wealth, great. He was convinced that such a marriage would enhance the standing of this extraordinary specimen of a recluse while furthering his own family's

stature. What could be more advantageous? Who could refuse such
an offer?

The Buddha did. He bluntly observed that the body "is filled
with urine and dung—I wouldn't touch it even with my foot."

Oooooff!

While the Buddha's response seemed to ring with personal re-
pugnance, he was in fact affirming, less than skillfully, a religious
principle that ascetics through the ages have striven to maintain.

When she heard about his comment, however, Magandiya,
who was unaccustomed to thinking in terms of principle, religious
or otherwise, took it personally. She was desirable in every way,
pursued by suitors left and right, and now this ascetic—who was he,
anyway?—rejected her in a most humiliating manner. Nothing more
than urine and dung! Right there and then, Magandiya conceived a
life-long hatred for the Buddha, a hatred that was to have disastrous
consequences.

Her parents had a different reaction. Her father, hence her
mother, soon enough realized they could offer a treasure even more
precious than their daughter: themselves. They became followers and
eventually left worldly life to pursue enlightenment. This meant that
not only had Magandiya been rejected by the ascetic but, as she gradually understood, she was losing her parents as well. She, the treasure
of the family, was thrice rejected.

All because of that miserable ascetic! She has cursed him repeatedly. He's called a "widow-maker" and a "son-stealer," but they
forget to say he's a hell-maker for daughters, too!

Deepening one's commitment to spiritual life is a long-term
process, and Magandiya's father needed to take things slowly. He had
familial obligations. Appropriately marrying off his daughter was
paramount among them. Ever watchful for an illustrious match, he
decided to reach beyond recluses; no one less than a king was worthy!
And he had a king in mind.

He sent a messenger to King Udena of Vamsa with a proposal
outlining the advantages of the marriage: a connection with an influential and wealthy family of brahmin lineage that traced all the way

back to the ancient legends, a clan whose ancestral home in Kuru country was just beyond the northwest boundary of Udena's own kingdom. Vamsa's prospects for expansion outside the fertile triangle of land between the Yamuna and Ganges Rivers were limited. To the north and southeast, two strong kings reigned; to the south, Udena's father-in-law. So if Udena had expansionist aspirations, they would have to be directed northwesterly. Relatives by marriage in that area could be quite advantageous.

The proposal put forth by Magandiya's father didn't crassly refer to Vamsa's possible territorial future, but it did emphasize other advantages of an alliance, and it extolled her beauty—a pearl, like all the stars in the night sky, like a whole field of flowers in springtime, like a celestial nymph born of the gods whose pride she was, a treasure of treasures. The messenger was instructed to repeat the proposal word for word, no forgetting, no changes.

Udena carefully weighed the matter. Vasuladatta, his queen, was then pregnant and, the gods willing, would present him with a son. But you can't be too careful in these matters. You can't have too many wives. All kings know this. He invited Magandiya's father to visit and to bring his celestial daughter with him. So it happened that Udena took a second queen into his hearth and home. Magandiya was fifteen and the king, twenty-three.

Then came the third wife. What a black day! Almost as beautiful as Magandiya herself, Samavati was a lot sweeter. She wasn't a brahmin, just a lowly merchant-class girl, yet everybody, including the king himself at the beginning, was falling all over her. To make matters worse, in Magandiya's view, in time Samavati not only bore children but became a follower of the abominable recluse. The constellation of her hatred solidified.

Magandiya writhes in her bed now, she beats the cushions, wads the bed linens. She sweats and heaves. Finally, exhausted, she lies still. Where from here? Her eyes snap open. She is rocked by a radical thought. It will be her ultimate plan.

CHAPTER 9.

THE ULTIMATE STRATEGY

ovember 3. His right leg doesn't keep pace with the rest of him as he trudges along. It's like struggling through mud. He used to enjoy these walks at dusk, the pastel sky softening the colors, everything slowly going dark and sometimes the bright moon face playing hide-and-seek in the leafy canopy, feeling so near you could touch it.

Not this evening, though. The moon is just a sliver and, even if it were full, Candana wouldn't be looking. He's shrinking. Day by day, he feels he's growing smaller. It seems to be the main activity of his life—this diminishment, slowing down, a shuffling gait that doesn't let him inhabit the largeness of movement that has always been his.

He stops in his tracks. I could end up the size of a six-year old! Maybe it's normal, he thinks. Maybe that's what happens to aging bodies, especially after an extra long almsround like today's. My chest is getting congested, a cold is coming on.

He gropes for a painless explanation. But no. Of course not. He stares at a large downed tree by his feet. It used to be a giant, like me. Envisioning it shriveling and shrinking within until it is unrecognizable, he thoroughly scares himself. He shakes his head like a dog shaking off water. His awareness is too sharp to let him wallow in unreality for long. The nightmare fades, and he stands a little taller. The tree, too, returns to its full, fluent length along the ground.

Candana wonders for the thousandth time why this is happening. A physical imbalance? Bhagava talks about that. But physical imbalances are a form of bad karma, aren't they? The result of unwise actions in this or past lives. It would have to be from a past life because his heart is pretty much at ease about this one. Of course, there are little things, little trespasses like all people have, but nothing serious enough to warrant this...

Suddenly, nothing. That's the answer. He needn't have done anything in this life or another to have caused the palsy. It is simply an expression of the flow of existence!

Candana is stunned. What makes some trees fall in the forest during the rains—even strong, deeply rooted trees like this simsapa, its smooth grey bark peeling in strips, while others stand for decades? It's just the way of existence. It's not a condemnation of any particular tree. This one didn't do anything evil. But then how do you reconcile that with the law of karma and rebirth?

Candana knows that the question stands in perilous relationship with the ancient wisdom and with his own teacher's Dhamma. Does karma not apply to trees? Or to worms? And if not and you're reborn in a lower realm, how do you ever get out? Condemned to be a tree or worm lifetime after lifetime? Not that there's anything wrong with a tree or worm. He is convinced beyond words that they have perfectly good lives in their own terms and that, in a deep way, we're all the same. Still, he doesn't want to be reborn as one.

It's a quagmire. He's been at its edge many times, for he has heard this Dhamma often and has repeated it himself when teaching. But he's never been fully convinced, not really. Something about karma keeps slipping away. It refuses to make sense. Or makes too much sense—it's too neat.

Well, I don't need to puzzle it out now. I've got enough to worry about. Someday I'll ask Bhagava again.

For now, he lets go of the conundrum and plods on with a small sense of relief, which, at least, is something to be grateful for.

Magandiya is also outside walking tonight. In the serenity of the garden behind her residence, her thoughts drift back to her childhood, to those golden days so long ago, another world...

As the only child of brahmin parents, pampered, wealthy and beautiful, she lived in innocent arrogance, basking in the promise of a fabulous future. She remembers her favorite uncle, her father's younger brother, Culla Magandiya.

Uncle was unmarried then, and he would laughingly take the little girl on his knee and tell her stories about ancient battles in which their ancestors played illustrious roles, and about gods and supernatural beings with their hilarious and sometimes cruel antics. He had a large imagination. How she loved those stories and begged for more. Such happiness! That's how things should be!

Her thoughts plummet back to the present. Everything has gone wrong. Another childhood memory flashes to mind: a story Uncle Culla told her featuring an avalanche unleashed by angry gods in the Himalayas—ferocious, uncontrollable, sweeping everything before it. He embellished its horror, and the little girl shivered. She never forgot it.

That's my life now, she thinks, an avalanche. She imagines gods of fearful visage glaring at her, then laughing evilly. Why? What did I do in a past life to merit this? Anger erupts. I can't be responsible for what I don't know! How can they punish me for that? Then for an instant, just an instant, Magandiya wonders, What about this life? Could I have done something differently? Was there another way, maybe? The image of Samavati intrudes, and the fragile moment of introspection is obliterated.

The arrow fiasco did it. The clumsy oaf! she curses her husband again. Clearly she needs to handle things herself. No slipups that way.

So now, all these years after the storytelling, Magandiya and her uncle are at it again. Culla Magandiya is frequently in Kosambi on some business or another, and because he has no proper residence in town and it would be unseemly for the queen to visit him, Udena has made an exception and has let the man visit her at her residence from time to time.

"I won't allow this often, mind you," the king had warned. "And I must be informed and agree to each visit."

Magandiya had smiled sweetly, agreeing with a demur nod. "Of course, my lord." But she had her victory.

Two days ago when Uncle visited, they created a new story. It's a story of how, once Samavati is gone, she will be the king's favorite. Vasuladatta is easily ignored; the king has been doing just that ever since Kumara died. It's as though he blames the mother for the crown prince's death. Yes, she, Magandiya, will be the favorite, and when that happens, she will generously reward her dear uncle with influence and great wealth, all he could ask for.

To divert suspicion from herself, Magandiya will have to be away at the time, of course. She'll visit her uncle's family in Benares, for Culla Magandiya and his wife are the closest things she's got to parents. Her own mother has died and her father is a blasted monk in the recluse's order. She hasn't seen him since she married. The last she heard, he was roaming somewhere near Savatthi. 'His treasure'— what dung! She believed the treasure line when she was a child, but now, when her father's often repeated endearment comes to mind, she knows the truth: It was flower-decked, jewel-ornamented, stinking dung!

He doesn't even care enough to visit me! By now, he probably thinks I'm dung, too, just like that imposter, his teacher. As she walks in the garden tonight, the unbearable pain of having been abandoned by her parents claws again at her stomach and pounds in her head.

Focus, damn it! she commands her thoughts, oblivious to the serenity of her surroundings. The pain of what is unbearable fuels her resolve to actualize what is possible.

She and Uncle have agreed to the plan. It's brilliant, even simple, but a few critical points still need to be worked out. She stops on the path as if to find answers. And she does.

How to make sure Udena is away from the palace? When he goes, a large retinue of servants and guards will accompany him, and Uncle and his men will be freer to do their work. Discussing the matter with Uncle Culla two days ago, Magandiya commented, "We'll go ahead in either case, whether he's here or not, but it would be much better if he weren't."

The problem is they can't wait until Udena leaves to act. They are going to say her dear aunt's health is failing, and above all she wants to see her niece. Since Auntie is unable to travel to Kosambi, Magandiya must go to her in Benares. That city, however, is a hundred miles away, a sixteen-day journey by ox caravan. The departure date needs to be announced in advance and preparations, made publicly and deliberately so as not to appear suspicious, especially in retrospect. But there's no way to predict her husband's movements that far ahead of time. He doesn't know them himself.

But predict they must. The pleasure park is their answer. With disgusting frequency, Udena spends days—and nights—there, north of town, with new mistresses. He usually explains his absence by saying he needs a break from the rigors of governance. Everyone understands that it's only a matter of time before he goes again.

How to nudge matters toward certainty? That's been her preoccupation. What leaps at her now, as though springing from the smooth, sandy path where she stands, is a certain needy brahmin couple with a very beautiful daughter. Introduce the girl to Udena, and he's guaranteed to be bewitched. Her face alights in triumph. From there, it's easy. The timing of his ultimate rhapsody can be arranged.

She envisions it: inviting the family to her residence, letting them know that their circumstances touch her heart and that she wants to help, and then making the proposal. Any qualms about proffering their daughter will be capped by their relief over the recompense. They'll be pathetically grateful. Brushing aside their thanks, she'll magnanimously stress that the longer the king's ardor is held at bay, the greater his royal generosity afterwards.

The family won't wonder about her motives. The king's prodigious sexual appetite is well known. His subjects take pride in it—an appetite befitting a king. They'll assume she's doing her duty to please her lord and husband. In fact, she'll say as much.

"It should be just about right if the assignation can be put off until after her next monthly period," she'll advise. Then she'll tactfully inquire as to the date of that biological event.

Ahhhhh! A lot of jabbering and maneuvering, but here's the point: Here she and Uncle can make their calculations. They can determine when to implement their plan. He'll have time to arrange

for a caravan in a seemly manner, and she'll be able to leave town before everything happens. It will serve Udena right when this hits him
while he's dallying! She turns toward her house with a smug smile.

November 12. Although Ghosita is often at the palace attending to government business, this is the first time in all the years since Samavati
married that he is visiting her. Until now, she has visited her steppar-
ents at their home, sometimes bringing the children. She has been
careful not to call on them too often, for she doesn't want to arouse
her husband's jealousy.

There is history here. Udena first saw Samavati when she was
sixteen, and he was immediately besotted. He proposed marriage.
Ghosita, who was already royal treasurer, not to mention a banker
and the wealthiest man in town aside from the king himself, was appalled, and he refused. The king retaliated by seizing his treasurer's
house and possessions and firing him from his royal post. Samavati
took the initiative to resolve the intolerable situation by agreeing to
his proposal on the condition that her stepfather be re-instated and
his possessions returned. It was double blackmail. Not a good way to
start a marriage.

The king and his treasurer have managed to work together
since then, but it has never been easy. Their relationship hasn't been
sweetened by the fact that Ghosita is patron of Ghosita's Park and
supports the bald-pated ones, those charlatans and spies. Though the
king frequently makes caustic allusions to the bhikkhus in Ghosita's
presence, he carefully avoids the confiscation topic. It is still raw between them.

When Ghosita heard about the arrow incident—word had
spread quickly—he was frantic to talk with his stepdaughter but knew
that now, of all times, she was unlikely to ask for permission to visit.
Then, he heard that Magandiya's uncle was allowed to visit her at
home. He chuckled silently at the transparency of the conflict that
played on the king's face when he made his request.

Does Ghosita know? Udena wondered as his treasurer stood before him that morning after council meeting, with a carefully composed neutral expression. Samavati and her stepfather hadn't met since the arrow incident, but that meant nothing. He's no fool. He must have heard. Then too, he would have heard that I asked (well, begged) Samavati for forgiveness.

As this little interior drama was unfolding, Ghosita very reasonably pointed out that a kinsman of the second queen was allowed to visit at her residence, so there was a precedent; it was the same thing. Except, he added to himself, the bastard tried to kill Samavati.

"That's the trouble with precedents," Udena grumbled. But deciding more was to be lost by denying the request than by acceding, he agreed. Ghosita nodded.

Now he sits on a low chair in Samavati's parlor, his granddaughters standing before him, his grandson on his lap and Samavati smiling from a low seat across. He has brought gifts, gold bangles for the girls and a toy for the prince, who is laughing and waving it in the air while trying to wriggle off of his grandfather's lap.

"I want one like Jina's!" Uppalavanna whines, eyeing her sister's bangle.

"Uppa!" her mother exclaims, "Where are your manners?"

Jinadatta sticks out her tongue at her older sister, who grimaces back at her. Samavati ignores the exchange, while Ghosita smiles and thinks, I knew I should have brought them alike.

The prince, meanwhile, who had suckled moments before his grandfather took him, stops. His eyes glaze and, arm motionless in the air, he vomits the milky contents of his stomach on himself and on Ghosita's fine robe. His nurse rushes apologetically to scoop up the child and hurry him off to the nursery, and the maid, who was serving sweetmeats, scurries to fetch a damp cloth. Samavati also apologizes, explaining that the prince has had an upset stomach since yesterday evening.

"As you can see, things are busy around here."

Ghosita waves her quiet and laughs. He loves it.

"All right, girls," Samavati says, turning to her daughters, "go on out to the garden and play now. Your grandfather and I want to talk."

She motions with her head to Mutta, who is in the room. Samavati and Ghosita watch in silence as the girls, still arguing, and maid depart. At the door, Uppalavanna turns suddenly and waves goodbye to her grandfather. He waves back, smiling. He will remember this wave in later days. He at dabs at his robe with the cloth provided by the other maid, hands it back, and gazes at Samavati as the woman departs.

"I've heard, of course."

She nods and sighs.

"You can leave and come with me. I'll protect you. Always."

"And the children?" she asks simply.

He nods. There's no way the children could come. How many times he has rethought this dilemma! No way, not without the royal guard, the whole army if necessary, on their tail. And she would never leave without them.

"The bastard doesn't deserve you!" He grows silent for a moment, then says, "I'm sorry, my dear. So, so sorry. I let it happen. If I'd been braver, if..."

"Shhh, Baba, shhhh. It was my decision, and I'm glad I made it. I have four wonderful children. They're the light in my life. What would I do without them? And there's you and Mata. And Khujj. So much love. So much good fortune."

What she isn't saying is present like an elephant between them. A murderous brute of a husband, a palace rife with fear and jealousy, Magandiya. Samavati has only hinted about Magandiya. She hasn't shared the half of it. His eyes fill with tears.

"Just say it and I'll arrange it," he concludes helplessly.

They smile sadly at each other. This is their karma, and they have no choice but inhabit it.

They work fast. Single-minded in her preparations for departure, Magandiya snaps out orders and counter-orders that send her maids scurrying. They are all too familiar with the stunning range of their mistress's distressed states, but they have never seen her like this. She is as taut as a bow strung too tightly. It is as though she were preparing for war, not Benares.

What's going on? Concern for her auntie's state of health doesn't seem to be the reason. If she's so concerned, then why in all these years has she never visited her or even talked much about her? Besides, when has the queen ever displayed love for anyone except herself?

Something doesn't make sense. And why is Culla Magandiya staying in town if his wife is so sick? The queen told one of her maids that he'd be detained here a while. And isn't it odd that the queen and her uncle have been meeting frequently when no female member of the king's family should be alone with a man other than the king himself? Does the king know?

Gossip is a favorite sport among servants. As Magandiya's maids toss the ball to and fro, word gets around the palace. Soon all the servants are speculating about the queen's strangeness.

Jenti is particularly suspicious. Though the queen hasn't shared the plot with her, Jenti is smart. Always ready to see angles by which she could benefit from her mistress's plans, she has more than once accepted generous bribes to help carry them out. Now she's wondering how to take advantage of whatever is happening.

Magandiya understands her maid's mind—how could it be otherwise when their minds are so similar? Jenti knows far too much. Magandiya has occasionally considered getting rid of the woman but has thought better of the idea: Jenti gone would be a greater danger than Jenti here. So she keeps the maid close. When she leaves for Benares, she'll take Jenti with her.

December 10. The royal caravan has been traveling for a week, jolting over the narrow, dusty ruts of hardened clay that serve as a road, for there isn't a major trade route between Kosambi and Benares. The four open ox-carts, a covered wagon and a small contingent of armed guards on horseback creep through countryside so monotonous it seems like they're going nowhere. A few days ago, the caravan ferried across at the confluence of the Yamuna and Ganges at Prayaga. It was a laborious undertaking. Now with the lethargic Ganges on their right, they plod through the flat terrain where all features are bleached white under a sun so fierce one has to squint. Flies forever assail them and farmers pause from their labors to gawk.

Magandiya, sitting with Jenti in the covered cart, listens to the squeaking axles and endures the bone-wrenching experience with ill grace. She'd be glad to never see another farmer. Or fly.

Tonight, the caravan is parked again by the roadside. Nighttime offers little respite from their travels because the tiny villages that dot the route can't accommodate a queen. It's winter and it's cold at night, so Magandiya and Jenti lie on a thin straw mattress in the covered wagon, huddled together under blankets for warmth, like children of a poor peasant family. The drivers and guards bed down in the open carts and on the ground, apparently impervious to the chill. The oxen and horses are hobbled nearby.

Now, after midnight, the only sound is the peacefully flowing river. The high moon, waxing, dispassionately surveys the little encampment below where all are asleep. All except Magandiya.

It is not the moonlight or the itchiness of the mattress or her maid's body odor and light snoring that keep her awake. Tonight is *the* night. Her mind is fixed on the drama now unfolding at the palace, envisioning it as though she were present herself. She wonders if the king is at the palace or at his pleasure park with his new mistress, the whore. She decides to trust that matters are working as planned.

She imagines her uncle's two lackeys stealing into the grounds using the secret entrance that has been opened in the wall behind her residence. They are crossing the short distance to Samavati's residence, their path lit by the moonlight.

Even the moon is on my side!

One stumbles on a protruding root. 'Dung!' he says.

'Chutt! Shut up, you idiot!' whispers the other. They walk on in silence.

Since no walls obstruct the way between the queens' houses, the route is easy. They are stealing over to Samavati's garden shed, where yesterday Uncle saw to it that vessels of oil, cloth, and unlit torches were stashed. No one ever looks in the shed except the gardener, and Magandiya made sure that he'd be called away for a few strategic days.

Now the men are getting the supplies from the shed, which is unlocked, and move toward Samavati's house, which they have been assured will also be unlocked. Though the harem's quarters in the women's building *are* locked at night—as much to keep the harem in as to keep intruders out—there is no need to lock the queens' residences and ancillary buildings. The grounds are securely guarded, and Udena knows that his queens won't escape and that no man in his right mind would try to violate them.

Because there are several jars of oil, lugging them and the other supplies from the shed to the residence requires two trips. But now all is ready for entry. The trespassers have never been in Samavati's residence, but they know the floor plan. Magandiya, who has never been in the house either but has her way of obtaining things, provided a sketch.

They transfer the supplies inside, and then, as per plan, stealthily move from one designated location to another, draping cloths on furniture, around posts and elsewhere on the ground floor of the wooden structure. Then they dowse the cloths, taking extra care to move the heavy clay oil vessels quietly.

Magandiya envisions them stealing into the kitchen area, each with an oil-soaked torch in hand and putting it to the embers in the hearth. These take an age to light—dung! The men fear it's not going to happen, that their plan will be ruined. But now, success! Ready. One slip at this point and they'll set the whole place on fire, themselves included. There are no slips.

They are stealing into the central area on the ground floor and—now!—quickly, quickly setting fire to each group of rags. No more silence. "Run, run!" they shout as they dash along their escape route to the door and safety, not caring if they wake up the sleeping women on the second floor or the children and their maids on the first. It's too late.

The ground floor and the stairwell, well doused, are in flames. There's no way the women can run down to safety. The windows are high, designed to let heat, not people, out. Jumping from a second floor window would mean probable death.

Oh, yes, the children! Magandiya remembers them, and the sequence unfolding in her mind stops. She has avoided thinking about them. Now though, for a moment, the heart of the mother she is not aches. Such sweet young things! Then she moves on. It can't be helped, it's their karma.

Switching to the scene on the second floor, Magandiya wonders who wakes up first. Samavati? Probably not. Probably it's the witch Khujjuttara. Now, it's only a matter of seconds, flames roaring up the stairwell, bursting into the women's quarters. Everything is on fire—walls, furnishings, women's clothing, bodies. She sees the panic—women running wildly, screaming, living torches. She focuses on Samavati—where is all that sweetness now? A smile crosses Magandiya lips as Samavati's panic and the women's screams linger in her twisted mind.

Samavati, two of her children and members of her household are immolated. Princess Jinadatta alone survives. The nursery and children's quarters on the main floor were aflame in seconds. Mutta, who loved the princess as her own child, shielded her. When a flaming splinter landed on the girl's shoulder, Mutta brushed it aside; then she put the child on her shoulders so that she could reach one of the high windows and scramble out. She was small enough to wriggle through. The area was aflame before Mutta and any of the others could escape. Jinadatta will bear the burn scar on her right shoulder to the end of her life, a reminder of her grievous losses on that terrible night, the details of which she can't remember.

Magandiya's last thoughts before she falls asleep on the itchy mattress next to Jenti are about the fetish she placed in Samavati's bedchamber many weeks ago.

And I thought it was a failure. Silly me! It's done its work.

CHAPTER 10.
THE TASTE OF ASHES

December 10-11. The palace grounds are pandemonium when Bharadvaja arrives. He was notified by a panicky messenger shortly after the fire erupted, and he raced to the palace from his mansion a few blocks away. Servants are shouting and rushing to the burning structure and halt at a distance before it, large-eyed and helpless. Many heard the women's screams—sounds that would ever haunt them. By the time Bharadvaja arrives, there are no more screams, only the collapsing structure and the smell of burning everywhere, burning timbers, burning bodies. Nauseated by the horror and stench, they stand frozen, as does Bharadvaja, unable to speak or even think.

There are no adequate means to combat the blaze. It's too late to save anyone. Bharadvaja, who recovers quickly, realizes that the fire will burn itself out without further damage because it is a windless night—thank the gods for that! As he retires to his office in the main building of the palace, the flames still roaring, his outrage mounts. In the king's absence, he, the chaplain, the first among royal ministers, is responsible for the efficient running of the palace and for the safety of its inhabitants. He has failed!

He is not a man to let emotions interfere with strategy. Once in his office, he summons a messenger to carry the news to the king at the pleasure park. Then, sitting on the single chair in the sparsely furnished room, he closes his eyes and, gently pinching his lower lip between thumb and forefinger, thinks.

One sharp knock on the door of the royal bedchamber arouses Udena from the warmth of his new mistress's body. They have been enjoying each other in the seclusion of the pleasure park for two days, but now his servant bursts into the room. "Great king, great king!"

Udena jolts upright.

"The queen, Queen Samavati, your children...they're... a fire... everybody...," he stutters incoherently, mumbling his way into silence. His shocked face tells the story.

In the flickering glow of the torch held by the servant, the two stare at each other blankly. Then the king manages to croak, "What? How?" while the woman beside him reaches for the bed cloth to cover her nakedness.

Jumping from bed and grabbing his cloak, Udena follows the servant down to the foyer where the palace messenger is waiting. He listens to the man, then mutters, "I must go. I must go." He doesn't feel like a king. He wishes he could curl up in a bed and let somebody else act for him. He wishes this weren't real. He wishes...

But no. Like a king, Udena turns to his servant, who is standing behind him and instructs the man with a steadiness he doesn't feel to have the carriage prepared immediately. As he hurries toward the bedchamber to collect his clothes, he throws a further instruction over his shoulder, "And make sure someone escorts the lady home safely."

In his distress, he has forgotten his new mistress's name. Nor does he think about her for weeks afterwards, and when he does finally, she's so closely associated with the tragedy that he doesn't want to see her again. She and her family, who had been anticipating the benefits of a royal liaison, lament the calamitous timing. When it is discovered two months later that the girl is pregnant and has to be hastily married off to save the family's honor, they petition the king, and he grants the newlyweds a generous stipend to assist with the child's upkeep. So all is not lost.

Bharadvaja sits in his office nearly motionless. That this catastrophe occurred on his watch is intolerable. He never approved of Samavati's Buddhist convictions, but he will avenge her death and that of her children and servants, no matter what the cost. He devises a plan.

It doesn't take much thinking. Volatile as the king is and despite the fact that he recently tried to kill his wife, Bharadvaja is certain Udena didn't instigate these murders—and he's sure that this *is* murder, not an accident. Magandiya. Manipulative, jealous, desperate. Everyone knows her hatred for Samavati. It takes no subtlety to surmise that she so aroused Udena's suspicions that he was driven to rash action in the arrow incident. In many ways, he's a very simple man. Of course she's behind the fire! Who else could it be?

In this supremely important matter, they need to proceed carefully. It must be concluded in a manner that leaves no doubt about the king's sovereignty and his uncompromising demand for justice. And no doubt about the culprit.

He will advise the king—no, no, he will *consult* with him—about the best way to trap her into confessing, and they will decide the appropriate punishment once she does. In fact, he already has the punishment in mind. He is sure Udena will agree.

Soon they will send a messenger to recall her. There is no point doing that now because a messenger on horseback would overtake the caravan, which should still be on the road. That would be awkward logistically, and it would alarm her. What would she do? Run? Maybe. He will dispatch the messenger after she's reached Benares; the party will return at normal pace and in full dignity—and he will be waiting, like a spider in its web.

When, two and a half hours later, the royal carriage pulls up to the main palace entrance, Bharadvaja meets his sovereign. Udena emerges bent like an old man. He is shocked and incoherent and is in no condition to make plans, as Bharadvaja had foreseen. They move into the palace, the king leaning on his chaplain's arm, their heads together, already in consultation.

They walk up to the king's private chambers. It's the first time Bharadvaja has been here. After offering condolences, he wastes no time. "Great king, it's clear that Queen Magandiya is responsible for this atrocity." Udena nods, having come to the same conclusion.

Cool and precise as usual, Bharadvaja explains, "She must confess, but without being forced. Once she does, you must make an example of her that all will remember. Such a blow against your honor, such an atrocity against your family, cannot be tolerated."

He argues forcefully that the safety of the whole kingdom depends on how the king handles this outrage. The people must be assured that their sovereign is just and is in control. He outlines his plan. Udena listens and nods.

"I'm only sorry that such drastic punishment needs to be levied against a brahmin," Bharadvaja adds. Brahmins are regarded as sacrosanct and by tradition are exempt from corporal punishment.

Even in his shock, enough of a politician is left in Udena for cynicism. Right, he'd rather the culprit were from my class!

The chaplain guesses his king's thoughts but says nothing. It would serve no purpose to mention the enduring rivalry between the two dominant classes, brahmins and warriors.

Cynicism notwithstanding, Udena appreciates that he, a warrior king, will soon flaunt Vedic law and exercise his power over brahmins. Yes! And he'll deal once and for all with that sorceress in his midst—as a great king, a maharaja, should.

But what kind of maharaja am I? he wonders as desolation reclaims his heart. On one night, I've lost a wife, a greatly beloved wife, and two of my precious children, including the little prince. Bharadvaja has informed him that Princess Jinadatta escaped.

After the conference, the king retires to his bedchamber, and there for the first time in years, he cries. At sunup, a broken man visits the site of queen's residence. A scattering of servants is present;

some are crying quietly. As the king approaches, they part to let him pass. He stays only briefly.

Returning to his quarters in a daze, Udena allows himself to be bathed as usual by his servants, all of whom are struggling against tears. He doesn't notice. Then, he sits in a chair in his bedchamber, lost in a vacuum until the noonday meal is brought to him. He can't eat. At mid-afternoon, a servant arouses him. He is to attend the emergency council meeting that Bharadvaja has convened.

December 11. It began with the smell that spread like a disease. Now the smell of catastrophe is everywhere. Word flew among vendors bringing their goods to the just opening markets, and then among the awakening households, neighbor to neighbor in town and in the suburbs.

Stunned, people move into the streets, needing to talk and share their confusion. How could this happen? Though most have never seen Queen Samavati, all know of her and her children. They know of her goodness, her beauty, her devotion to the Buddha, and of course they know her as mother of the new crown prince. The king is the essence of the state, and they pay homage to him as citizens must, but the queen, *this* queen, represents continuity and all the qualities of the heart that they cherish. Samavati, they love. There is weeping and lamenting among all classes. The business of the day nearly comes to a halt.

Ghosita is preparing to go to the business district and is wondering about the odor that has seeped into the house when he hears shouts and someone banging on the door downstairs. A servant opens to see the neighbor's young son, standing pale and breathless.

Hearing the boy's stammered news, the servant leaves him on the doorstep with the door open and rushes up to his master's chamber. "Master, Master, Queen Samavati..." he begins. He pauses for breath, then starts again, "Master, last night there was a fire at the palace and Queen Samavati..."

Ghosita hears no more. He knows. His breath stops. He drops helplessly onto the bed and puts his head in his hand. His wife rushes into the room. Still in her nightclothes with a shawl around her shoulders, her long greying hair tumbling down her back, she sits beside her husband. Together they listen as the servant tells them what little he knows. Together the couple weeps, holding each other closely. The servant is embarrassed. Such intimacy between husband and wife is not to be viewed by others.

Though Samavati was their adopted daughter, Ghosita and his wife love her as their own. She and her parents came to Kosambi seeking refuge from the plague that was devastating their town in 449. Shortly after their arrival, both parents died of complications caused by the plague, leaving Samavati, then fifteen years old, orphaned and vulnerable. No woman is safe without a male protector, and a young, unmarried woman, especially a beautiful young woman, is in great danger.

Shortly after she was orphaned, Ghosita happened to meet her and was touched not only by her beauty, but also by her intelligence and sensitivity. He adopted her, as was the custom of the day. He informed his wife after his decision rather than consulted with her, patriarchal prerogative also being the custom of the day. He relied on Sakula's loving nature and strong maternal instincts to welcome Samavati, and he was right. She immediately took the frightened young woman into her heart.

Not so all their children. There were three children in the Ghosita family, two sons and a daughter, all teenagers. The older son, at nineteen, was newly married and lived with his wife in his parents' home, which was large enough to accommodate a small town. He immediately accepted the orphaned girl as a sister and grew fond of her.

His younger brother and sister, however, felt threatened. Always close, they allied against their new sister, although subtly, for there was too much love in the Ghosita household to permit overt jealousy. The boy, a year younger than Samavati, was at the age when rich boys of his class were beginning to fixate on women, the age when there was still much bragging but little action. Samavati's presence made him feel his youth and awkwardness. How to relate? The daughter, meanwhile, was deeply jealous. Samavati's beauty and sweetness, so far outshone her own that she felt positively ugly, for she was too young to know that her own beauty would blossom in a few years. Moreover both brother and sister feared that Samavati's presence in their family would reduce their eventual inheritance, though as the offspring wealthiest family in a very prosperous city, they stood to inherit fortunes worthy of royalty, new sister or not.

Samavati felt their covert hostility and tried to win them with kindness. She succeeded with the younger brother. He began to feel less awkward as his masculine powers developed, though he would always regret that his stepsister could never be the object of them. The daughter, however, grew more jealous, for even as her own feminine beauty budded, she was no match for Samavati.

In any event, Samavati counted herself supremely lucky to be where she was. No one could ever replace her own parents in her affections, but she grew to love her adopted parents. Sakula, who was as efficient at running her household as her husband was at banking, saw to it that Samavati lacked for nothing, and both parents, as far as was in their power, surrounded her with affection.

Now, having delivered the ghastly news, Ghosita's servant leaves his master and mistress to their grief and returns downstairs. Finding the neighbor boy gone, he starts to shut the door when the king's messenger arrives. He brings news of the calamity and of an emergency council meeting this afternoon. The servant assures him that his master knows about the former and that he'll inform him of the meeting. Neither considers it amiss that the envoy isn't granted access to the treasurer.

Still, palace residents stand, viewing the horror, the heart-wrenching absence of those who hours ago made their lives here, the cruel, cruel vacancy. A few observe in muted voices that the gods' protection kept the fire from spreading to Queen Magandiya's residence. Vasuladatta's mansion probably wasn't in danger because there was no wind, but if there had been? What would have happened to the whole palace then? The prospects are too awful to think about. Most, however, can't yet bring themselves to talk or think much. Soon there will be remembrances, but now, now, they are locked in shock and tears and wordless grief for Samavati, her children and their friends and dear ones who were maids in her household.

They are joined one by one by members of the king's council. Ghosita, who has canceled business for the day—and will do so for several days hence—arrives with Sakula. Three other ministers are already here, standing amid the servants. The ministers nod to each other but don't speak.

As the sun barely surmounts the horizon, a lay adherent who lives nearby rushes to the monastic park and bangs loudly on the massive wooden gate. "Venerables, news, news! Let me in!" Although the monks rise early to meditate, they usually don't unbolt the gate until they are ready for almsround. Now, two of them hurry to open. Candana hears the commotion and steps onto his portico. He waits and watches as the two monks and householder hasten toward him with their terrible burden.

Candana slept little last night. A sense of foreboding enveloped him. What was this? Was his palsy showing in a new way? The uneasiness didn't feel connected to the disease, but what did he know? Maybe this was a natural progression—from uncontrollable physical symptoms to uncontrollable emotional ones. The growing intensity of the smell confirmed his unease. Something was very wrong.

Hearing the news, Candana crumbles inside for a moment. It's too much to take in. Samavati's frightened expression the last time he saw her flashes before him. Her hurried, whispered request for a meeting. How he wishes he could have talked to her! Maybe he could have averted this tragedy somehow.

He looks away from the monks and householder and then back. What can he say? A few forlorn words that are supposed to convey wisdom and comfort, which he himself doesn't feel?

He simply nods and, as they leave, he absentmindedly watches their backs and wonders if Samavati had been afraid of Udena. That's possible. The man is insensitive to the point of cruelty. Candana knows the arrow story—who doesn't—and he wonders, Now what? Only three things are clear to Candana: He needs to send a message to the Buddha. Asoka, who is eager to travel, will surely carry it. And he must get on with the day.

On almsrounds, the bhikkhus encounter horror-stricken towns-people, who repeat the story over and over. And they ask questions. How could their devout and beloved queen have such bad karma? Why did the children have to die? What does the tragedy say about the royal family? Is it cursed? And what about their own lives—what's the karmic lesson for them? The bhikkhus can't answer, but towns-people don't really want answers. They want consolation, and this the monks provide in abundance.

Because most of the bhikkhus return to the monastic park well after noon, they decide to bypass for today the monastic rule requiring that they finish eating before noon. Compassion takes precedence over rules. Even Pindola agrees here.

December 11. Members of the king's council gather in the palace council hall. The mighty of the kingdom are subdued as they talk among

themselves, awaiting the arrival of the king and Bharadvaja. When Ghosita arrives, they offer sympathy, which he accepts with a nod, barely aware of the exchanges.

Ghosita is frozen. He is locked onto one subject: Udena. The murderous bastard! The swine! Who else could it have been? Hatred smothers him like a beached fish smothered by air. Follower of the Buddha or not, Ghosita intends murder—the consequences of the act in this lifetime or another be damned!

Udena enters the council chamber with Bharadvaja following behind. The ministers rise and bow. They are shocked. They've seen their king in many moods—boisterous, demanding, inflamed with anger, even dead drunk (in fact, frequently dead drunk), but they've never seen him like this—absent. The man simply isn't here. Like a husband who has lost his beloved wife and two children.

Udena takes his seat without glancing at any of the ministers and continues to gaze at nothing, while leaving the conduct of the meeting to his chaplain, who is calm, cold as Himalayan ice.

Bharadvaja states that there is no business today, no agenda beyond expressing the grief they are all experiencing. All nod. In fact, however, the chaplain has an unacknowledged aim: To set the ministers straight. Though the thought hasn't occurred to the king, Bharadvaja knows that they might justifiably suspect him of the crime. One look at the man will dispel that notion. Udena is his own best defense.

Ghosita realizes that regicide won't be necessary, after all. For the first time ever, he recognizes a common bond with this man.

Bharadvaja also wants to affirm that the fire wasn't an accident. Wooden structures often burn in the Middle Land—it only takes one spark from a kitchen fire in this dry season to start a blaze—but that's not what happened here. The chaplain wasn't surprised when his suspicion was confirmed earlier today.

"An oil container was found near the back door of the queen's residence," he discloses. "Before this is over, there will be further evidence of criminal activity—there's no doubt about it."

With the king ruled out as perpetrator, there is only one obvious candidate. Bharadvaja has no intention of disclosing that he and the king are already convinced that Magandiya is responsible and that they have a plan to trap her. This must remain entirely confidential. He simply warns the ministers against public speculation about the matter.

"Be assured, honorable sirs, we will pursue this! We will find the perpetrators and punish them to the full extent. I'm sure you appreciate the delicacy of this matter. It's of critical importance that you don't engage in loose talk. That would harm our chances of resolving the case in a just manner, and I know you all wish for a just resolution—you wish it personally, you wish it for the sake of our late, esteemed queen, and you wish it for the stability of the kingdom. So we need your full cooperation and discretion."

Bharadvaja seldom resorts to eloquence, for he assumes the cogency of his points needs no enhancement. But on this occasion so fraught with emotion, he chooses to broaden the force of his appeal. He looks intently from man to man, eliciting their assent.

He closes the meeting, "Sirs, we've all experienced a great shock. The king especially is in need of solitude. We'll adjourn now, but we'll keep you informed."

As the king leaves the chamber, followed at a respectful distance by his ministers, Bharadvaja approaches Ghosita and says, "Treasurer Ghosita, may I have a word with you? Just a moment," raising one precise finger.

Ghosita follows him to a corner of the chamber. The chaplain turns to him and says in a voice that is almost compassionate, "I want to express my condolences and sympathy."

Bharadvaja has considered how he would feel if one of his sons were murdered. Of course, they're different cases: Samavati was a female and an adopted daughter and, even though she was a queen, she was from the merchant class. So is Ghosita. Still...

"My sincere condolences," he repeats, then, looking Ghosita in the eyes, declares, "I assure you we'll find the culprits. It may take some time. Please be patient. We *will* find them and bring them to the king's justice." He purposely uses the plural, for clearly more than one person was involved. "I'm technically responsible, you know. In the king's absence, I was responsible for the safety of palace residents, and I will not rest until this matter is justly resolved."

His voice is steely and his eyes, hard. Ghosita, who has never been on friendly terms with him, is sure he will fulfill his pledge, and he's relieved. That's all. At the moment, he's too numb for thought.

In the late afternoon of this terrible day, Udena instructs one of his maidservants to bring his daughter to him in his private chamber. The woman, whom Jinadatta doesn't know, fetches her from Vasuladatta's residence where she has been staying since last night. She enters the chamber, bewildered and frightened. She has never been here and isn't sure how to act. It's as though her father were a stranger. As Jinadatta stands hesitantly in the doorway, the maid at her side puts a gentle hand on her un-bandaged shoulder and nudges her forward, but the girl resists shyly. Udena rises from his chair, goes down on one knee and extends his arms. Jinadatta runs to him, "Daddy!"

Udena has hugged his children, but never like this. For a long time, they hold each other in a wordless embrace; then, he takes her small hands in his, and he talks and she talks, and it doesn't matter what they say. Before Jinadatta leaves, her father promises her, "I'll take you to see the horses as often as you like—how does that sound?" The child nods gravely and emphatically.

December 12. Asoka's ankle has healed. Sirivaddha has given his approval: He is fit to travel. He would have left a couple of days ago but for the fire. Now Candana's request adds a sense of mission to his

travels. He's leaving today with something helpful he can do in this calamity. Maybe my accident happened so I'd be here to carry the message. You never know when bad things lead to good, he muses, unaware that instead of simply viewing events as they are, he is concocting an appealing meaning in which he is the centerpiece.

Word has it that the Buddha is at Jeta's Grove, the large monastic center outside of Savatthi, two hundred miles to the north. In these days when writing isn't in general use, wandering monks serve as messengers, verbally conveying the whereabouts of their brothers and other important information. A haphazard system, it works remarkably well. A couple of monks passing through Kosambi recently reported that the Blessed One was at Savatthi. So that's where Asoka is heading. He'll walk along the trade route that runs north-south through Kosambi, the route that has helped make that city the important metropolis that it is.

Parting is a sadness for Asoka and Candana. Who knows when they'll meet again? Monks learn to accept such partings as teachings. They are the kind of loss that life regularly presents, and, when accepted with grace rather than grasping, they are small steps on the path to liberation. Both take a small step when they say goodbye at the gate, performing anjali to each other, equal to equal, friend to friend.

Asoka's step is a lot smaller than Candana's, though. He is eager to leave. The fire has deepened his aversion to Kosambi. *The place has bad karma—I knew it before I got here!*

Too bad the city is situated on the trade route, he thinks as he walks out the gate. *It'll be hard to avoid in the future. Unless I go around and walk through the jungle.* Being city-bred, he can't gladly embrace that animal-infested prospect. He vows to make future stopovers in the area brief and, like before, will stay at Kukkuta's Park. Candana will hear, of course, and that will be hurtful. He sighs. *Kukkuta's Park isn't much of an improvement, anyway. Some of the monks there participated in the mess fourteen years earlier.*

Well, it can't be helped. I'm just sorry about Candana. I'll miss him.

But as he exits the city's north gate, his face set toward Savatthi bearing a message for his teacher, Asoka leaves Kosambi and his sad thoughts behind. He is a happy bhikkhu. On the road again!

December 15. "Minister Ghosita!" Candana moves out onto his portico. He has just finished an afternoon nap and is carrying his sitting mat. He planned to meditate in the warm, angled, winter light. Now, watching him approach, Candana inquires softly "Anupama?" using his first name.

Ghosita says nothing. He mechanically steps up onto the tamped-earth porch, and Candana, raising a palm in a one-moment gesture, goes back inside for the other mat. They sit. Still Ghosita is silent. Candana waits.

Few townspeople come to the monastic park on days like today when there is no public talk, and they almost never arrive in the afternoon. Ghosita, however, is welcome any time.

Finally in a pinched, low voice, he says, "I did it. It's my fault." He speaks haltingly as thoughts that have been long buried grope their way into audibility. He caved in under the king's blackmail. He was afraid, not strong enough to say no. Recrimination mounts and his words gain velocity and volume.

"I let her marry him. I knew it would bring no good, I knew it! It was a disaster from the start, but I sacrificed her anyway! I killed her, my daughter! That's what I did, killed her!"

Candana knows the story. Everybody does, and no one blames him.

Gripped by self-condemnation, his body is rigid. At last, words exhausted, he slumps with his elbows on his knees and his face cradled in his hands. Tears flow and flow.

When they subside, Candana speaks. He could say, "Friend, it's your karma, it's the consequence of your actions, and these you must bear." But he doesn't. Instead, he say, "It's not your fault. It's the fault of being alive. Living means we must act and there are consequences to our actions. If you hadn't agreed, your family would have been driven into poverty and maybe would even have been in physical danger. She knew that. She wanted you to say "yes." You had no good choice. Leave off with the guilt, Anupama. Guilt only harms you. It will devour you like a tiger does its prey. Grieve, as you must, but be kind now. Be kind to yourself first of all, my friend."

Ghosita, with his head still in his hands, doesn't reply. They sit for a long time. Finally standing with effort, he anjalis, takes one step backward in deference, then turns and walks away. Candana gazes at the departing figure, shaking his head.

Surely there's something I could have said to ease his heart. He reminds himself that people hear only what they're ready to hear, but this bit of wisdom makes no headway against the knot in his belly.

Ghosita's feet automatically take him along the well-trod path to the simsapa grove, the place where he often retreats for solace. He wanders there, stopping to peer at the ground, as though comfort might materialize amid the dappled light and brittle leaves under foot. Then he retraces his steps aimlessly, enters the assembly hall and sits while, in the oncoming evening, bhikkhus file in for meditation. Some nod to him. He doesn't see. Surrounded by the robed ones, Ghosita passes the next two hours neither present nor not present.

December 21. Once the ruins were cold, palace groundsmen searched for human remains. It was sad, sad business, and messy. They worked in the oily sludge that used to be human and charred bones. If they'd been Vedic priests, they might have theologized, saying the bodies had been consecrated by the holy flames of Agni, the fire god. That is, in fact, the priestly pronouncement. There are no bodies to cremate; the remains are to be regarded as holy relics.

Being simple men, however, the groundsmen had no comments. There was only desolation, and they were often overwhelmed as they worked. They knew Samavati's maidservants and were kin to three of them. They loved the gentle queen and occasionally saw her children playing in the garden.

From time to time amid the digging and sifting, workers found themselves in tears or simply standing vacantly. The brother of one of Samavati's maids, a young man, stopped frequently. He took refuge on a nearby stool, which hadn't been touched by the fire, and sat clutching one of the shiny river stones that were scattered nearby, squeezing it as if to squeeze his sister back to life. Others came to him and put a hand on his shoulder, trying to comfort him. They spoke with their supervisor who excused him from this duty. The others continued, helping each other through. They tried to be thorough at the grisly work, but long afterwards, though the smell disappeared, bits of bone would be found here. No one blamed them.

While some of the children's remains were identifiable, there was no way to tell which were Samavati's. So all the remains, those of her eight servants included, are to be equally honored. To hold them, the bone fragments as well as what seems to be ashes, eleven wooden coffins, small boxes really, have been hastily constructed and a simple wooden altar is erected at the site and fenced around.

This morning a royal memorial ceremony is being held. Several horse-drawn carriages bearing the king, Queen Vasuladatta and her two daughters, Jinadatta, Bharadvaja, Ghosita and other government ministers and dignitaries solemnly make their way to the ghat where the ceremony is to occur. Queen Magandiya is absent, having only just arrived in Benares. Bharadvaja calculates she won't receive the command to return for another four or five days. Just as well.

Heading the royal procession is a carriage bearing only an ornate funereal vessel holding token remains. The vessel is prominently displayed so that citizens gathered along the route can pay tribute. The import of the carriage is underscored by the fact that it is drawn by the white stallion, which all recognize as the state horse.

Because the citizenry was informed in advance, the number of spectators grows rapidly as the procession moves through the streets toward the south gate. Unlike most gatherings, this throng is subdued.

Their destination is the sacred Yamuna River. Immersion in its waters is, as all know, an act of purification, a cleansing of contaminating influences. It is here that the funereal urn is to be buried.

The royal family and dignitaries leave the carriages and descend to the lower steps of the ghat, while citizens at the head of the crowd surge onto the upper steps and others fan out behind. Those on the steps are kept at a respectful distance from the illustrious ones by royal guards.

Once all are in place, the penetrating voice of the chaplain soars in Vedic chants that command silence. Even rowdy urchins in the street are brought to a standstill. When the chants cease, the Venerable Candana, who was invited in honor of the queen's devotion to the Buddha, utters prayers. And two Vedic priests have been rowed in a skiff to the middle of the river where, intoning prayers, they scatter flowers; then they immerse the funereal vessel, thereby symbolically blessing not only these remains, but all of them.

During the past few chaotic days, Udena has conceived a memorial plan of his own, grander, more visible, more enduring than this one, like nothing there has ever been before. He is bursting to announce it to the assembled crowd and the assembled dead, whose presence oppresses him like a mountain sitting on his chest. He needs to demonstrate that he loved his wife and children and that he is a benevolent king who cared for all in the queen's service, down to the very least of them.

But he must wait. He must wait because announcing it now would jeopardize their scheme for trapping Magandiya. So he, who is unaccustomed to restraint even in trivial matters, stands on the ghat silently watching the funereal urn sink beneath the water's glittering surface and feeling that he can't endure one more moment of this pressure.

Candana, too, is struggling. He walked to the palace early this morning, He won't eat until after the ceremony, which will probably be well after midday. He asked Sati to set food aside for him. At one time, fasting was a strength, like an extra muscle he had developed. If food weren't present, he didn't need to eat. But as he ages and with the palsy eroding his energy, he needs food regularly, even if it means eating after noon. Monastic rules makes allowances for sickness, and Candana thinks wryly, I fit into that category.

By the time he reached the palace this morning, Candana was tired. Then he, Bharadvaja and the two priests occupied the same carriage. Monastic rules stipulate that bhikkhus must travel by foot except in the case of illness, when ox-drawn or hand-drawn carts are permitted. There is no mention of royal horse-drawn carriages. It was unthinkable, however, for Candana to refuse to be part of the procession.

The ride is Candana and Bharadvaja's first face-to-face encounter in years. Neither relish it. Aside from the fact that both men are members of the great Bharadvaja clan, they have little in common.

There's much suffering in life, Candana reflects, invoking the Blessed Ones' first noble truth as he sits in the carriage across from the royal chaplain, who is studiously averting his gaze.

Rather than bonding them, their common clan heritage is a divisive factor. While being a Bharadvaja is central to the chaplain's worldview, Candana has outgrown clan identification. The chaplain can't forgive him that. Equally he can't forgive Candana for adopting the Sakiyan's Dhamma. In its opposition to blood sacrifice and its disregard for class distinctions, it undermines key elements in the sacred Vedic traditions. It's an outrage.

Maybe the worst affront of all, however, is that Bharadvaja feels, without an iota of justification, that Pindola's decision to go forth as a bhikkhu, to adopt the same unspeakable heresy, is Candana's fault. Even though he recognizes political advantage for himself in his son's choice, he can barely contain his jealousy. He suspects that this recluse has more influence with Pindola than he does.

Candana is grateful for their silence. As they ride to and from the river, he hopes his infirmity doesn't show. By the return trip, both of his hands are shaking. Tremors in his right hand have been lurking under the skin for weeks, and now, in his exhaustion, they've broken through for the first time. Will Bharadvaja notice? Or is he too involved with his own thoughts? He buries his hands in a fold in his robe and tries to relax. He has learned that tensing up, willing stillness, only produces greater trembling. More urgently, however, he is concerned whether he'll have the strength to endure the private ceremony that is about to take place on the palace grounds.

The royal procession, shorn of the public component, gathers at Samavati's altar. The remainder of the relics was ritually washed with water from the Yamuna, then placed in the coffins. With lids now closed, these are lined up around the altar, and next to each, a hole has been dug. One by one, amidst more chants by Bharadvaja and prayers from Candana, the coffins, two of them tiny, are buried. Udena places the first shovelful of earth, then the groundsmen, still on duty at this terrible site, quickly finish the job as all watch. Here the coffins will disintegrate over time, as will the bones they contain.

Udena takes such comfort as he can from the knowledge that this burial is temporary. His glorious plan, which he'll soon reveal, will change all this.

As the ceremony wears on, Candana feels increasingly faint. The energy behind his prayers dwindles. His voice softens, and he has to make an effort to project. Bharadvaja notices his struggle and experiences a frisson of gladness for whatever has caused it.

Afterwards Candana accomplishes the walk back to the monastic park more by will than muscle. Too exhausted to eat, he lies on his cot. The calico cat comes around and patiently waits, sitting in boat position next to her water bowl under a shrub near the hut. Noticing her, he smiles.

"What? Hasn't anyone fed you? Or do you just like coming around here?" He goes out, gives her some of the food the bhikkhus have brought for him; then he eats the rest.

He can't remain abbot much longer. This is clear. An abbot doesn't often have days like today, with its exertion and departure from routine, but even this one day has made the point: He's not up to it. His thoughts turn toward naming a successor.

CHAPTER 11

A SPLENDID ILLUSION

*D*ecember 25. She has been at her uncle's house for only a few days when the king's messengers arrive. It is morning and there are two of them, big, burly men. Udena, who had recovered enough to think, didn't want to take a chance by sending only one. You never knew what hazards might be encountered on the road. The less grimy of the pair now walks to the door, while the other waits on the road, holding his horse.

When she hears the message, Magandiya feigns horror, but she is terrified. She didn't expect to be called home! Her thoughts had jumped from the fire to the delicious part: Udena's gratitude to her for dealing with his murderous wife. Now, instead of an adoring husband, here is his command. That's what it is, a command—there's no arguing with it. She is to return as soon as possible. She is to take her maid and only her most essential baggage. The rest can follow.

Still tired from the journey, not to mention the tension, Magandiya wants to gag. She is being treated like a child. No, like a prisoner!

Magandiya's aunt, who is in the room, is oblivious to her niece's agony as well as to her own reputed ill health. She anxiously inquires about her husband. "He should have been here by now. Did you overtake him on the road?"

Magandiya told her that Uncle had been detained in Kosambi for a few days, but would be arriving soon. "It's been so long since I've seen you, darling, that I went on ahead. I had to come. I've missed you, and the king is generous. He always grants my wishes." And with a wistful smile, "You are my dearest family, you know."

Auntie was surprised. Since when? Where did this affection come from? She has never been fond of her niece, who, in her view, possesses the warmth of a snake, but you never know. Snakes change their skin; maybe Magandiya has changed, she reasoned rather imprecisely. In any case, being a good-hearted and emotional woman, she pulled her niece to her broad bosom and hugged the poor dear as though she were her own daughter.

Now, though, hugs aren't on her mind. Auntie is concerned when the messenger replies in the negative. Has something happened to him?

Magandiya is panicky. If he's not on the road, where the hell is he? This gets worse and worse. She stops listening as the man outlines his orders. Details about procuring carts and so forth—all of which should take a few days; then they are to start out immediately. She barely hears Auntie's handsome offer. While they are here, they can stay in the servants' quarters, she says. Her house, though not grand, can easily accommodate two more. Housing a queen and two of the king's messengers is an obligation Auntie happily assumes.

Magandiya's thoughts scramble one on top of the other like a troupe of monkeys after the same banana. What if Udena suspects? Or—oh, gods!—what if he knows? Maybe the intruders were caught and confessed. Maybe Uncle was imprisoned, too! Stay calm! Stand straight. Hands at your side. No expression on your face, she sternly commands herself. But disobedient thoughts clamor, Run! Run now while you can! A frantic glance at the messenger informs her this is not a viable option.

And once back in Kosambi, then what? The secret entrance behind her house takes on new significance. That's my route. What about doing it before I see him? Afterwards could be too late. Uh-oh! If the intruders were caught, wouldn't they have confessed, secret entrance and all? Yes, of course they would—craven bastards! Magandiya is sure that Samavati's agony when she burned in the fire couldn't have been worse than what she is experiencing now.

December 29. The Venerable Asoka's happiness isn't long-lived. Just outside Saketa (modern Ayodhya), he stumbles. His ankle gives way and he falls to one knee. As he rises and puts weight on both legs, pain bursts in the ankle and makes him twist unnaturally. Oh no! The back, too!

He tries but can barely stand. Walking isn't an option and sitting is no better. So, continuing the downward trajectory, he cautiously rolls onto his back and lies still. Better.

From this prone position, he looks around. Now what? No one else is on the road. But, he thinks optimistically, someone's bound to come along sooner or later. Aloud he asserts, "My back is strong—most of the time—and the ankle has always been sound, at least until lately. They should heal quickly. After two accidents, it's time for good karma. Right?" Then he shouts as if to convince the universe, "Yes, right! It's time for good karma!" He thrusts a fist into the air to seal the assertion. He winces.

Above, the tree canopy and deep sky are serene. Gazing at them, Asoka is struck by the preposterousness of his situation: A puny human being, flat on his back, unable to take a step, alone on the road, is commanding the universe! How like us, all of us. We think we're so important! He laughs. Carefully, so as not to hurt his back.

Then he realizes, I could die here, right by the side of the road, and who would know? One more dead man, this one with an orange robe and bald head. On the road to Saketa of all places! Why does this seem funny?

Asoka hasn't thought much about where his life might end. He has vaguely assumed it would be at Savatthi or Rajagaha, at one of the large Buddha monastic centers, the two places he loves best—where there's always plenty of activity, lots of comings and goings. Saketa has never been a consideration. He has heard tales that told of sacred events that anciently occurred in Saketa, but what use is the past to him? His life is about moving forward. His careful laughter subsides.

Now remembering that he is carrying a message for the Buddha, he is suddenly filled with urgency. I can't die now! The message must get through! Somebody must come along, somebody with a cart to take me to town and help me find a bhikkhu, so I can pass it on.

And soon it is so. A peasant with an ox-cart who is leaving town comes by and, though not a follower of the Buddha himself, he knows of a wealthy man who is. He kindly turns the cart around and, helping him to painfully ascend, drives Asoka to the man's home.

The master of the house offers to care for the disabled bhikkhu, to provide him with a room, food and medical treatment while he recovers. Such is the respect that laypeople have for religious wanderers, Buddhist and non-Buddhist alike. It is a respect buttressed by the universal belief that acts of generosity to recluses produce great merit, tangible rewards for the giver in this and future lives.

According to Buddhist monastic rules, bhikkhus are expected to lodge only with other bhikkhus, but in emergencies like this one, exceptions are allowed. Asoka is very grateful to this householder.

December 30. Asoka's benefactor has put word out that the injured bhikkhu was on his way to Savatthi with a message for the Blessed One. Within a day, a monk travelling through town and bound for Savatthi arrives at his bedside. He finds Asoka flat on his back with his knees elevated on cushions, as the doctor who saw him this morning advised. His left ankle is splinted.

Relieved as well as reluctant, Asoka entrusts the message to the young bhikkhu. Asoka hasn't met him before. He remarks to himself, It's a sure sign of age when most of the brothers are younger than you are and you don't know them. Can these young ones be relied on? At least, he muses, looking at the bright side, this bhikkhu is strong and will arrive without mishap, probably.

The necessary having been accomplished, he relaxes on the fresh bed linens, which cover a cotton-stuffed mattress on a bed protected by mosquito curtains. The room is more luxurious than any he has inhabited. He now has all the time in the world to heal and to think.

January 16, 431. The party left Benares less than a week after the messengers arrived. The return trip was worse than Magandiya had imagined. At least, she persuaded her aunt to drop the idea of accompanying her. The woman had insisted that her niece needed a chaperone. She would want no less for her own daughter, she had explained. She was also anxious to check on whereabouts of her husband, but that was understood.

Magandiya had always found her aunt's well-meaning chatter a strain. Enduring it while cooped up in a cramped wagon for several days and not knowing what faced her at home was unthinkable. So she replied, "Darling, my husband needs me. He wants me to return as soon as possible, and we've got to travel light. I came alone. I can go back the same way. Don't worry. I'll be well guarded."

Once Magandiya saw the newly hired guards, though, she had doubts. They looked like brigands, but she decided she couldn't worry about them.

She hardly noticed the journey. All the way back to Kosambi, her thoughts writhed in a blur of pain. Afterwards, she remembered only that she had wanted it to be over immediately, and at the same time she hadn't wanted it to ever end.

They arrive in late afternoon with a clatter, two guards, three ox-carts and Magandiya issuing instructions about unloading. Her maids rush to the entranceway to greet her. They express joy (so to speak) for her safe return and inform her, several talking simultaneously, about the fire. Chattering monkeys. She nods and doesn't listen.

One maid observes her mistress' glazed expression and assumes she is exhausted. She offers to help her up to her room.

"What? Uh, no, no. I need fresh air." As though she hadn't spent the past seventeen days in fresh air. She hurries through the house and out the back door. The maids exchange perplexed looks. More inexplicable behavior.

Still there or closed up? Remembering discretion—you never know who is looking—she slows and walks through the garden in a seemingly casual stroll. She eventually arrives at the back wall, where she moves in close to admire the shrubs.

Yes! It's there! Uncle is still unaccounted for, but the intruders weren't caught. Neither was he. She wants to weep. Instead, she makes her way across the garden to the site of Samavati's residence.

She had contemplated its destruction for weeks beforehand, but seeing the charred ruin is shocking. It's so real. So final. And the altar—what about the altar? And the memorial ceremony? Her servants jabbered something about a public consecration ceremony and the private burial of remains afterwards.

Trying to quell rising panic, she reasons, Of course, of course, he had put on a good show for the public. But an alarming thought counters, No, he really is grieving for Samavati. And he's looking for the one who did it—you! Shuddering, she turns and hurries back to her residence.

January 17. She didn't sleep last night, and now, this morning, she holds her breath as she listens to the royal messenger, who is standing in the entryway. He informs her that the king will visit tonight. If he suspects, wouldn't he have commanded my presence at the palace? she ponders. Or sent guards to arrest me? A nighttime visit suggests intimacy. So maybe he doesn't suspect. Maybe he wants solace. All the rest of the day she swings wildly between hope and profound dread. Opting on the side of hope, she decides not to run.

A maid enters the parlor where she is seated so as to be seen at advantage when he enters. She wears a gorgeous sari, and a ruby, a special gift from him, hangs at her forehead from a rope of pearls. The maid announces him. Her attention is riveted on the doorway. This could be my last night on earth! Do I run now? There's still time.

He appears and she sees: Solace. It's solace! Ahhhhhhh!

A tsunami of relief inundates every cell of her body. She rises so hurriedly to greet him she is in danger of fainting. He rushes toward her and enfolds her in a strenuous embrace that keeps her upright. In fact, she can hardly move.

He whispers in her ear, "My dear, dear wife, my cherished one! You are safe. Thank the gods for that!" He squeezes her harder, then loosens his grip and kisses her tenderly on the forehead, next to the ruby. He can feel its hard edges against his cheek. The servant discreetly leaves. She will have something to report to the others.

He releases her and sits on a low chair. Beckoning her to take one close by, he pours out the story as though he had been waiting all this time just to confide.

Skipping details of the calamity, he focuses on the awful possibilities. What if there had been a wind, if her residence, the whole palace burned? Oh, how happy, immensely happy, he is that she, his beloved Magandiya, was out of harm's way. The gods were indeed watching over her, over all of them. But the children. He grieves for them, he always will, the dear young ones, but he quickly switches subjects, lest a catch in his voice betray too much emotion. He knows children are her sore point.

"She's gone!" he proclaims. "The murderess, the unfaithful wife, the whore—she's gone! What if she'd succeeded? I can't even think about it! Chaos. I've been saved from chaos. The kingdom's been saved. We're rid of her! Thank the gods, thank the inscrutable, just gods!"

He uses the word "inscrutable," having carefully rehearsed it. He thinks this whole charade is inscrutable.

Magandiya has imagined these words (minus "inscrutable") so often that now that they are spoken, they seem entirely genuine. Overwrought, she doesn't detect the bathos in his voice. He rises to embrace her again, and she flows into his arms, closing her eyes, savoring the sweetness of the moment, all the more intense for the torture she has endured. She gazes up into his earnest face, and emotion doesn't prevent her from thinking, I *knew* he wouldn't turn to Vasuladatta, that cold fish! I'm the one—I haven't lost my touch!

"You are my comfort, my darling, my only comfort. I've missed you so very much," he rhapsodizes as he gently guides her up to the bedchamber. On the stairs, he muses casually, "I wonder who could have done this for me."

He's not looking for an answer. It's as though he recognizes that the gods, inscrutable or not, need humans to carry out their will. "It could only have been someone who loves me very, very much." They enter room, and he begins to undress her.

After they make love, first violently, then tenderly, Magandiya snuggles next to him in her fragrant bed. She is content but reveals nothing. Not yet. A small qualm called self-preservation keeps her from speaking. There are still the disturbing matters of the altar and the consecration ceremonies. Why did he do that? She needs to be quite certain that what he is saying is real.

January 22. He visits again tonight. After entirely satisfactory lovemaking, they lie curled on her bed in dreamy contentment, her back against his chest, his knees against the back of hers and his right hand on her breast. He murmurs into her ear, "I'm happy, so boundlessly happy, that you, my dearest, are in my arms." He gently caresses her breast.

A moment of silence, then he says, "I only wish I knew who saved my life from that demon. Not only mine, but the kingdom. He preserved the peace. It must be someone who loves me beyond all others! I'm in his debt, and I intend to bestow a great boon on him."

The Magadhi language that Udena speaks contains no personal pronouns. Person is signified by verb ending, and in this patriarchal culture, the third person singular ending is generally understood to refer to a male. Which is exactly the implication that Udena means to convey.

It isn't a man! She puffs up like a cat being praised. A small, happy smile plays on her lips, she almost purrs. She's sure now. She turns over. Her head cradled in the crook of her elbow, her face very close to his, and, in the soft light of the single ghee lamp, she confesses.

"My lord, my dearest husband, my life, I'll tell you now. I did it. I was the one. I did it for you because, my darling, I love you so utterly." Now started, she babbles, "The gods told me that it was up to me to do this for you, to relieve you of that terrible woman who was betraying you daily. It wasn't easy. It took so much courage, but I had to obey their holy command. You see, there's nothing in the world I wouldn't do for you, my dearest.

Yes!

"Oh my treasure, my dearest one, I've never fully appreciated your devotion. I've been a blind man!"

He lifts her hand and kisses it reverentially. Then, aroused, he moves on to other parts. Though he has just used the despicable "treasure" word, under the circumstances, she hears it more than gladly.

When they stop for breath, he declares, "I must reward you, dearest—no, no, not just you, your entire family because you're their jewel. I want them to see how a grateful king honors his beloved wife."

Seemingly carried away with his own largesse, he continues, "Yes, we'll celebrate your devotion with a royal festivity. We'll invite them, all of them. Let them come and rejoice in our happiness and our love for each other! And I'll bestow a royal boon upon each of them."

Oh, he thinks, this is so thick! But he takes sly pleasure in knowing what the boon will be. To Magandiya his words are honey.

Husband and wife spend more ardent hours in her flower-decked bedchamber. Broken-hearted or not, he must carry out the plan and, truth to tell, this isn't such a bad way of doing it.

During their love-making, her old hope revives: Now that she has shown her unparalleled devotion, maybe now she'll be rewarded with pregnancy. That's how it should be!

He likes this new Magandiya—or rather the old one, the one he first knew—the passionate, beautiful woman. And she's beautiful still, though the blossom sits more heavily on its stem. It's too bad, he thinks. Too bad about reality. It stands in the way of fully enjoying her. He wishes it different.

He leaves before dawn. The manservant, who is drowsing outside the front door, leaps to his feet as the king exits. He reaches for the torch next to him in the stone entryway and lights it from a ghee lamp left burning through the night. Then leading the way, he and his sovereign proceed on the familiar path from the queen's residence back to the palace.

Now we've got her! he gloats. He weighs the strange game he's playing—sleeping with a murderess, the woman who murdered his beloved Samavati, and actually enjoying it.

How can I do this? It's repulsive! Because I'm king, that's why. I'm safeguarding my kingdom. This is what it means to be a maharaja.

Though it certainly wasn't his idea of a maharaja when he was a boy. How he hates his father! In the gloom before dawn, his thoughts flit like winter birds from topic to topic. The maharaja—his arrogant father, who was ever disappointed in the son who adored him.

No matter how hard I tried, I wasn't good enough! Starting with my height—too short. And it still is, he sighs discontentedly. Samavati. She understood. She was the *only* one who understood, and she loved me even though. Now she's gone. Tears almost fill his eyes. This isn't how I wanted things to turn out. What a curse! Did Magandiya do it because the gods commanded? Or was it demons? He's afraid it's the latter. My household, my reign, me—are we all cursed?

Entering the palace, he moves up to his chambers and begins an uneasy day. He is too distraught to notice the knot that sits in his belly like bad food.

CHAPTER 12.

THE BUDDHA'S ARRIVAL

The next several weeks are the happiest of Magandiya's life. She spends intimate nights with her husband, as she did when they were newly married, and she constructs a list of relatives to be invited to the festivity. Having been woefully under-employed all her married life, she embraces usefulness with zeal.

The invitation is simple. Bharadvaja composed it: "Udena, Maharaja of Vamsa, invites you and your family to celebrate the unparalleled devotion expressed by his beautiful wife, the illustrious Queen Magandiya. He wishes to share his joy and gratitude by bestowing a royal boon upon the Magandiya clan. Festivities will be held in Kosambi on March 20th. Provisions will be made for your accommodation." Mention of a boon might be considered a bit crass, but Bharadvaja wanted to insure their arrival in case the hardships of travel seemed off-putting. He assumed greed, if not curiosity, would prevail.

Devising the list of invitees is not so simple, however. Magandiya hasn't seen most members of her extended family in years and many, never. She had never paid much attention to the web of family relations even before she became queen. Since then, she has been otherwise occupied, and the naturally occurring changes have largely slid by without her noticing. She consults Uncle Culla, who is better informed. He is back from wherever he went. (He is vague, and Magandiya doesn't press him. It doesn't matter now.)

They make a working list—aunties, uncles, cousins, their children and grandchildren. The only one intentionally omitted is her father. He wouldn't come, Magandiya thinks bitterly. She doesn't want to be rejected again. As for her mother, she died several years ago from the rigors of monastic life to which she was ill-suited.

Udena and Bharadvaja have simplified the undertaking by excluding relatives in Kuru country, the clan's ancestral seat. The area is over four hundred miles away and with no major trade route linking the region with Kosambi, travel to and from is long and challenging and would mean postponing the celebration until after the rains. Udena and Bharadvaja don't want to wait.

Neither does Magandiya. Royal generosity will be magnificent without her Kuru relatives, for many others live within a three-week journey, which is the travel limit set by the king and Bharadvaja.

The messengers bearing the invitation will need to be detectives. The addresses, even the town in which some relatives live, are guesswork. They will have to rely on information from family members and add names as they proceed and drop those who have died.

Bharadvaja has selected three messengers, all intelligent men with good memories, for they have no written record to work with. They must carry the list in their head and are being instructed in a crude tally system to keep track of people contacted. Because tracing everyone would take an inordinate amount of time, the chaplain has limited the messengers' time in outlying areas to six weeks. After that, it's anybody's guess as to whether additional family members will receive the invitation informally through family connections and, if so, whether they would have time to prepare and travel to Kosambi.

Aside from the list-making, Magandiya and her uncle enjoy themselves. Still meeting privately at her residence, they giggle at their good fortune. Magandiya asks him to tell her stories like in her childhood, and she hops onto his lap—just for a moment because nosy servants are everywhere. The fire is unmentioned, as though it never happened. Now is now, and Magandiya is happy.

She has acquired a new mynah, and, when not busy with preparations for the celebration, she enjoys teaching it to talk. This is a good thing because another pastime—sitting on her balcony and watching Samavati—is done. In fact, she doesn't sit on the balcony at all these days. The ruins, which aren't fully cleared yet, present a rather depressing prospect, and she thinks, *It'll be a long time before*

I go out there again. As it happens, she never will. In the meantime, however, the mynah gets a lot of attention.

Servants who observed or heard about the queen's conduct before the fire wonder at the goings-on now. Who can understand the behavior of royal masters and mistresses? None dare reveal their suspicions to the king or, more to the point, to Dasama, the king's barber.

Dasama has ready access to his lord because he daily shaves the royal face and tweezes body hairs. The king's toilette is almost as elaborate as his harem's. Udena trusts the man more fully than many of his ministers and occasionally has him attend meetings to which the ministers aren't invited. Taking advantage of his privileged position, Dasama acts as a channel for petitions. He has grown quite wealthy and very fat.

It is serious business to accuse a queen to her husband, and the servants hesitate. Jenti especially has considered speaking out. Dasama owes her. With reluctance and just the right amount of deference, she could tell him about her mistress's private meetings with her uncle. She would protect herself by admitting that, while she doesn't know for sure, while she didn't hear it with her own ears, but could it be that they were hatching a plot? Everybody knows that her mistress didn't like Queen Samavati. There would be no need to mention her own role in the queen's various schemes—like how she, Jenti, bribed one of Samavati's maids to place the fetish in her bedchamber, or how she once had a cook put hair in Samavati's soup thereby making it ritually unclean, or any of the other things. No need for that. But she could relate how jumpy Magandiya was before her departure and while traveling, too. Jenti has never seen her so nervous. And no one is naïve enough to think that just because her mistress wasn't in town at the time of the fire that she couldn't have put her uncle up to it. He *was* in town.

Prudence prevails, however. It would be stupidity to say any of these things when the king is so lavishly bestowing favors on her mistress. Jenti is no fool. She wants to be on the winning side. She'll use the Dasama option another time.

January 431. Asoka has been becalmed like a ship on a windless day. The doctor told him to lie on his back and not to move, except for the necessary. This is the hardest period in his monastic career.

Before he ordained, Asoka had been unhappily married. His wife ministered to him in ways large and small as was expected by society, but she was insensitive and her intelligence, limited. Beyond sharing a marriage bed, they had little in common. She was satisfied to have married a man who didn't beat her, who, in fact, was kind. She had mothered a son and lived in comfortable circumstances. Society held these conditions to be the height of a woman's felicity, and she wasn't one to question social norms.

So she didn't understand why he was unhappy. They had a good life, didn't they? They had a son. What more did he want? But Asoka couldn't relate to her in ways he yearned to. He barely articulated these to himself, but he did know something was missing. Both grew querulous.

When she died in childbirth along with their infant daughter, Asoka grieved, but he was relieved. Like a prisoner on the day of his release, almost. For there was still his son, whom he loved dearly. Soon after the boy's marriage, Asoka left home, rejoicing in freedom at last. He happily ordained in the Buddha's young order and shed forever his peevishness, along with his worldly possessions.

For each of the nearly twenty years that he has been a bhikkhu, Asoka has regarded his annual nine months of travel as a celebration of independence. He is a man with wanderlust in his feet. He craves new places, new people and not knowing what the day will hold. During the rains retreat, when bhikkhus are settled, he eagerly anticipates being back on the road.

"Freedom" refers to more than the freedom to wander, according to the Buddha's teachings. Asoka knows this, but his has been the satisfactory position in which his passion coincides with religious norms. Contented as a dog snoozing in the sun, he has felt little need to inquire more deeply.

Now, however, the happy coincidence has come undone. His body isn't cooperating. He has always known that someday his body would begin to fail and he would have to curtail and eventually end wandering. But that would be someday, not now.

So during the long, lonely days in his bed in Saketa, as Asoka rehearses countless versions of how he will set out again before the rains and where he will go, his fantasies invariably collide with the unavoidable truth that, even if he manages to travel again this year, he can't continue indefinitely.

How many years do I have left? The force of the question germinates in his belly and becomes a large, heavy knot. If he were a woman, he might think himself pregnant. Other questions follow.

What has all my travel amounted to? What do I know now that I didn't know twenty years ago? Words, yes, many. But do I really understand them? How have they changed me? I've wasted my time, he concludes.

In despair, he overlooks the many ways in which the wisdom of the Dhamma has transformed him. It has been a subtle process, like the falling of mist, and he is unaware that he has gotten wet. But now, finally, he is beginning to examine what he ignored during the happy, heedless years of travel. Finally, he is doing the work of a bhikkhu.

February 4. He's here! The Buddha has arrived at Ghosita's Park, accompanied by two bhikkhus.

Years ago, Ghosita had a special hut built for him, and whenever the Buddha visits, he stays there. At the Buddha's insistence, the hut isn't much different from the others: a wooden structure plastered with baked mud, consisting of a single room and portico under a thatched roof. It is slightly larger than most and situated at a suitable distance from them.

Last week, a junior monk opened and dusted the hut and swept it clean of droppings. The job is considered a great honor, and the bhikkhu performed it carefully. In the Buddha's absence, geckos made the hut their headquarters, so there was plenty of work to do. The monk carefully put the little creatures outside in accord with the Dhamma of non-harming, a teaching that includes all living beings, no matter how small. When he finished, he propped the boom, twigs tied to a long straight branch, by the door in case a last-minute sweeping were necessary, and he placed three sitting mats on the floor, instead of two.

Outside, a gardener pulled weeds around the hut so the area would be tidy. The gardener is one of several workmen hired by Ghosita to maintain the monastic park because the prohibition against killing includes plant life. This means bhikkhus aren't permitted to garden.

Pulling weeds was difficult because the yard hadn't been tended recently and in this dry season, only tops of plants could be yanked off; roots didn't yield. Now a few hardy shoots have reappeared. Still, the area remains acceptably clear—a sandy patch, not to say dusty, awaiting the footsteps of the Illustrious One. No one doubted his arrival.

Although Asoka had been nervous about giving a message of such importance to an unknown bhikkhu, the monk was glad to serve—thrilled, in fact, to have a chance to speak with the Blessed One. Traveling on the trade route linking Saketa and Savatthi, Venerable Girimananda set a fast pace and arrived in Savatthi six days after Asoka bequeathed the message to him. There, shyly and with respect, he delivered it in person. The honor was one of the highlights of Girimananda's yet brief monastic career. Long afterwards, he would tell the story to his monastic brothers.

Two days after he received the young monk's message, the Buddha began the journey to Kosambi. Each morning during the journey, he and two companions walked in the cool of the day, begging for food along the way.

Among all acts of generosity, those that produce the greatest merit is generosity to the Buddha, the Exalted One, the most virtuous of beings. So it is believed. The Buddha and his companions don't lack for food or other necessities.

After their midday meal, he and his companions continued walking until it grew too hot; then they rested and meditated in the shade of trees until evening when local people, excited to have the Teacher in their midst, gathered to hear the Dhamma and ask questions. At night they slept under the trees or in shelters provided by supporters.

The Buddha stopped for two days in Saketa, where he spoke with adherents and briefly visited with Venerable Asoka. Finally, late this afternoon, the travelers, enter the monastic park grounds. They are bathed in sweat and their saffron robes are soiled. Even so, as the Buddha, tall and upright, enters the grounds of Ghosita's Park, a stillness emanates from him that distinguishes him from his two companions. A few resident bhikkhus who happen to be near the gate, spread the news, and suddenly the common area is filled with quiet, happy commotion.

Candana almost runs to greet his teacher. He prostrates himself and touches his head at his Buddha's feet. Then he stands before him, palms joined and his face illuminated with a large smile. "Bhagava!" So much has happened since they last met. Candana senses this will be a momentous visit, but for now they stand silently looking at each other, wrapped in the joy of welcome.

Pindola wedges into the group. Shouldering aside Venerable Udayi, he positions himself next to the Buddha. He would have prostrated himself, but bending is a major effort and conversation is already underway. He hopes for special notice from the Teacher. Being the widest among them, it's hard not to notice him.

Udayi, now standing behind Pindola and looking at his expanse, shakes his head imperceptibly. As a senior bhikkhu, Udayi knows there's no end to the maneuverings of young monks. Learning what is meaningless—it's all part of the training, he reminds himself.

Will this bhikkhu grow up? Envisioning Pindola twenty years from now in all his port, he shudders. This one could cause a lot of trouble.

Disappointed not to receive the kind of attention he feels he deserves, Pindola tries a concentration tactic, looking at the Blessed One intently, willing him to speak directly to him, or at least settle his gaze on him. When that fails, he tries smiling bigly, like Candana did.

Little escapes the notice of these bhikkhus who live with each other. They know the truth behind even subtle gestures, and Pindola's are hardly subtle. Harika looks at him in disgust.

Venerable Uttara is also watching the young monk. It wasn't so long ago that he, Uttara, was similarly hungry for the Buddha's attention.

Ah, the old days, he thinks. How glad I am they're gone! Not merely the passing of the old days but, more specifically, the disappearance of his ambition to be abbot and his jealousy of Candana—that is what Uttara is glad about.

I was never cut out for that kind of leadership. Strange how deluded we can be, he muses, not for the first time.

Uttara feels the suffering in Pindola's yearning as though it were his own. Tenderness for the young monk surges through his chest, and he recognizes it as compassion.

The Buddha looks at Uttara and smiles. "I'm glad to see you friend Uttara," he says quietly.

Bhagava understands! Uttara performs a small anjali. The gesture hides a heart bursting with joy.

Greetings continue and the Buddha shares news of Venerable Asoka's mishap, about which they'd already heard.

Then Candana says, "Venerable Sati will accompany you to your hut, sir. And he'll show you, venerables, to yours," nodding to the two who traveled with the Buddha. "We are glad to welcome you."

Sati has been dividing his attention between the greetings and the matter of accommodations. The Buddha's hut is clean and ready, and guessing that Venerable Sunakkhatta, the Teacher's attendant, would accompany him, he also had Asoka's recently vacated hut cleaned. That was easy. But where to put Cittaka? There was no point cleaning a third hut if only one monk would be traveling with the Buddha. I'll figure it out on the spot, Sati decided. And this is it, he tells himself as he walks with the Buddha and the two bhikkhus.

By the time they reach the Buddha's hut, Sati has a plan for Cittaka's housing, but while deliberating, he wasn't attentive to the Buddha's comments. Now he hears him say, "...not meeting with the bhikkhus tonight. I'll stay in and rest."

"Yes, Bhagava," Sati assents, nodding his head. What else did he say? In any case, it makes perfect sense to Sati that the Buddha will stay in his hut tonight. When you're tired, you rest.

And the Buddha is tired. Though he is remarkably fit, having walked across the breadth of northern India for decades, at fifty-eight his body has a growing need for kind consideration. The Buddha readily gives it, though always within the bounds of the rule of the Vinaya.

By any measure, the Buddha's life is austere. He observes disciplinary code that he prescribes for the bhikkhus, claiming no exceptions for himself. The rules pointedly exclude rigid ascetic observances, for, as a young man searching for liberation, he uncompromisingly engaged in many austerities, including starvation. Eating only a handful of grain or one piece of fruit a day, he became so emaciated that, by touching his belly, he could almost feel his spine. His hair rotted, and his limbs became dry and knotted, "like bamboo joints," he later described them. Finally, near death, Siddhattha Gotama—that was his name before he became the Enlightened One, the Buddha—realized that emaciation doesn't produce liberation. Torturing the body doesn't vanquish the ego; it reinforces it. For when starving, he was preoccupied with his body's crying need for food and his ego's determination to subdue it.

At that point, in his despair, a radical insight arose to Siddhattha: There was another way to the release the ego's hold, a middle way. He shifted his practice, and not long after, he attained release from the illusion of self, freedom from suffering, supreme awakening, Buddhahood.

While Sati thinks that the Buddha's decision to rest tonight is reasonable, Venerable Bhaddaji doesn't. Bhaddaji has been unhappy for all of his fifteen months at Ghosita's Park. He suffers from a respiratory weakness. Dust, which in the dry season coats all things, animate and inanimate, makes him cough and wheeze; thus, he is unable to range across the region like most bhikkhus. He needs a protected environment where, when necessary, he can take refuge within a hut or hall. He spends much of the dry season with a kerchief over his nose and mouth. He hates it.

Endowed with the passionate temperament of youth, Bhaddaji is convinced that progress toward liberation happens in proportion to the degree of asceticism of one's practice. He tries to compensate for his physical limitation by being rigidly ascetic. He proudly eats only one meal every other day, a very large meal, and is oblivious to the damage he is inflicting on his body long-term. He has become a stickler for the disciplinary rules and painstakingly observes them down to the most minor protocol.

Before he lost respect for Harika, on the occasion when that bhikkhu declared breaking the law a good thing, Bhaddaji had hounded him, asking questions and checking his own knowledge of the Vinaya. Though Harika no longer hungered for such adulation as he had in earlier years, in truth, he was a wee bit flattered by the young monk's attention and feels the lack of it as loss. Nonetheless, he understands now that no one becomes enlightened because he knows the disciplinary rules.

Harika has imparted this fact to Bhaddaji, but to no effect. If he can't be ascetic in ways that others are, Bhaddaji is determined to do it in those available to him, and nobody is going to stop him!

That's why Bhaddaji doesn't believe Candana, either. Candana has repeatedly stressed that strict asceticism can be an impediment, not a means, to liberation because it promotes a sense of ego, a self who is proud of his own restraint. He has pointed out that the Buddha's

Dhamma is called the Middle Way; it is, among other things, a path between rigid austerity and indulgence.

As far as Bhaddaji is concerned, their counsel makes both Harika and Candana suspect. And now the Buddha, whom he is meeting for the first time, has joined their ranks. The Blessed One isn't living up to his own teachings! Bhaddaji is a very confused and unhappy bhikkhu.

"It's indulgence." Bhaddaji issues this bold criticism through the kerchief that covers his nose and mouth as he walks this evening with another young bhikkhu to the assembly hall, the hall from which the Buddha will be absent. "Sheer indulgence!"

His companion is startled by his outspokenness, and he is impressed but says nothing.

February 5. Tonight the Buddha is ready for the large assembly of bhikkhus and townspeople that is gathering in the hall. Bhikkhus are arriving from the two monastic centers outside town, and many plan to stay for the duration of their teacher's visit. Sati has lodged most of the visiting seniors in the vacant huts with the understanding that they must clean the premises themselves. Juniors may camp in the common area.

There is a noisy bustle as lay friends and neighbors from town, mainly men but not entirely, arrive and greet each other. Although they lack precision instruments, these people have a keenly developed sense, governed by the sun and long habit, which enables them to be where they are supposed to be more or less on time. They've also cultivated an ample supply of patience for those whose interpretation of timeliness needs honing. Stragglers are not a problem.

Everyone is eager to see the Buddha. It has been more than two years since his last visit. Bhikkhus are already seated on their mats at the front of the hall, and townspeople, behind in happy disorder. Latecomers who can't find space in the hall, sit on the ground outside. The wooden structure is a pavilion with bamboo partitions, which are now rolled up.

Several relatives of Samavati's servants as well as some members of the palace staff are present for the first time. Their mood is more somber than that of the rest. Rituals performed by local priests have been unsatisfactory. It's too late for rituals.

Conversation stills as the Buddha enters. In the light of ghee lamps affixed to the wooden pillars, they watch as he takes his place on the mat on the raised dais at the front of the hall facing them. He sits cross-legged, closes his eyes and without a word begins to meditate. All follow. There isn't a sound from the large group except for an occasional cough and some quiet squirming among those for whom meditation isn't a habitual practice. An hour later when the Blessed One ends his meditation—to the great relief of the squirmers—the crowd shifts. People stretch their legs, but all remain hushed. They wait for the Blessed One to speak.

"Greetings, bhikkhus and householders. Greetings to those of you who frequent Ghosita's Park and those who are new as well. I've come at this painful time at the request of Venerable Candana." He nods at Candana, who is seated next to him.

Without further preliminaries, he begins, "Queen Samavati, her maids and two of her four children have died. This is a great, great sadness. The fire has caused immense suffering in the palace and the whole city. You are grieving your losses. But you can take some comfort in this: Queen Samavati was a worthy and revered queen and mother. Respected by all, she was foremost in lovingkindness among laywomen followers. She reached a high level of spiritual attainment. So, too, each of her trustworthy servants were spiritually advanced. None died without attaining the fruits of spiritual practice. Remember this even while you grieve. Moreover, there is something else you can do."

Not another prayer to the gods! Some townspeople new to the Buddha's teachings sigh. And probably for a hefty fee, like the priests.

"You can reflect, bhikkhus and householders. Pay close attention. What do you think? Is there anyone in this city who has not lost a relative or friend? Anyone not ever touched by death?"

For many, the month and a half since the fire has dulled the razor edge of grief. The Buddha senses that they are ready to move to a more impersonal level of understanding. If they can grasp the truth of impermanence, they will achieve a softer, less painful relationship with their grief.

"No, there is not. There's not a single person who has never lost a relative or friend. Such is the fate of all beings."

The father of one of Samavati's maids, a newcomer, isn't ready for this. His grief is still a knife, and his nature is argumentative. He interrupts. "It's true, Master Gotama, everybody dies—we all know that. But most die in old age. The queen and my daughter and the other maids and the children, they were young. All of them. Why did they have to die? They died before their time!" His hands, which are doing violence to the air, and the strenuous side-to-side movement of his head underscore his outrage.

"Yes, householder, they were young. This is true. But who are you—who is anyone—to determine a person's time to die? Do you understand all the forces at work? Do you know what each did in this life or in past lives? There are no untimely deaths. 'Untimely' is a human view, an unwise view. It's born of expectations based on what is considered a normal lifespan. But death doesn't obey a law of human expectations. It happens according to the law of karma."

Most people, whether followers of the Buddha or not, understand the principle here, a principle that operates within one's life as well as over lifetimes. But it's one thing to understand it, and another to accept its application to one's own life. The father truculently crosses his arms over his chest. His daughter was virtuous—he knows that—and he is certain the queen and her other maids were, too. There's no need to doubt the virtue of the children.

He is about to retort when Sati speaks up with the question that's on everybody's mind. "Bhagava, you've just said Queen Samavati was your foremost laywoman follower in lovingkindness. So why did she have such bad karma? Why did she and the others die in this horrible way?"

The assembly is silent.

The Buddha nods and explains that in a past life Samavati was a queen and her maids were noble ladies-in-waiting. Bathing on a chilly day, they set fire to a nearby stand of shrubbery for warmth, and only after the blaze had started did they realize the foolishness of their action: A fire in the dry season could set the whole town ablaze. Listeners in the audience nod knowingly; the same could have happened this time.

The story continues. Then to their horror, the ladies noticed that a recluse, deeply absorbed in meditation, was hidden amidst the shrubs. Panicking, they decided not to try to save him because, if he survived, he would probably reveal that they had started the blaze, and they would be severely punished. The recluse did survive and didn't inform others, but their intention, initially innocent though thoughtless, had turned evil. "It bore fruit in this lifetime."

So that it explains it! No one doubts the Buddha. They are sure he knows. Even the argumentative father is a bit mollified: At least his daughter was a noble lady-in-waiting in a former life; she even had spiritual attainment, whatever that is.

"Therefore, carefully examine your actions and your intentions," the Teacher continues. "Guard against misconduct whether in your thoughts, words or deeds. Do only good, harm none, and have compassion for all living beings. Then, you will live serenely and obtain a fortunate rebirth."

More silence. The concept of rebirth isn't questioned, but that one's own behavior, not divine favor, determines results is radical. It takes some getting used to. Many would rather believe that Vedic ritual or that listening to the Blessed One's teachings and being in his presence work like a lucky charm, that they confer sure-fire protection. But the Buddha isn't letting them doze in that cozy place.

He caps his comments, saying, "Heedfulness is the way to the Deathless; heedlessness is the way to death. The heedful never die, but those who are heedless are, in effect, already dead."

Some with a literal cast of mind, wonder whom he's talking about. It's clear that Queen Samavati was heedful, even if she had harbored an unfortunate, murderous intention in a past life. But who's the heedless one? Who caused the fire? Theories have been circulating in town, and most are betting on Queen Magandiya. Even as the Buddha continues to speak, they are traveling in thought down speculative lanes, unaware that this perhaps is heedlessness. Candana however feels a strange sense of compassion for the heedless woman whom he has never met, but of whom he has heard much. Cruel, yes; possibly deranged. Caught in circumstances she finds intolerable, she has chosen the path of evil—Candana assumes it was she who caused the fire—and Bhagava is saying that she has died before she dies. Candana is reminded of a man he once saw when on almsround: The man was in the streets, slobber dribbling from his mouth, gesticulating wildly and cursing; he didn't know what he was doing, a dead man. Poor, poor man.

CHAPTER 13.
ASOKA'S SPRING

February 5. For several evenings afterwards, troubled townspeople flock to Ghosita's Park to hear the Buddha speak and to ask questions. The quick-tempered father is among them, and he brings his wife. After their third visit, they declare themselves adherents of the Blessed One. They are not the only ones.

Candana is also turning to the Buddha. He must talk about his condition. He can't put it off any longer. There are practical matters, especially the matter of a successor, that need to be dealt with.

What Candana doesn't want to talk about is how he is handling the disease. He's not doing a good job. He has managed to only feebly shine the light of the Dhamma on that red-hot topic. It's not so much that he's afraid of death—he has come to terms with that. But of decline, of losing control of his body and possibly his mind, he is terrified. How do you accept such things? Already his body is changing. Who is he, anyway?

Despite having counseled people for years, many in dire circumstances, now, when it comes to himself, he hasn't been able to bring the wisdom home. He has had equanimous moments, it is true, but mainly he feels like an ox pulling too heavy a load. He'll keep trying, though! He's determined to succeed before he talks with his teacher. If he were to reveal his struggle, the pathetic poverty of his spiritual attainment, the Buddha would be deeply disappointed, he's sure of it.

What would Bhagava say? That I'm experiencing fear because I haven't adequately observed the precepts in this or past lives? Or that I haven't meditated enough or don't possess sufficient insight? What have I been doing all these years, if not working as hard as I can to follow his example? The image of the straining ox flashes into his mind again. Engulfed in self-pity, the last thing Candana feels able to bear is his teacher's condemnation.

The Buddha's attendant, Venerable Sunakkhatta, arranges individual meetings with the Blessed One. Candana however is an exception: He is free to speak with him whenever he wishes. It's a privilege he's careful not to abuse.

Now, as he makes his way across the common area, around bhikkhus encamped there, he rehearses his strategy. This isn't about me. I won't be selfish. This is business, about the future of Ghosita's Park, and now's the time to talk about it.

The door is ajar, and he knocks lightly on the frame. From within the Buddha says, "Welcome, Candana." He has been waiting.

Stepping into the room, Candana anjalis and sits stiffly on one of the mats, a stiffness born of his distress as much as his physical condition. After a few pleasantries and with what he hopes is dispassion, he begins. He speaks of his disease, describing his symptoms, then relates, "Sirivaddha says it may not be the shaking palsy at all. Maybe it's something else. But the truth is, he doesn't think it's something else. Neither do I. And if it is the shaking palsy, it will gradually affect all the rhythms of my life, bodily as well as mental. All of them. There's no telling how the disease will show up or how long it will take to run its full course. Possibly years—but, but..."

Before emotion unnerves him, he pauses. He reaches for the support of his breath, inhaling deeply, then continues. "Though there's no way to know how rapid the decline will be, it's happening already. I've noticed changes."

So has the Buddha. He nods gently. The fire is only one reason he came to Kosambi. There are two others, and both have to do with Candana. Now, as they sit across from each other, the Teacher wants to give him all the room he needs in this discussion. He will want to talk about the disease and its practical consequences, but what about the other aspect—his fear? Will he be honest enough to talk about that? This bhikkhu is on the brink of a deep spiritual opening—if he can step over the edge of fear and self-delusion.

"This is indeed sad, sad news, Candana. So painful, so hard to hear."

To Candana's relief, instead of launching into a teaching about impermanence and transcending suffering as he had feared, the Buddha offers him compassion. He embraces him with words of understanding and care. The Buddha teaches that compassion, a tender regard for those who are suffering, is a heavenly mindstate, and right now he is embodying it.

"If I were to remain abbot, Bhagava, some people will criticize my decisions even *before* my clarity is compromised—that's for sure. Even if my mind were as clear as an October sky, if they don't like my decisions, they'll say the disease is at work and is impairing my judgment. I'll wonder about it myself. That's not good for our community or for the order as a whole. And it isn't good for me. I need to retire. I need to become an ordinary monk now, before my condition gets too serious and my judgment really is impaired."

"I hear you, friend, I hear you, and I agree. You do need to retire. But, you know, it's too late."

Too late? A pulse of despair contracts his heart.

"Too late to be ordinary. You no longer are, no matter what your role."

The Buddha is acknowledging that Candana is an *ariya*, one noble in spirit. Training in the Dhamma involves exposing to the light of awareness the automatic, reflexive reactions that crimp one's life. It's a crucible that progressively refines the spirit and expands awareness.

At one time Candana would have heard this comment with satisfaction and would have known the truth of it, but not now. He looks at his teacher dubiously. He hardly feels like an ariya.

"That means someone needs to step in and assume my duties," he continues, ignoring the comment.

The Buddha doesn't insist. "And whom do you have in mind?" As if he didn't know.

Candana has thought this through well. The Venerable Musila would have been perfect, but the Buddha knew that, too, which is why, a few years ago, he asked him to be abbot at Kukkuta's Park outside of town. Candana has missed him. Musila was his closest friend at Ghosita's Park and, though they still visit occasionally—in fact Musila is here now with the contingent from his monastery—it's not like before.

"Sati, sir."

"Ah."

"I know. There's the matter of his offense. He's only just finished his penance. And there's question whether he's still a 'thera' now that he's been demoted. Many people would hold his offense against him, but," he asserts, "they'd get over that. And we could reconfirm his status as a senior—maybe not right away, but very soon. No one else is suitable, you see.

"Udayi would be, but he's old and unwell. He doesn't have the energy for the job. Uttara," he says, moving on to the second senior, "has become a deeply compassionate bhikkhu—many of us are grateful to him." (Candana can't know how grateful he will be in years to come.) "But he has no talent for administration. He's the first to admit it.

"As for Harika, he's deepened greatly in his understanding of the Dhamma, but he's still prickly. He has an edge that antagonizes people, and he lacks the wisdom to lead.

"And Kappa," he says referring to a monk who ordained with Sati at Ghosita's Park years earlier, "is a fine bhikkhu, but he's only been back a year. He's traveled a lot and hasn't had the administrative experience that Sati has."

Nodding, the Buddha remarks, "I could send someone who's experienced, who could handle the job well."

"No!" he replies sharply, then immediately pulls back. "Sir, sending a bhikkhu from outside would be resented by members of this sangha." As I was, he thinks—for Candana was resented long after the Buddha sent him to Ghosita's Park to promote harmony in the contentious community. He is convinced his presence was a major factor triggering the schism.

"We need someone from this community, someone known and respected by all. Which Sati has been and will be again once the recent, unfortunate matter is well past. And Ghosita likes him," he adds.

"Ah, relations with the court—there's a sticky subject. Chaplain Bharadvaja is a realistic man and no doubt recognizes that his son is too young for the duties, but he wouldn't easily accept Sati. There was history between him and Sati's father, wasn't there? No love between them. We'd be inviting tensions with the court, even if Ghosita supports him."

"There'd be tensions anyway."

A patent truth. The Buddha smiles.

It's significant that they don't cite as a disadvantage Sati's past among outcastes. The royal chaplain had a hand in crafting that past. Bhikkhus and townspeople alike are aware of Sati's youth spent among fisherfolk, as well as of his noble birth. People make it their business to know each other's class background—it's an inquiry as natural a breathing. As a result of his noble origins and his estimable behavior as a bhikkhu, however, most have come to overlook the irregularity of his early life.

"I agree with you, Candana. I support your choice."

Candana exhales in relief and anjalis. "We need to talk with Sati, of course. It's probably going to take some convincing, but I'm sure he'll come around. Assuming he does, when do you think we should announce it to the sangha?"

"Wait a bit. Give him a chance to be at ease with this first."

He nods. I should be happy, he thinks. Both my points have been accepted. But he doesn't feel happy.

"Tell me," the Buddha says, switching topics. "What about you, Candana? How are you handling all this?"

Resistance rises like a wall. I can't say it. Can't say I'm afraid, that I'm not the bhikkhu he thinks I am.

"I'm ready," he responds evenly, as though misunderstanding what's being asked. "I've been ready to let go of these duties for a long time. Though now it looks like it's going to happen for a different reason than I expected." He smiles wryly.

The Buddha sighs at his dodge and gives him another chance to talk about himself. "What will you do? Will you travel? Stay here? Maybe move to another center?"

"I'd like to travel. It's been so long, but my body is weakening. Sometimes even almsround is tiring." Self-pity wells up again. He steps on it.

"No," he continues reasonably. "I'll stay here—advise Sati and teach as needed. This has become 'home' to this homeless bhikkhu."

The Buddha nods. "We'll talk about it again, before I leave." It is clear the meeting is over.

Candana anjalis and rises, but inside he wails, Leaving! You're leaving? Of course he is, you fool, his inner voice retorts. He's got to leave; you know that. But I haven't done it yet! I need more time! How much longer will you stay? I need to talk to you!

He respectfully backs out the door.

February 5. Another hard, empty day. Ghosita sits alone in his garden at twilight. No amount of activity masks his loss. Samavati is gone, and his guilt has intensified in the weeks since she died. Candana's counsel has passed with hardly a trace. A fool, a sniveling fool masquerading as a follower of the Blessed One, that's what I am! Attached to position, status, wealth, all the crap.

His thoughts expand to include the bastard, one of his favorite topics. It is a habit that his new sense of kinship with Udena doesn't disrupt. He despises the man in whose government he serves, and he loathes himself for serving.

At this moment Sakula quietly joins him. She sits next to him on the garden bench, her shoulders wrapped in a shawl against the cool evening air. He turns, and puts his head on her breast and begins to weep. She doesn't try to cheer him or alleviate his guilt, or even speak. It's not the time for words. Stroking his hair, this good woman cries, too. She didn't argue when he capitulated to the king's blackmail. With family in mind and of a practical nature, she believed he made the right, though terrible, decision, and she cries now for her husband, for their lost daughter, and in sheer outrage at having been forced into an intolerable choice.

She waits until his tears are spent, then whispers, "My dear, there is something you can do."

He pulls back and looks at her, brows raised. He brushes his cheeks with the back of his hand.

"I've been thinking. Nothing would have pleased her more than to have a center for nuns here in town. Monastic centers for bhikkhus are springing up all over, but there are few for nuns. You could do it. You could find a place, I'm sure, and convert it into a residence for *bhikkhunis*." She looks at him questioningly.

His eyes narrow and he gazes past her into space. The he looks at her with light in his eyes for the first time in weeks. "As long as you promise not to join them!"

She smiles, profoundly relieved to see a sign of revival. They have been wandering in a foggy land and missing each other. She reaches for his hand.

February 10. Asoka has been well taken care of by his benefactor, who considers his presence a blessing for the entire household. Under the skilled attention of the family's doctor, he has spent many days on his back—far too many for his liking. He thought he would go mad from the boredom. A bhikkhu can only meditate for so long at a stretch. But his back has now healed, and his ankle is well on its way, and he, who was always lean, has gained weight from the inactivity and sumptuous food brought to him by servants at midday. It would be insulting to refuse any of it.

On most evenings, he teaches and answers questions. At first, when he was confined to bed, family members came to his room, where he would lie with the mosquito curtains raised and offer the

Buddha's teachings. It was very uncomfortable. The family's presence in his room, women included, was an intrusion, not to mention an infraction of monastic rules.

He hadn't shared his living space with a layperson for twenty years, but being unable to move and immensely grateful for the care he was receiving, he decided to regard the situation with flexibility and good humor. He took the Buddha's visit to his bedside early on as sanction for the irregularity, which it was.

They are a large family—the master and mistress, in their mid-forties, their eldest son and his young family, and their youngest as yet unmarried son. Their second son, who lives nearby, also attends. Like many people, they are accustomed to living in close quarters, though theirs are more luxurious than most. It didn't occur to them that their presence in his room was inappropriate. They had no precedent. Eventually his back healed enough so that he could walk to the parlor, and he was relieved.

There, he sits on a chair, crutch at his side, while listeners sit on lower chairs or the floor. The benefactor and his wife initially insisted that their grandchildren attend, for they wanted them to be blessed by the bhikkhu's presence. But the young ones were bored and wriggly, and the grandparents soon deemed them adequately blessed and left them in the care of servants or their daughter-in-law, whose interest in the Dhamma is tepid. She is happy to be absent from the gatherings.

In the parlor, Asoka welcomes company, which occasionally includes bhikkhus who are passing through Saketa. The monastic communications network effectively spread news about his indisposition. There was talk at Ghosita's Park about bringing him back to recuperate, but when the Buddha arrived, he capped the discussion. "Leave him where he is. He's getting what he needs." Harika's legalistic mind objected—it's a violation of the Vinaya—but he said nothing.

He has, however, been mostly alone and has come to relish the hours of solitude. This has surprised him. "What's happening to you, Asoka?" he has asked himself aloud.

A ripening is happening. A great hush is blossoming within. Unwilling or unable to touch it, he watches, as though from a distance, as the process unfolds. This morning when he awakens, the hush and heaviness in his belly are larger than ever. Again he wonders, What's happening to you, Asoka?

After rising and washing, he moves out into the garden amid the jackfruit, mango and ornamental trees and flowerbeds, where he walks daily. Fragile signs of spring are everywhere. He steps off the path to examine a young flame tree and draws a branch close, looking for buds that will in time ignite into glorious flower. He stands for a long moment, neither thinking nor not thinking. When he turns to continue his walk, he stumbles on an exposed root and falls to his hands and knees.

As he straightens, silence envelops him. It is utter. There are no sounds. But the absence of sounds isn't the essence, nor the absence of everything else—for everything else *is* absent. Rather, the essence is a fullness so complete that it is unfathomable, a crack in space that is wholeness.

It lasts just a moment. At least, reviewing later, he thinks it was just a moment. Then it's over. Sounds burst upon his ears—birds sing, a child calls from inside the house, street sounds clatter beyond the garden walls, and all returns to normal. Yet nothing is normal. Asoka has become a stranger who hasn't heard or seen any of this before. Or he has: He has seen it all, but not like this. It's as though, until this moment, everything was black and white, and now, for the first time, he sees colors.

He walks in a daze back to his room and finds that it, too, is new: familiar, yet unfamiliar. Something's wrong with me, he thinks. But he knows that nothing is wrong. It's simply gone, his old sense of himself and the world is gone, and who or what he is, what the world is, is a bright mystery. It is the first day of the rest of his life.

He stands in the doorway looking into the room he has occupied for several weeks. For a moment, there is grief for what has been lost, which is everything. And fear. Then, slowly, a deep-down laugh is born. There is a shaking of his shoulders, and the music of his laughter rises and fills the room, and the heaviness in his belly has disappeared. A servant passing in the hall gazes at the back of the orange-robed monk. She pauses and smiles.

February 12. Ordinarily bhikkhus ask their Dhamma questions in assembly so all may benefit from the response. Pindola, however, considers himself an exception. That is, he has an exceptional need to impress his teacher, who hasn't yet given him the attention he feels he deserves. It's time to make some headway, he has decided.

Venerable Sunakkhatta said "yes." The Buddha's attendant knows who Pindola is and agreed to his request for a private meeting. Now, this afternoon, he is sitting in the Buddha's hut, and having exchanged polite preliminaries, his teacher is silent, waiting for him to speak.

"Bhagava, I'm confused about the nature of consciousness and no-self. What is consciousness, and how is it that I am conscious since there is no-self?" He deliberated long about this question. It must be suitably complex. It must reveal the depth of his inquiry and practice.

The Buddha regards him thoughtfully. His searching gaze makes Pindola feel naked. "Bhikkhu, don't come to me privately with such questions. This is to be asked in assembly."

He feels like a child again, being scolded by his father.

"But since you're here, listen closely. There are six forms of consciousness, each associated with one of the senses—eye consciousness, ear consciousness and so forth." The Buddha' teaches that the sixth sense is the mind. "When a sense object impinges on a sense organ—the sound of a voice on the ear, for example—the corresponding consciousness activates. When the sound ceases, ear consciousness likewise ceases. There's an ever-changing flow of sense objects impacting sense organs and the arising and passing away of their corresponding consciousness. An uninstructed person identifies with the sense organs and their consciousnesses and believes 'I am the one who is experiencing this. This is me and mine.' But the view that self is in the body is a false view. It's a foolish view."

No one has called him "foolish" except his father, who made a habit of it.

"Such a belief would mean that, if one lost the use of all senses except the eyes, then the self would reside only there, in the eyes and eye consciousness. So what do you think, Pindola? Does that belief make sense? "

"No, venerable sir." Clearly this is the required response.

"Then, is it correct to believe that the self exists in a shifting heap of sense organs and sense consciousnesses?"

"No, venerable sir."

"Even so, bhikkhu," the Buddha concludes.

'Even so'—what does that mean? He heard the words and followed their meaning, more or less, but he still knows himself to be a person. How could it be otherwise? "Marvelous, Bhagava," he says, performing anjali, his face shining with gratitude.

He is about to stand and leave when the Buddha says, "Pindola, eat less. A lack of self-control is an obstacle to liberation, and that's the reason to go forth, the reason one becomes a bhikkhu, isn't it? To be liberated." There is a near smile on his lips. "And remember, you're not the only one whom your gluttony affects. A bhikkhu who lacks self-restraint undermines householders' confidence in the monastic sangha."

The abrupt shift from elevated abstraction to a very unpleasant specific is jarring. He anjalis but says nothing. If it were easy to do, he would have, long ago. His father has been haranguing him about restraint since he was thirteen.

Pindola spends the rest of the afternoon not so much trying to understand consciousness and no-self, nor committing to weight loss, but evaluating progress in his relations with his teacher. He concludes, Overall, not bad. Even his remark about my weight shows he cares. I've made some headway. But the Buddha's comment about foolishness still stings.

February 20. "It's healed, but you have a long journey ahead of you, venerable. You want to be sure you're strong enough. Give it a bit more time," his doctor advised recently.

This time Asoka is listening. It *will* be a long journey, and he needs to prepare. The extra weight has to go. With a courteous explanation to the servants, he declines some of the abundant food offerings, and leaving his benefactor's garden, he begins to take lengthy morning walks in the city that he has been so un-fond of.

What a surprise! There is nothing wrong with Saketa. It is like any other city! Even more surprising is the discovery that the city itself never was the problem. His prejudice was, and that has disappeared, along with a lot of other things. How did it happen? He didn't do anything. Now, there is a freshness to Saketa that makes his moments in town joyful. It's amazing!

In addition to amazement, a question preoccupies Asoka: Where will I go? He has asked it countless times since he was bedridden, but now he knows that, wherever it is, once he gets there, he won't be leaving, at least not in the way he did before, when he traveled free as a bird for nine months each year. He is at peace with this knowledge. What kept his feet compulsively moving over the great breadth of the Middle Land, his easy assumption that wandering was freedom, has evaporated as well.

Jeta's Grove in Savatthi and the Bamboo Wood in Rajagaha are the two most obvious choices. Either would provide a fine home base for an aging monk, he thinks.

Asoka becomes a familiar sight in the neighborhoods. Many wonder why this bhikkhu isn't carrying a begging bowl. Word spreads that he is staying at Mahanama Migara's home and is teaching the Dhamma there at night. The doors are open. Evenings at Migara's become something of a civic event. The Buddha's adherents as well as the curious come, men and women. Many begin to consider him their own special bhikkhu.

He is a fine teacher. When bhikkhus teach, they recite the Buddha's words, which they have memorized. Asoka's facility with words and his sharp memory enable him to do so more accurately than some. Moreover, listeners notice in him a quality that is compelling, something they can't quite identify, and his answers to their questions are deeply insightful.

Especially attentive are Bakkula, the youngest son of the house, and his cousin. They listen with grave attention. The benefactor and his wife exchange glances, alert to the signals. Young men all over the region are attracted to the Buddha's teachings and are leaving home to go forth into homelessness.

It's time, Migara thinks, for the venerable to be on his way. And he reviews a list of prospective brides.

Still, both parents are deeply drawn to the Dhamma, especially the mother. She knows that if it weren't for family obligations, she would become a bhikkhuni. Bakkula's mother begins to make room in her heart for the possibility that their son may want to go forth. Because no son lightly contravenes parental wishes, she considers, in her thorough way, If he comes to us, I'll speak on his behalf. She will remind her husband that their two older sons are carrying on the family and will suggest very sweetly, "If Bakkula really wants to leave, should we prevent him? Should we not be happy for him? Shouldn't we give him time to make up his mind and, if this is what he wishes, let him go with our blessings? Think of the merit he would accrue for the family."

Thus it happens that this morning, when Asoka is walking in the garden before he sets out for the city, Migara joins him. "May I speak with you, venerable?" he inquires, looking intently at Asoka, his palms joined in anjali.

Asoka nods and they walk together.

Knowing that Asoka is planning to leave soon, he diffidently asks him to postpone his departure. "It would be a great blessing." He explains that his youngest son and nephew are showing interest in going forth. Asoka has noticed. He states that he and his wife want the young man's highest good, and they want to give him time to become clear about his desires. "One doesn't go forth lightly. My nephew needs time, too," he adds. "And if Bakkula decides for it, we'll need to have family gatherings to say good-bye. We'll want to properly honor his leave-taking. It would require a few weeks."

Asoka is silent. The father looks at him apprehensively.

At last, Asoka says, "You've given me very good care, Mahanama. You've been extremely generous, and now my body is healthy. I'm ready to travel. But I'll return. I'll come back in a month and a half and, if either young man wishes to go forth, I'll take him with me. It can't be later than that because they'll need to be in robes before the rains. There aren't ordinations during the rains retreat."

The father nods. Then his voice drops. "If it comes to it, would you look after my boy? Keep him safe on the journey—and afterwards?"

CHAPTER 14.
EXECUTION

March 18. The family is arriving. Fifty-seven relatives, so far. Culla Magandiya and his wife (whom servants note shows no sign of illness) and another uncle, auntie and their children are staying with Magandiya. Those not lodging with relatives or friends are housed with wealthy strangers as guests of the state.

For the past several days, a squad of royal guards has been secretly preparing the celebration grounds. This is a pleasure park just outside the city owned by Gopaka Phagguna, a wealthy merchant. Phagguna was honored to let his king use the park for his outing. The prospect of a royal reward brightens his days.

He doesn't mind that he has been forbidden to visit his park while improvements are underway and was delighted when, five days ago, he was invited to view the pavilion, which was almost finished. Located at the park's entrance, it is an impressive addition, though larger than anything Phagguna and his family will need. More recently, invitations to view other improvements haven't been forthcoming.

In a well-tended field surrounded by trees, where deer frequently graze, guards have been digging one hundred holes, each five feet deep. Bharadvaja has made a generous guess about numbers, to be on the safe side.

Today the digging is done, and the guards cart in wagonloads of straw, placing a large mound and a shovel next to each hole. Then, after parking ten plows at the far end of the field, they leave, tired but satisfied that they've finished on time. The king will be pleased. They weren't told the purpose of this assignment, but it's not hard to guess. They avoid talking about this and try to not to think about it.

Because of the need for secrecy, the digging has been done just after sunup. Even so, the movement of ten men through town and its outskirts at an hour when street vendors are setting up shop have attracted attention. Though in work clothes and traveling in ones and twos, the men are known to be royal guards. Word has spread, and some townspeople come by the park to look. To prevent them from entering, Bharadvaja, ever thorough, has sentries posted along the frontage and the inner perimeter as well. The curious are told, "The public will be invited to the celebration on the twentieth. Come back then."

March 20. The first official event is held at the palace at noon. The entire family is present. All sixty-eight of them. They are dazzled by the banquet—a great array of meats, grains, vegetables and sweets, served in bowls of gold and silver with servants, barefooted, in royal livery noiselessly attending to every need.

Elders eat lounging on divans while the rest sit cross-legged or with legs folded to one side. Young children, with tacit parental permission, scamper around the royal dining hall as though it were their parlor at home, getting in the way of the servants and creating clamor. Udena, who is honoring the guests with his presence, smiles benignly on the chaos from his decorated divan.

After the meal, the children are temporarily confined to their parents' side, where they fidget while the king addresses the assembly. He welcomes all and reminds them of the happy reason for the occasion—his beloved, Magandiya. He extols her devotion, her beauty, her family lineage. She is one of the jewels of the kingdom, a treasure.

Of the illustriousness of their lineage, the family needs no instruction, and one look at the kingdom's treasure impresses upon them the truth of all his other praises. She is adorned like the queen she is. Her sari, the finest Benares muslin, is the color of fire like a flame tree. Gems set in pure silver and gold blaze on her fingers, at her ears, and on her wrists. At her forehead is the large ruby the king gave her when their marriage was young. Dangling from a rope of pearls wound through her hair and held in place with exquisitely worked hairpins, it glitters when she moves her head. Flowers, also in her hair, and costly scents envelop her in fragrance. Nor is her beauty, even with her advancing years, outshone by the magnificence of her attire.

Yes, her family is convinced. So is Magandiya, who is flushed as she reclines on a divan at her husband's side. A regal smile graces her lips, which like her hands and feet, are dyed with red lac, and she dips her shining head in acknowledgement of her husband's praise.

At the conclusion of his comments, Udena invites, which is to say, commands, the assembly to attend a special sporting event. A servant explains that carriages will transport them from the palace to a pleasure park outside of town. The servant doesn't mention the nature of the sport, and no one asks.

Having feasted and refreshed themselves, laughing and dressed in their finery, a kaleidoscope of color, the family leaves the palace and enters the carriages for the twenty-minute journey to the park.

Not all are happy, though. Magandiya's thirteen-year-old cousin whines as she rides with her family, "But I don't want to see a sporting event. I'm sleepy! I want to go back to auntie's and go to bed." She's been sulking all afternoon because her mother wouldn't let her wear her favorite sari.

Her father chastises her, "Be quiet, child. This is an experience of a lifetime. You'll look back on this day when you're married and tell your children."

The girl grimaces. She leans against her mother's shoulder and closes her eyes. *At least I don't have to look at this horrid yellow sari— nobody can make me!*

The weather is ideal, sunny and still cool enough to be enjoyable. As the carriages move through town, citizens, who are alerted that something special is happening, gather along the route. They play drums and cymbals and shower the procession with flowers, a brilliantly colored rain. All are glad for the excuse for a holiday. Royal agents, casually dressed, are stationed along the route whispering the news for those who may not have heard: A royal sporting event is being held at Gopaka Phagguna's park; the public is invited. The crowd grows and moves like a giant amoeba through the streets to the city's north gate. Most have never been to a pleasure park, but locating this one isn't a problem since it has been well scouted.

The queen and her family are driven to the newly constructed pavilion at the park's entrance. The rectangular structure is built of twenty-four tree trunks sunk into the ground, framed by wooden girders below and above, and topped by a thatched roof slanting down from a ridgepole in the style common to the Middle Land. The side facing the park's entrance is open, but the other three sides are covered with bamboo screens that are dropped to the floor and reach three-quarters of the way up, an arrangement that allows for cross-ventilation while providing shade and, not incidentally, blocking the view.

No one thinks much about the screens as they excitedly move into the pavilion to await the king's arrival. For the convenience of the elderly, a few cushions have been scattered on the tamped-earth floor along the perimeter, but most people mill about and talk animatedly. Included in the crowd are three young men from town who joined the family on a dare and entered the pavilion, laughing and unnoticed. Children run everywhere within. One of Magandiya's cousins is silent for a moment and inhales deeply; she loves the smell of fresh thatch.

Magandiya's five-year-old cousin wanders away from his mother's side. He peeks under one of the screens, then rushes back. "Mamma, Mamma, lotsa men out there!" he squeals, pointing urgently to the screen.

"Shhh, darling, shhh. The king will be coming."

"But..." She draws him close and puts her arm around him. He clings to her, burying his face in her leg until, comforted, he pulls away and joins other children. He doesn't return to the screens.

Magandiya's auntie, Uncle Culla Magandiya's wife, is immensely proud of her niece. To be honored by the king for unparalleled devotion! Her significant, bejeweled bosom heaves with emotion. Neither she nor anyone else knows how Magandiya displayed the devotion that so won their sovereign's gratitude, and Magandiya has prudently refrained from explaining.

To Auntie, then, and to all her relatives except the sullen teen, this moment is good. Very good. To its sweetness is added anticipation of the royal boon. They've naturally been wondering. The banquet would have been an appropriate occasion for the announcement, but maybe it will happen now, before the sporting event.

Magandiya and Auntie catch sight of each other across the pavilion and exchange a sweet, secret smile. Several female relatives admire her peacock fan, which Jenti has brought from the palace. They gather around, and a cousin whom Magandiya hasn't met before asks timidly, "May I hold it?" She graciously hands it to her.

Standing and talking, pleasant as it is, is tiring. People are getting restless. The children are becoming bored; being confined inside the pavilion isn't so much fun any more. Everyone would like to move on with the afternoon. Where is he?

Finally, the royal carriage arrives. Udena has waited to give the good citizens who are walking time to reach the park. They are now milling about on the road, prevented by guards from entering just yet. The throng deferentially parts to enable the carriage, drawn by the magnificent state horse, to pass.

The king strides into the pavilion accompanied by his royal chaplain, who as usual is dour. Whispers pass among the assembled as to who this personage is. The Royal Chaplain Bharadvaja, the most exalted brahmin in the kingdom! They savor their brahminic connection, even while aware that their great families were historically rivals.

The presence of the two august ones quickly imposes order. Parents call to their children, seated elders stand, and the family arranges itself before them. Amidst the group is a cousin who is a follower of the Buddha. Enjoying a full belly and practicing loving-kindness, he looks benignly at the royal one and at the man who presides over state-sponsored animal sacrifices that are so at odds with the Dhamma of non-harming.

To allow a little extra time for latecomers among the public to arrive, Udena makes more fulsome remarks about his queen. This nauseating charade is almost over, and he is immensely relieved—and also keyed up.

Biding for time, he bestows the much-anticipated boon upon each head of family. It's a generous gift that sends all exclaiming and performing repeated anjalis to this most benevolent of sovereigns. They talk excitedly among themselves. The king nods his head in royal acknowledgement. Such easy generosity! He waits patiently for the outpouring to die down.

Finally he says, "Esteemed family, honorable brahmins, it is now time for the sporting event. You will be escorted to the field just beyond the trees. It's but a short walk; however, if anyone needs help, let us know. Someone will assist you."

One of the screens at the back of the pavilion is dropped, and the family cheerfully moves through the opening and emerges blinking in the sun. Four very elderly people, each supported on the arm of a younger adult, step out unsteadily. The day's events and the waiting have over-taxed them. They would rather be home. It's almost over, though—they only need to walk a little way, then they can sit and doze through the sport.

A guard appears at Magandiya's side to escort her to the king. She didn't expect this, but his presence makes for a nice bit of pageantry; he'll walk in attendance as she and the king process to the royal dais. There is, though, something in his manner: polite, but not deferential. It jars her a bit, as though this were a military manoeuver, not a sporting event. She'll reprimand him if it continues, but for now, too much is happening to bother.

As soon as most people are outside, guards surround them, while another contingent, armed but polite, enters the pavilion at the front and conducts the last ones out.

The family looks around uncertainly. What's this? A few try to make light of the situation. Everything else about this visit is unprecedented, why not this, too?

Still in the pavilion, Magandiya now stands apart with her husband and the royal chaplain, the guard at her side. She frowns at the sudden intrusion of the troops.

As all are escorted through the grove—the king, queen, Bharadvaja, family members and the three uninvited youths—a troupe of monkeys swings from the tree canopy and chatters loudly in serenade. Several of the children, including the child who peeked under the screen, are afraid of the bold creatures and grab a parent's hand.

The five-year-old is crying and his mother reassures him, whispering soothingly into his ear, "It's okay, darling. The monkeys won't hurt you. Shhhhh." But she is becoming nervous. This is all so strange! She glances apprehensively at her husband, who is walking next to her, frowning.

Leaving the chattering monkeys behind, the company emerges from the trees, and stops. The field in front of them is pocked with holes and guards are interspersed among them, holding unlit torches. A moment of confusion, then realization.

Shouting, panic and struggling begin. Most cling to family members in huddles of desperation, frantically clutching at each other as guards wrench them apart. A few people try to break free and run but are restrained.

An unearthly roar slams into Magandiya: the sound of her universe collapsing. She starts to turn somewhere, anywhere, but her guard's hand clamps her shoulder and shoves her roughly forward. She is to walk a few steps behind her husband and Bharadvaja, neither of whom looks back at her as they proceed to the dais. She stumbles, then her body, regaining its balance, obeys and moves forward, but her mind has taken leave.

The dais, which is very large, was constructed in the shade of trees edging the field. Vasuladatta, ministers, high administrative councilors and a few others stand at its base awaiting the king. Mercifully, Princess Jinadatta and her two teen-aged cousins, Vasuladatta's daughters, have not been required to attend.

Udena mounts the dais and takes his seat, the highest, in the center. His two queens are seated beside him, Vasuladatta to his right and Magandiya, his left. Her guard squats at her side. Bharadvaja and the other notables mount the steps and are shown to their places on low individual sitting platforms that are placed closely together.

Four servants stand behind the king. One holds over his head the white parasol symbolizing royal power. Two others, standing on either side of the parasol-bearer, will fan him and wield a whisk to brush away flies. The fourth servant stands off to the side bearing the royal standard of black, red and yellow, which flutters in the gentle breeze. Sculptors of another era might have modeled their stone bas-reliefs on just this scene, which latter-day viewers would presume was joyous.

Unable to bear the brutality under way, Vasuladatta rises to leave, but Udena puts a hand on her arm and restrains her. She must be present. The full weight of official and familial support must stand behind this royal decision. Reluctantly, she sits again. She locks her gaze onto the wooden floorboards and cries. The whole afternoon her tears hardly stop, nor does she raise her eyes.

Now seated, Magandiya is rigid. She grips her fan so tightly that the diamonds and rubies at its base bite into her skin.

The public, which streamed into the park in high good humor, was directed along the same path and was also serenaded by the monkeys. Then, as people caught sight of the macabre scene, revulsion, excitement or both, depending on the individual, seized them. Guards politely instructed them to sit on the ground and formed a cordon to keep them at a distance from the doomed ones. No one is inclined to move closer. Nor, it is clear, are they at liberty to leave. Latecomers on the road, hearing the screams, quickly change their plans and hurry home. News of horror spreads through town even as it is underway.

From the royal dais, Magandiya, Udena and the other notables have a full view. People are struggling, screaming the names of loved ones and futilely reaching toward them as they are being marched or, in some cases, carried, to their destination. A few, including the woman who loves the smell of fresh thatch, wordlessly gaze at family from whose grasp they've been pried, then move to their death with a resigned dignity, which, while unnoticed by anyone in the midst of the chaos, speaks, perhaps, of a bigness of spirit that has graced their lives.

The Buddhist cousin isn't one of these. A large man, he fights with his guard until a second man steps in to help subdue him. The teen in the yellow sari is hysterical and doesn't realize that the guard who is carrying her is groping her. Remarkably, a younger cousin, a quick-witted eleven-year-old at the far edge of the melee, manages to escape. Unnoticed by any except several spectators, who say nothing, she darts into the woods, then creeps through the trees and joins the crowd, which protectively closes around her.

Jenti, who is standing near her mistress at the dais' base, is seized by a guard. She gesticulates wildly, exclaiming that she isn't a family member. "I know that, Jenti," he says through gritted teeth. He knows Jenti's second cousin, who is also a member of the royal guard and who has often spoken of her proudly. This isn't easy for him, but when she tries to bolt, he steels himself, grabs and carries her thrashing.

Jenti's guard isn't alone. This is the most terrible assignment of these men's career. Digging the holes was nothing, just manual labor. But what they are doing now, the hideous annihilation that is underway, the agony, screams and death, will torment them hereafter, never will they escape its horror. They arrived on this field as strong men; they will leave defeated.

Magandiya faints. The fan drops from her hands and isn't seen again in public. The guard crouching by her side, moves in front and splashes her with water from a bowl at his feet—he is prepared. She revives. When she closes her eyes, he twists her arm, "Open your eyes!" Cruel, cruel man!

Each person, young and old, is buried to the chest, and straw is piled on top of the earth. Six children, infants, are permitted to stay in their mothers' arms, and, in consideration, the women are buried only to their waist. One woman, far along in pregnancy, who shouldn't have risked the journey, aborts her fetus when the weight of the earth presses on her belly. Her screams are lost in the din.

The guards light the torches and, quickly walking from hole to hole, set each ablaze. Culla Magandiya's hole is last. The screams of terror and resistance change now into shrieks of mortal pain. Those who were human beings only minutes before become writhing masses of pain beyond bearing. The guards retreat to the edge of the field.

Magandiya's mind shrieks as well: Anything, anything but this! To be away, gone, dead! She faints again. And again.

When water isn't sufficient, her guard slaps her face, and she revives to see mean, narrowed eyes, just inches from her face, glaring at her pitilessly. Her world becomes those eyes and the slaps, and they are kinder than the one beyond.

Eventually, the shrieks from the field subside into unconscious groans, and life ebbs. It is time. In a loud voice, Udena declares Magandiya's crime. "Queen Magandiya has confessed to the unspeakable crime of murdering Queen Samavati, her children and her household. She planned the fire at the queen's mansion, the fire that killed all the residents except my daughter, Princess Jinadatta. She planned this crime, which is of a magnitude we've never witnessed in Vamsa. We've never seen its like before, and, as long as I am king, we never shall again.

"As protector of my people, I am responsible for maintaining order in this kingdom and for ensuring that justice is carried out impartially everywhere. That includes within my own family. Especially in my own family. As even in village councils, when a council member is guilty of serious wrongdoing, the entire family is punished, so too we cannot, we must not, do less in the case of a queen. To exact a lesser punishment would mean that I have failed in my divinely ordained responsibility to protect all the subjects of my realm! But I have not failed! I, who am a just and benevolent king, a maharaja, who cares for the well-being of every citizen, I am carrying out justice."

Magandiya is only vaguely aware of his words. She doesn't try to listen. There is no need.

For the benefit of citizens who might be unable to hear his voice, several officials have moved behind the guards who are detaining the public. They repeat their sovereign's words. The king wants everyone to be very clear why this execution is necessary.

The royal proclamation and the gruesome scene have imposed silence on the crowd. Even the monkeys are quiet. Many people watch and listen transfixed, while others bury their face in their hands. The stench of burning bodies drifts over all. Some onlookers are nauseated and vomit.

Whatever their individual reactions to this nightmare and to being involuntarily subjected to it, all the citizens understand their king's decision. They have a precise appreciation of the circumstances under which an entire family is legally punishable for the wrongdoing of a single member, and the seriousness of this crime is beyond dispute.

Brahmins, the priestly class, the only class anciently privileged to celebrate religious services, are sacrosanct and consequently exempt from corporal punishment, including the death sentence. The exemption will have the force of law in a later era, but even now it is widely observed. Yet in this case, this extraordinary case, most people don't need to argue pros and cons. They unanimously endorse the execution of this brahmin family. Disregarding the fact that the majority of the executed didn't live in Vamsa and so weren't the king's subjects, most citizens, even though appalled, don't think the punishment extravagant.

Bharadvaja, who is seated next to Vasuladatta, is impassive. Having presided over animal sacrifices for years, the royal chaplain is accustomed to the screams of dying creatures. Is this so different? Animal sacrifices are holy, and so too, he has persuaded himself, is this.

The king must ensure political stability and collective prosperity in his kingdom, or he forfeits his divine right to rule. If Magandiya's grave crime were not sternly dealt with, the cosmic balance would, according to Vedic wisdom, be jeopardized.

There's further significance to today's proceedings, something Bharadvaja doesn't disclose: At one blow, he has crippled an eminent brahmin family that historically was rival to his own. Brahmins are sacrosanct, true, but there are exceptions! Today's is an event of legendary proportions, to be sung through the ages to come. Like a prince in the great epics, he is a servant of destiny, taking revenge for ancient betrayals and calumnies, thereby showing reverence for his ancestors and protecting the Bharadvaja clan.

At last the groans fade, and all is quiet in the field. Magandiya's guard, who was standing in front to revive her, now steps aside as instructed. Ten bullocks are being hitched to the plows at the end of the field, and she watches as they begin to plow the corpses into the ground. She faints again.

This is the moment Udena has been waiting for, the moment to announce his plan, and he wants Magandiya to hear it. With a sideways nod in her direction, he signals the man to do his duty.

Once she is revived, the king proclaims, "My people!" The officials, still in place behind the line of guards, repeat loudly, "Maharaja Udena says, 'My people!'"

He continues, "Our late, beloved Queen Samavati, the mother of the heir apparent, was a queen of the highest virtue. She has been taken from us most cruelly. We cannot restore to life this loyal wife, this queen of queens, but we can remember her always and honor her as she deserves to be honored."

As is common among those who have lost a dear one, Udena focuses on the bright memories. In his praise, he forgets his past suspicions and jealousies. Forgotten, too, is the fact that only four months ago he tried to murder her. He wouldn't have harbored unworthy suspicions in the first place if it hadn't been for Magandiya's conniving. He realizes this now. The executions and the grand plan that he is announcing are his expiation. Never again need he regret his earlier behavior. In fact, he needn't think about it any more. So he has counseled himself.

Udena pauses to give the officials a chance to relay his words and to check out Magandiya's state of consciousness. She's alert but is staring into the featureless sky. Does she hear?

"I will build a monument to our beloved queen, a monument the size and splendor of which has never been seen in all the land! In this way, our queen will be remembered forever." It needn't be mentioned that the monument will also attest to his stature as a maharaja, a wheel-turning monarch. His father would appreciate this moment.

Bharadvaja is looking at him, surprised. This isn't part of our plan!

The crowd, hearing their king's words, cheers dutifully, but with little heart. Bharadvaja is concerned: Samavati was a follower of the Buddha, and the plan will aggrandize the recluse. He doesn't approve.

Ghosita, seated on the platform some distance from the king, has been so sickened by the spectacle that he has retreated into the numbness that became home after Samavati's death. Udena's tribute elicits a cynical thought from the frozen mass: At last! At last, the bastard sees her worth. Too bad it's too late. And a fleeting thought to the stupendous cost of the king's plan—he is treasurer after all.

"The monument will be built in merchant Nanda Mendaka's beautiful pleasure park, which has recently become royal property," Udena proclaims. "It adjoins these very grounds so that the execution and the justice we have witnessed here today will be hallowed forever by the presence nearby of our revered and beloved queen. Those grounds will become a public park, open to you all, the good citizens of our great kingdom of Vamsa."

Dead silence. Then a hum of voices as people turn to each other in confusion. How to respond? With their mother's milk, they have absorbed an abhorrence of pollution and the need for ritual purity. Granted, the memorial will be adjacent to these grounds, not on them, but it will be close. Too close. In their minds, the king's plan mixes the un-mixable.

Gopaka Phagguna, who was immensely proud to be invited to sit among the august ones, is experiencing shortness of breath. His hands rigidly grasp his sitting platform to brace him against the shocking events. Adding significantly to this calamity to his way of thinking is the fact that his park has been despoiled forever, and, anyway, it is no longer his. The king has claimed it.

As though picking up on Phagguna's thoughts, Udena turns to him and announces, "Our esteemed citizen, merchant Phagguna has graciously allowed us to use his park. He will be compensated. We will bestow another beautiful park upon him for his and his family's use. His is an example of citizen loyalty that we happily acknowledge and honor."

Phagguna lets loose the sitting platform. He joins palms in an-jali and bows his head to his sovereign as all look on. In later days, after the horror—or justice, depending on your viewpoint—is over, he decides that the new pleasure park, though considerably smaller, is much the better part of the deal.

Udena isn't finished. Now for the final, brilliant stroke. Turning back to the public, he declares, "Let it further be known that the remains of our great queen, my dear children and her household servants, which are currently buried at the altar at her former residence on the palace grounds, these will be transferred to the new site. And fountains, a tank, and beautiful gardens will be constructed, as well as a large pavilion to provide shelter from sun and rain. Any who visit the memorial shall receive Queen Samavati's blessings of lovingkindness. She generously bestowed them upon all she met during her lifetime. Now, she will bestow them upon you, good citizens of Vamsa. You will be blessed by her forever."

The long-restrained emotions of this volatile man are being directed toward this splendid gesture. He is outdoing himself in eloquence. To his credit, he now recognizes that at the heart of Samavati's many virtues was lovingkindness. His own supply may be nonexistent, but he has at last noticed hers.

Bharadvaja doesn't hear the eloquence. Every brahminic instinct in him is in revolt. To place next to this polluted ground the remains of the honored dead, remains that have been consecrated in the holy waters of the River Yamuna—it's inconceivable! In people's mind and in his own, it will be as though they were interred in this very ground. Bharadvaja has never thought much of the king's judgment, but this tops it all. How did he come up with such an abominable scheme?

The answer is that, beyond his need for personal atonement, Udean is fighting demons. It is a battle that takes priority over all others. His plan will silence gossip that evil spirits caused one of his queens to murder another and will put paid to the suspicion that his reign is cursed. He hasn't actually heard the gossip—who would dare speak in front of a king?—but he knows, he knows. The palace and town are abuzz with it.

Worse, he's afraid the gossip may be right. Daily he is tormented by malevolent voices within shouting that his royal house and he himself are cursed. He won't permit it! He, ruler by divine right, regulator of the seasons, embodiment of state power, insurer of prosperity in the land, he will fight these demons like the noble warrior he is!

That is what he is doing now. Enshrining Samavati's ashes in the ground close to Magandiya's corpse and those of her family will, in the eyes of demons, gods and men, reunite his family that has been so tragically torn apart. In death, his two queens shall be united in peace—under his royal auspices. His people, his ministers, everybody will bow in love and awe before him, the maharaja.

Bharadvaja stares at the king. A new and alarming thought occurs to him: Is the man mad? Has he cracked under the strain? Has he become a danger to the very state that he heads?

Absorbed in his declaration, Udena doesn't heed Bharadvaja. People always stare at a maharaja. One stare means nothing.

The maharaja now turns to Magandiya's guard, signaling him to perform his penultimate task. This scene has been well rehearsed. The man glances at the queen to make sure she's conscious. She is. She's still involved with the sky.

Her silent shrieking has stopped, come to a dead halt in the whiteness. A numb mind. She surrenders, yielding finally to the truth that is waiting for her, just a moment away. A peace she has never known descends. The gods' embrace Magandiya at last.

She is hardly aware of the guard who, having stepped in front of her, is stripping off her jewelry and placing it in a bag he carries for this purpose. Then he moves behind, puts hands on her temples and firmly turns her head toward the king, her lord, her husband, the man she has made love to, lied to and manipulated a thousand times.

She, who is the occasion of the carnage, the centerpiece of it all, regards him vacantly. His heavy jowls, balding head, lips compressed in a grim line, hard eyes trained on her, discharge an unmistakable message: Now it's your turn.

CHAPTER 15.

SATI'S PANIC

*M*arch 20. Breaking his pledge to remain silent, this morning Ghosita informed the Buddha about what was to transpire at the pleasure park. He didn't want to do it. He wanted to spare his teacher and the other bhikkhus knowledge of the massacre. But they would have learned afterwards, and his allegiance to the Buddha's order is greater than his vow of confidentiality as a government official. Besides, he assumes the Blessed One knows, anyway.

So it is that throughout the afternoon, the monks at Ghosita's Park are gathered in the assembly hall, offering prayers and compassion. The Buddha is meditating in his hut.

Some of the younger bhikkhus chafe at their inability to take action. They yearn to help those who are suffering. Others, more senior, have come to peace with this fundamental monastic constraint. The Dhamma, which they offer freely, teaches men and women in the dusty world to act wisely and compassionately so that they may alleviate their own suffering. And, as on this afternoon, their silent meditative offerings are, they believe, a powerful, if intangible, force for good. The Buddha teaches that bhikkhus are a field of merit for the many.

Field of merit or not, all in this hall today are profoundly distressed by the slaughter that is unfolding. It is as though the screams of the dying are shattering the silence and ravaging the very air in the hall. They bless these screams, these people, with hearts of compassion.

March 20. Though no Dhamma talk was scheduled tonight, townspeople flock to the monastic park. They are turning to the Buddha

and his Dhamma like children reaching for their mother's hand. First the fire, now this. Usually cheerfully outgoing, tonight most of those assembling are too shocked to speak or even think much. There are among them, however, a few experts at distancing themselves from emotion.

"Bharadvaja didn't come out of that too badly, did he?" A sardonic smile.

"Don't be snide, Dona. Just because you don't like him. How could our most high and holy chaplain have done wrong?" Another sardonic smile. These two are cousins.

A third companion chimes in, "It's like antiquity came alive again." He was present at the massacre. "The old enmity between the Bharadvajas and Magandiyas, right in front of our eyes."

The other two look at him. What else are we discussing?

"What?" the third asks, glancing from one to the other uncertainly. "What did I say?"

Yet, as they engage in their usual banter, all three, being wealthy brahmins, feel a little less secure. On this point, they *can* get emotional. Maybe they and theirs aren't exempt from punishment, after all. Not that they're breaking any laws.

A fourth man, brother to the first, is sitting nearby and interjects over the heads of a few people, "Oh, stop quibbling! It's done! What about what's not yet done—the king's plan to build a sanctuary next to the charnel ground? It's an outrage!" He wags his head energetically and waves his arms, coming precariously close to hitting a neighbor. "That's what it is, an outrage! That's what we need to think about. How do we get around that?"

Such comments will erupt in town like a plague over the next few days, but right now, the Buddha's entry into the hall silences everyone. He has been fasting and meditating in his hut. Taking the seat prepared for him at the front, he meditates again. All join, or at least imitate the posture, and some find invoking the discipline of meditation to be grounding.

Afterwards, the Buddha speaks. Even knowing that, for most of those gathered, his words will bounce like raindrops off a roof in a hard storm, for hearts are too raw to be comforted. Nonetheless, he talks of lovingkindness and compassion. What else is there to talk about? "People of Kosambi, you are confronted with great suffering. Men, women and children died today like animals, without knowing why they were being slaughtered. Most were not residents of this city, nor even citizens of this land. They were not your kin. But they were human beings like you are, and though none of us can do anything to restore them to life—they are gone—you can open your hearts. Recognize the preciousness of this human life. It is precious and brief, for death comes to all, sooner or later. Honor life. Don't cause harm. Don't create suffering. Don't deceive anyone or despise anyone anywhere. Do only good. Cultivate a heart that is free of resentment and hatred, a heart that embraces all the world in lovingkindness. In your shock and sorrow, be kind to each other. Be like a mother who risks her life to protect her children. Towards all living beings cultivate a boundless heart. Practice this daily so that your mind dwells always in lovingkindness and compassion. May all beings be free from suffering. May all beings be happy."

He is silent for several moments. There is no movement among the assembly. Then he begins to meditate again, and they follow. The evening wears on, and, while the he remains immobile, people begin to stir. One by one, then in small groups, they silently get up and leave. The Buddha, the monks and a few laypeople remain in the hall until late into the night.

March 21. The Buddha calls a special meeting with the bhikkhus in the assembly hall this afternoon. After a brief meditation, he makes an announcement. "Bhikkhus, I'll soon be leaving. It's time to continue my travels. They can't be delayed any longer."

There is a rustling, a low groan or two and much tightening of jaw muscles. They had wondered what this meeting was about, for none but Candana knew. Another calamity! We need you!

"Much work is to be done here. The people of Kosambi need guidance and teaching. And you, bhikkhus, not I, are the ones to offer it. You, the bhikkhus here at Ghosita's Park, and at Kukkuta's Park and Pavarikambavanna," referring to the two monastic centers outside of town, "are well known by townspeople. They have generously supported you. They listen to you. And now, after these two terrible events, you are the ones to salve the anguish in their heart. Apply the medicine of the Dhamma. Help them take refuge, because of all the medicines in the world, there is none like this. Their wounds are deep and healing will be slow, but you have all you need to help bring it about. The Dhamma—remember, when you have that, you have the *Tathagata*." (The Buddha uses this term to refer to himself. It means "thus gone one" or "enlightened one.") "The Tathagata is here with you."

Sati is panicky. The prospect, still unannounced, that he, as abbot, would be significantly called upon to respond to yesterday's horror has brought his mind to a standstill. The Buddha and Candana talked with him a few weeks ago and, against every inner defense, he allowed himself to be persuaded. Now, however, there's the execution, topped by Bhagava's news.

It's too soon to leave—the people need him! I need him!

After the meeting, he practically sprints to Candana's hut and fidgets on the portico, waiting. When he sees his mentor approaching, he rushes forward.

"Sir," he says without preliminary, "I can't do it. I can't be abbot. The people and the bhikkhus need comfort, they need wise advice. They need a real senior—they need you. They don't want me. I can't do it."

His husky voice cracks as it rises to a register beyond its range.

"Control yourself," Candana commands.

Silently and deliberately, Candana walks into the hut. Sati agitates at his side. Spreading his sitting mat, which he carried back from the assembly hall, Candana says quietly, pointing to the other mat "Sit down, Sati."

Once seated, Candana pauses for a moment, then says firmly, "Yes, you can do it. You ..."

Sati interrupts, his voice rising again, "I can't! What would I say? I don't have the wisdom. Or the seniority. Many people call me an outcaste. I lied for ten years. I've done penance in front of everybody. I've been demoted."

"Forget about the lie! It's over. Penance is done. Your status as an elder will be reconfirmed for the benefit of anyone who questions it. We've talked about these things. We've gone through all of that. Yes, this is a terrible time, a great ordeal. The suffering is profound. Neither Bhagava nor I wanted it to start like this for you, but here it is. He sanctioned your appointment, so did I. You *will* be abbot."

"Even if I convinced myself that I'm abbot, what about everybody else? Who would listen to me? Nobody wants me. Nobody's going to accept me! It hasn't been announced yet; there's still time to change things."

"Everybody must accept you, and sooner or later they will."

They sit in silence for a few moments. Then Candana, knowing how hard it is going to be, assures him in a softened tone, "I'll be there, Sati. I'll advise you. You won't be alone."

"After Bhagava leaves, will you give the talks? Will you meet with people?"

"No, I won't. You *must* take the lead. I'll be there to support you, but you must lead. That's important."

Sati's body sags.

"You can do this. You *do* have the wisdom. Bhagava knows it and so do I."

It's over. Sati rises, turns his back and walks out the door. He doesn't bow.

Candana is distressed. Got to talk with Bhagava—and Udayi. They *must* reassure him. And he questions the wisdom of retiring now of all times. But how could I have known?

Then a thought: Bhagava knew. He knew the execution was going to happen, didn't he? Isn't that why he stayed all this time—so that he could be here when it did? And if he knew and agreed to my retiring, then he also knew that Sati could manage. With these thoughts, Candana allows his worries to drop for the time being.

March 22. Sati is collecting his bowl for almsround when Candana comes to his door. "Forget almsround, Sati. You're to meet with Bhagava this morning."

Sati nods and sets his bowl back on the shelf that holds his few belongings. The monks will share their alms food with him later. He says nothing. He didn't sleep last night. Almsround would have been taxing, but he's sure that talking with Bhagava is entirely beyond his capabilities. Yet somehow he finds himself in the Buddha's hut, sitting across from him.

The Teacher begins, "Candana told me about your conversation yesterday."

Obviously, thinks Sati sarcastically.

"And about your hesitations. Your fears are natural, friend. You lied, and a just penance was levied. Now it's finished. In the course of his monastic career, every bhikkhu does penance one way or another—if he hasn't, he hasn't made much progress. This was yours.

"If you weren't afraid and feeling inadequate at this point, you'd either be a prideful and unrealistic bhikkhu or else you'd be an *arahant*," referring to one who has reached a high level of spiritual attainment.

"And since you're not an arahant, I commend you on your modesty and realism."

Sati is surprised. He didn't know what he expected from the conversation, but it wasn't this.

"You're not in an easy position, Sati. This isn't the way either Candana or I wanted your new duties to begin," repeating Candana's comment from last night. "But this is what's happening. And you're right: People will remember your offense. They'll dismiss you as a junior monk and talk behind your back in town, even here at Ghosita's Park. They'll say you haven't the wisdom or maturity to lead. More than that, small-minded men will call you 'outcaste'."

Don't I know it! Pindola already has.

"People aren't to be judged by their class or lack of it—it's a basic principle of the Dhamma—you know that. But you, Sati, still get lost in others' judgments. You get entangled in the thicket of views, especially when they're about yourself.

"So I'll remind you because you seem to forget: First of all, you are not a junior. You're an elder. You didn't lose your wisdom or the title with the pronouncement of your penance. Even by the ten-year standard some bhikkhus hold, you've just passed the mark. Anyway, your seniority will be reaffirmed at the ceremony. Second, you were born a warrior, not an outcaste." The Buddha smiles at him.

"Learn to stick to the way things are, friend. And remember, that more important than what others say about you is what you say to yourself. Stop judging yourself unwisely. As long as you do that, others will too."

Sati is listening intently. He no longer feels tired.

"As you undertake these duties," he says, without giving Sati an option, "as you undertake them, you must remember that being abbot is not about you, Venerable Sati Abhaya. It is about the Dhamma, about relieving people of their suffering. What they say about you doesn't matter. Just do your duty, transmit the Dhamma as best you can, treat people with compassion, and forget your self-doubt. Do this, and the Dhamma will take care of you. It's very simple."

The Buddha stops and looks at him steadily, waiting. A silence blooms in the room, and Sati is drawn into it, settling like a stone tossed into a pond, except there is no bottom. He doesn't know how long he sits, but slowly it occurs to him that a response is required. He rouses himself, and without thought—there is no need to think—the response is clear. He nods. Yes.

The Buddha smiles. And Sati notices with wonder that he loves him. He loves the Blessed One like he loves no other, for the Buddha is like no other. It's taken me all these years to discover this! he thinks, amazed. He almost blames himself for thick-headedness, but instead he smiles back.

This evening, Venerable Udayi seeks out Sati, and they walk together in the grove before meditation.

"Psst, psst, Amba," Sati calls to her softly using the name Candana has given her—"Amba, mango," because she's colorful and sweet. Like most cats, Amba doesn't come at call. But in honor of their presence, she stops and sits at the edge of the path, and wrapping her tail neatly around her calico body, solemnly watches them pass.

"She's got a litter somewhere here."

Udayi laughs. "Why not? She's a smart cat. She knows a safe place."

They walk slowly because Udayi is frail. But his counsel is robust. He adds to the Buddha's assurances, based on his own long relationship with the younger monk.

"You can do this, Sati. Everything changes. We seniors grow old; new seniors follow, and among them are the clear-sighted and compassionate ones. You are compassionate, though you sometimes exclude yourself from its domain. And increasingly you're becoming clear-sighted.

"You won't solve all suffering. You can't, no one can. But you'll be a good abbot, and slowly—maybe not at first—people will come to appreciate and learn from you. And then, friend, years will pass, and your time, too, will be over. Over—such is the cycle of life."

By the time Sati enters the assembly hall this evening, his step is surer. He moves with a new perspective.

CHAPTER **16.**

THE NEW ABBOT

March 22. Candana lies on his cot, focusing on the day before him. His thoughts toy with questions. When is Bhagava leaving? Why hasn't he announced the transition? Sati's ready, I certainly am. What's he waiting for?

Suddenly he is ambushed. The fear he has so desperately been trying to conquer gallops out of a dark corner of his mind and tramples him. All this effort for nothing!

Fully awake now, he sits up in bed. He's been planning to tell Bhagava. Naturally. That's what being a bhikkhu means, being truthful in word and action, especially with one's teacher. He has just wanted to wait a little while—wait so he could come as a victor. Not this way. But he hasn't done it, and Bhagava will be leaving any time now, maybe even today. Maybe I'll never manage it, he laments.

Then through the murk, looming right in the middle of the road, a familiar shape blocks traffic. For the first time, at long last, he recognizes it: pride. Owww! What he thought was spiritual effort to overcome an impediment is pride, just pride! He has assumed that he, a senior bhikkhu, should be fearless, and he didn't want to speak until he was. He's not just a bhikkhu who is afraid. He's a *proud* bhikkhu who is afraid. He puts his head in his hands and cries.

It is a humble man who walks to the Buddha's hut after the midday meal. There's no fooling himself this time. This isn't monastic business. This is personal.

"Welcome, Candana," the Buddha says in response to the knock. Finally!

Candana smiles in spite of himself. This is how we started last time.

He explains. All of it—his fear, his efforts, his failure. Then a question he has long wanted to ask pushes forth: "What about you, Bhagava? Do you ever feel fear? Like when you're in a dangerous situation, maybe in a forest with a tiger nearby?"

"Of course."

Candana is amazed, and it shows all over his face.

The Buddha smiles. "Of course I do," he repeats.

"But you never said so!"

"No one ever asked."

"Oh."

"When there's danger, tightening occurs, a bodily alert." He puts a palm against his chest. "Most call it 'fear'. I call it simply 'tightening' or 'alertness.' The body reacting in a bodily way. That's how it protects itself. The mind recognizes the body's reaction and doesn't identify with it, doesn't call it 'my fear.' Non-identification happens without effort, without working at not grasping or not pushing away. This is what it means to feel no fear. This is purified bodily conduct. From here, a wise response, untainted by fear or delusion, emerges. When the tightening is present, it's present; the body is reacting. And when it's over, it's over, without remainder. There's no mulling about it afterwards.

"When most people face danger, they slip into a fear-filled reaction. We see it all the time."

Candana nods.

"They run, they fight. Sometimes that's necessary, but doing it automatically isn't the wise action of a noble one. And afterwards, the fearful ones carry the reaction around in their minds and bodies and gnaw on it like a dog on a bone. How frightened they were, what might have happened, and so on."

He pauses and smiles. "And when some bhikkhus experience fear, they blame themselves because they think they should be beyond it. They mull it over and over. Same thing—no mindfulness. In this case, it's attachment to a concept about the way things *should* be and aversion to the way they are. Don't get stuck in concepts, Candana. You understand the Dhamma well enough, the things I've taught.

Don't let conceptual understanding stand in the way. Penetrate beyond. Be with what's true in the moment, see things as they truly are, all of it. Then identification will loosen naturally, in its own time. You can't make it happen. In fact, fighting, like you've been doing, only adds more fear. Don't get ahead of things. Just trust."

Candana's mind is turning a somersault. "But you never said so," he repeats, filling in because his thoughts haven't caught up with this new understanding.

The Buddha sighs. He has faced this dilemma since he began teaching. "The Dhamma is subtle and hard to understand. What else have I been saying all these years? Except, granted, I haven't expressed it quite like this. Because no one ever asked like this."

"So..." Candana starts. "So, my body is going do things I can't control. It's probably going to make me dependent on others in ways I don't like." And in a rush of words—this is well-trod territory, "Until my mind gets so confused that I'm not aware of what's happening, of what I do or don't like, but at that point it wouldn't matter to me, because I wouldn't know. And maybe I won't get confused after all, but if it does start happening and before I'm completely mindless, I will know. Every inch of the decline. And I may experience fear all the way down, with each new little change. But..."

He slows, feeling his way. "But I don't have to push the fear aside. I don't have to fear my fear. Or blame myself for feeling it. None of that's necessary because..."

Nodding, the Buddha asks, "What do you think, Candana, is it possible not to judge what's happening to your body as decline? Can you see it simply as impermanence, a change in the way things are? Instead of comparing your present state to what you were at your prime, can you bring mindfulness and compassion, even interest, to how existence is expressing. Can you allow it to unfold as it will, rather than resist it? You have no choice about how it will unfold, you know, but you can dig in your heels and resist all the way. You can cause yourself great suffering. We're all going to die. None of us control death. Most people don't really know that. They think they know, but they don't. You do, however. And your illness will be an ongoing lesson in the great truth of impermanence. It will take you inexorably to deeper levels."

Candana is silent. His pride now seems to him a puny thing, like a little squirrel. It scampers off, out the door. No doubt, he will meet it again, but at this moment he knows that, while the way forward is dotted with fearful elements, they don't matter much.

March 23. After the noonday meal, when many would have preferred to sleep, the Buddha again called a special meeting. The bhikkhus assumed he would be giving a final teaching before his departure. Instead, he informed them that Candana would be retiring and Sati would be the new abbot.

The Buddha praised Candana—an exemplary monk who has offered great service to the sangha, facts of which all are well aware—and he stated that for health reasons, Candana feels it's time to relinquish his duties. He didn't elaborate. Candana will explain as he wishes. The bhikkhus have guessed at his sickness already, but of this other development, none knew, except Udayi and Sati.

The formal transition was brief. The Buddha and Candana had devised a simple ceremony, for there was no precedent. No abbot in the Buddha's order had retired and new one appointed because there are as yet few Buddhist monasteries and few abbots. By the time the meeting was over, no one felt like sleeping.

Now at this evening's public talk, before the Buddha speaks—this *is* to be his last talk—Candana announces the transfer of duties to the lay community. For the first time, Sati is sitting up front on the platform next to the Buddha and his mentor. He feels naked with all eyes on him. He quails.

There is muted hubbub among the townsfolk. The pause after the announcement and before the Buddha speaks gives them time to receive the news. Sati knows what they're saying; it doesn't take much imagination. He's the venerable who lived with outcastes. Yes, but he was born a noble. Strange history. Didn't he do some kind of penance recently—what was that about? Others provide details. Though the proceedings of Uposatha are confidential, word about major issues like Sati's offenses has a way of getting out. Some are scandalized anew. He's so young, and now that he's been penalized, is he even a senior? How can the Blessed One name him abbot? And most are sorry to hear about Candana. They plan to consult him for guidance, whether he is abbot or not.

Some of the monastic brothers who are looking at Sati are awed and surprised. A few look with the shut face of jealousy. Pindola is one of those.

Ghosita sits in the crowd and smiles encouragingly. Candana notified him today that the transition was official. Though Ghosita hasn't spoken to Sati about his new role yet, he approves. He doesn't consider Sati too young. Life is short. Nor does he begrudge Sati his offenses, being himself achingly aware of what it means to not live to the highest standard.

While the Buddha speaks, Sati struggles for equanimity. He remembers the Blessed One's words: "What they say about you doesn't matter. Just do your duty, transmit the Dhamma as best you can, treat people with compassion, forget your self-doubt. Do this, and the Dhamma will take care of you."

And he remembers, too, Udayi's wisdom and knows that he is part of the succession of people, monastic and lay, who practice the Dhamma and who will practice in the ages to come. The river flows almost visibly before him. He is not just an observer on the bank, but a tiny part of the flow. His time is now, he'll do his best, the years will pass, and his time will be over. Such is the cycle of life. He sits taller.

March 23. Pindola hasn't seen straight since the ceremony this afternoon. Now, after the evening meditation, as he walks to his hut, he a blind man, his mind darker than the night. His feet know the way, and he pays no attention to them.

How, he asks himself, could I have been so stupid? I'm an ass for not suspecting! Candana's been abbot forever. Damn! Who'd think he'd leave now, even if he isn't well? But why else has Bhagava stayed all this time? The fire's long over. There's only one reason—they've been discussing a successor, and they've disagreed.

Succession has been a paramount issue for Pindola before he took robes. He has discounted the other seniors. He reckoned that they'd be too old when the time came. It's always been either him or Sati.

He reviews his calculations, adjusted for present circumstances. Sati's a senior. How a bhikkhu who lied as he did could be considered wise enough to be called "thera" is beyond him, but there you have it. And in any case, he's just passed the ten-year mark, so "thera" he is—a thera with a tainted record. While my record is absolutely spotless. He considers the fact that he has not yet been designated a thera to be a witless oversight. His brilliance and more importantly his social status qualify him as an elder in any assembly of men. My family, my class, my preeminence against what? A fisherman! Why wasn't that the clincher? It's ludicrous! Mealy-mouthed, ignoble, nonentity, Sati—the abbot!

He resurrects another grievance: Sati is literate while he and everyone else he knows aren't. Sati doesn't talk about it. Why not? Could it just a rumor? A hoax to elevate himself? But if it's true, it would certainly set him apart, though it wouldn't have much practical value.

Directing his thoughts back into more certain territory, Pindola knows as surely as this night is dark that Candana wanted Sati for abbot, and Bhagava wanted him. Which is why Bhagava has been so distant all these weeks, isn't it? He hasn't wanted to show favoritism. And he conceded in the end only because Candana is his disciple and this is Candana's place—and because Sati is a senior. What else could it have been? Pindola indulges in the age-old pastime of concocting stories to fit his needs. He doesn't notice improbabilities in his logic.

He is almost to his hut now. His chest is tight and his meditation mat is clenched in his fist. His life-long curse has struck again.
Big brother gets the goods! To the resentment that he holds toward
his older brother and the law of primogeniture, he now adds outrage
at Sati and the monastic rule of seniority. For the rest of his life, he
won't let go of that resentment.

Sati could be abbot for decades, he fumes. By the time he dies,
I'll be too old. I won't let it happen! I'll bring him down, somehow.
No matter what!

And he thinks of his father, who will hear the news first thing
in the morning. Pindola doesn't know details of his father's involve-
ment with Sati's father, but he knows there was animosity. Yes, Father
will help me. I can rely on it.

March 25. Life in the palace is at a near standstill, the heart has gone
out of it. Udena and his ministers attend to necessary business, but
not very well. The royal cook and his staff prepare meals and everybody eats, but without appetite. Even children are subdued at play.

It wasn't only the execution. The seepage started with the fire.
That such a calamity could happen in their midst, to the royal family, to their beloved Samavati and her children, is unthinkable. And
afterwards, Magandiya's hectic gaiety, of which they've heard rumors,
and Udena's effusive praise of her, also rumored, seemed unreal.
Then the massacre.

In town, people are shaking their heads. "Everything's wrong."
Life is on the wrong footing, like a nightmare they haven't been able
to wake up from. They understand the legality—the taking of the
lives of an entire family for the wrongdoing of one—but legalities hold
no sway over the human heart. Moreover, the king's plan outrages
their beliefs about ritual purity. How could their king, their ruler by
divine right, have proposed this impossible scheme?

As for Udena, his certainty, his ringing declaration at the execution, has faded. It's hard to hold fast to a plan when everybody opposes it and when your grip was merely desperate in the first place.

Almost every evening, he visits Vasuladatta, the quiet woman who has been with him since the beginning of his kingship. She knows him like no other, and alone among all those in his life now, he can trust her, his first, his only queen. He comes not as a lover, though lovemaking is occasionally part of their meetings. It is the lovemaking of two survivors from a wrecked ship.

"Why didn't I see it coming? Why didn't I believe Samavati? She told me many times, but I didn't listen," he asks aloud, a king no longer, but simply a man overwhelmed by doubt and self-censure. Having no more pride to hide behind, he weeps in Vasuladatta's arms.

She doesn't assure him that it will be all right, but she holds his head to her breast, strokes his hair and rocks him like a child. And he returns night after night.

Tonight he asks, "Am I cursed by the gods?"

How often she has asked that very question about herself! Now she can answer with conviction. "No, my dear, you are not."

She attended Khujjuttara's teaching sessions for only a few weeks before the fire ended them, but, having traveled deeply into the land of suffering, she absorbed the Buddha's teachings like a parched plant absorbs rain. "The Blessed One teaches that everything is impermanent. Everything changes, sometimes they change in ways we like, and sometime in ways we hate. That's the nature of life. The consequences, the things we experience depend on our own actions, whether for good or ill. We ourselves are responsible, not supernatural beings."

She means this as good news, and she knows it is. Still, she's careful not to arouse royal ire by saying, "You are responsible. Your actions caused these things." He doesn't need more condemnation.

"And because we're responsible, at any time we can decide to take wholesome actions, actions that will bear wholesome results. "

Udena whose head is resting on her breast, draws back and looks at her surprised. How does she know this? When did Vasuladatta become so wise? Aloud he asks, "He does? The recluse teaches that?"

Vasuladatta nods and quietly explains that she attended Khujjuttara's last teaching sessions. Both are silent.

Here are two new things to digest—the Buddha's teachings and a wise wife. Like Magandiya, he'd thought her a nonentity, even if she was a princess and the mother of the late heir apparent.

The time is right. Vasuladatta says, "I want to hear the Blessed One's teachings." She doesn't ask it as a question needing permission. In her low, liquid voice she asserts an unassailable need.

"I want teaching sessions to start again for the women in the palace."

How can he refuse his first and only queen?

CHAPTER 17.

THE RETURN

March 28. Candana received the royal message yesterday, inviting him to the palace to resume teaching the women. Mention was made of Queen Vasuladatta's interest. This is a surprise, Candana thought as he listened.

The residents of Ghosita's Park learned about the messenger's presence before he exited the gate, and they speculated about his purpose. They speculated in a dispassionate manner, of course, because bhikkhus are not supposed to entangle themselves in worldly considerations. Pindola was irritated. Whatever it's about, I should have been the bearer—like before.

That evening, gathering in the assembly hall, the bhikkhus looked at Candana expectantly, but he wasn't forthcoming, and nobody asked.

He was sitting among the bhikkhus; Sati was leading the meditation.

Candana needed time to think. It's an honor to be invited to teach at the palace. It would mean starting over, mostly new women because...well. And Queen Vasuladatta! He doesn't know her at all, though it's understandable that she'd be turning to the Dhamma now—as if the death of her son weren't enough.

As Candana deliberates, it becomes clear that he isn't the one to conduct the sessions. Sati is. Udena will be surprised. He won't like having an unknown bhikkhu, and a young, handsome one at that. With a smile, Candana remembers how at the beginning, all the monks, including the Buddha himself, were unknown to Udena. And how early on, when the king invited the Buddha to teach the women, he refused and sent Venerable Ananda instead, he of the dazzling visage. Ananda was about the age of Sati now. Yes, he'll talk with Sati.

This afternoon after the midday meal, he goes to Sati's hut and explains. Sati listens with growing concern. Another challenge!

"Sati," Candana cautions, "You're young and the king is a jealous man. The queen isn't very much older than you are. And there will be maids from her household and probably members of his harem who are young and beautiful. You're a good-looking man, the kind of looks that attract women."

Sati blushes.

Candana thinks, Especially when they're trapped in the palace with that lecher. Well, nothing like trial by fire. If he can't handle this, he won't make it as abbot.

"There will be temptations, friend. You mustn't give the king reason to suspect you of impropriety. And believe me, it doesn't take much." Because it's important, Candana repeats. "There mustn't be any behavior that could be viewed as inappropriate. You understand this, don't you? You must retain strict custody of your eyes."

Sati raises his eyebrows in a mute question.

"Yes, of course, you can look at them. You must. You need to be natural and relaxed." It's a tall order, thinks Candana, who has fulfilled it many times. He smiles. "It won't be so hard if you remember what you're there for: You're there to teach the Dhamma, to give these ladies the most important gift of their life. You're offering them a path for release from suffering—and suffering is intense in that place. It's a hell realm, believe me. No one else is giving them that. Can you do it?" He concludes bluntly and looks Sati in the eye.

Both appreciate the size of the challenge. Before Siha, there was Samana with whom Sati had been infatuated when he was a very young monk. On just the whiff of impropriety, she, who'd been employed in one of the great houses that Sati visited on almsround, was dismissed in disgrace. Candana knows her fate, but he never told Sati. There would be no point. The stakes are even more far-reaching now.

He shifts uncomfortably. He's not sorry about his two years with Siha, especially now that he's done penance, nor about Samana, whose face he no longer remembers. He wishes them well. He includes them daily in his lovingkindness practice and he thinks of them without regret or physical longing, though he's by no means past sexual urges. Now his brows knit, and he silently considers what's before him.

"I'll try," he says in his husky voice.

"Good. I'll inform the palace and let you know the day and time you are to start. It's yours from there," Candana says and rises. Then he adds, "If anything comes up, even little things, talk to me." He leaves, silently sending Sati blessings.

April 25. This late afternoon, Sati and Candana are sitting on the portico of Candana's hut, hoping to catch a slight breeze, for the summer's heat is upon them. They are often together these days, discussing the running of Ghosita's Park.

Candana is more aware than Sati that, beyond advising on practical details, he is mentoring him, as he has since he was a boy of sixteen. The mentoring now though, is usually in the form of casual comments, not responses to formal Dhamma questions. Sati has, much to Candana's satisfaction, come increasingly to understand the Dhamma from within and to embody it. Candana, too, has changed. For one thing, his hands, both of them, noticeably shake, but he is no longer dominated by fear of this illness. Fear has its moments, but it doesn't govern.

Sati sees him first, walking down the path toward them. His body has lost its wiry look. It is as solid as a tree trunk; yet he walks with an ease of step. Yes—it's Asoka! Sati's eyes widen in astonishment. Candana follows his gaze. They see the man they know well, accompanied by two young laymen. They see him, and yet he is different and not only in bodily build.

Asoka turns to the young men and says something to them. They stop on the path. Then Asoka comes on, walking with a brightness that hadn't been there before.

As he approaches, Candana and Sati rise together, and Candana moves down the step to greet his old friend. His smile equals in radiance the one that illuminates Asoka's face. For a few moments, they stand in wordless community, in a light that envelops them both and spreads to all the world.

"You once said my welcome was unlimited. Is it still true?" Asoka asks.

"More than ever," Candana replies, and he bows deeply.

Sati watches them, and he knows with certainty that, more than the teachings of the Blessed One, profound as they are, this is it. This is the wordless teaching, and he wants it. He wants what these two have, this bright peace. It is for this that he has ordained, for nothing less.

BACKGROUND NOTES

Most novels need no comment; however, because *The Jealous Heart* deals with a remote era little explored in literature, because it recounts a legend virtually unknown in the West and, most of all, because it portrays one of history's greatest spiritual figures, the Buddha, I feel obliged to comment on some of the "whats" and "wherefores" of the tale.

Continuing the story of the Buddhist monk named Sati and carrying on with my intention of embedding the story within the history of his day, this second volume of *The Sati Trilogy* is structured around the legend of two queens. The legend is found in the *Commentary* to the *Dhammapada*. The *Dhammapada* is part of Buddhist scriptures known as the Pali canon. The *Commentary* was written later in what is now Sri Lanka, probably around 450 A.D., some eight hundred to nine hundred years after the Buddha's death. The legend in the *Commentary* that we are concerned with appears in E. W. Burlingame's *Buddhist Legends*.

Telling of the jealous Queen Magandiya who murdered Queen Samavati, a follower of the Buddha, the legend has little bearing on the *Dhammapada* verse it purports to illuminate. Nor does it have much bearing on historical fact, although the anonymous author claimed it to be history. He wrote at a time when the distinction between legend and history was murky and literary fiction was an unknown genre. Perhaps he, himself, didn't know the difference.

Despite its dubious historicity, the legend is the second best source we have about events in Kosambi in the fifth century B.C. (The best source, the Buddhist scriptures, relates the story of schism told in *The Kosambi Intrigue*, the first volume of this trilogy; those events probably did occur.) The execution of Queen Magandiya and her family, which is chronicled in grisly detail in the legend, is likely fictitious, but there was a custom whereby all members of a family might be punished for the serious misdeeds of one. The murder of a rival queen and her household, a horrendous crime indeed, would have called for a horrendous punishment. The belief that brahmins were sacrosanct and therefore exempt from corporal punishment is likewise historically accurate.

It has been intriguing to realize that I, at my computer in Charlottesville, Virginia, U.S.A., have a link with the ancient author, who was probably a Buddhist monk and who wrote on palm leaves in the tropics of Sri Lanka. But it is a tenuous link, for our purposes differ dramatically. The ancient author had an ax to grind: By the mid-fifth century A.D. when he wrote, developments might well have embittered him as he considered the great land to the north where his religion had arisen. The brahmin class was more firmly entrenched at the pinnacle of the social hierarchy than it had been during the Buddha's day, and early Hinduism, which had evolved from the Vedic tradition, had triumphed in many parts of the subcontinent at the expense perhaps of Buddhism. The legend reads as an indictment of brahmins and, by implication, Vedic orthodoxy.

My purpose, on the other hand, has been to portray a remote, little known era; to show the universality of spiritual aspiration; and to illustrate how the Buddha's teaching can relieve suffering in daily life. To be honest, though, I, too, began with an ax. I wanted to redeem the reputation of the monk Sati, who was, I thought, unfairly maligned in the Buddhist scriptures. Although the narrative of the trilogy is considerably subtler than that of the legend, by the end of the third volume, my ax will have been ground, my point made.

Several of the monks portrayed in the first volume, *The Kosambi Intrigue*, appear as central figures in this novel—Sati, Candana, Harika and others. Because the characters are numerous and the names, difficult for many readers, a glossary following these notes helps keep things straight.

In the absence of historical documentation, I have set the tale fourteen years after events in the first volume. The monks continue to face challenges. Life at Ghosita's Park, which is far from peaceful, is complicated by tragedies in the royal family.

In this volume, I have introduced new monks to Ghosita's Park, most notably Venerables Asoka and Pindola. I love Asoka, who is imaginary. He exemplifies the transformation to which the Buddha's *Dhamma* (teachings) point, a transformation from the limited, pain-filled perspectives that burden people's lives into a truer, awakened, more joyful way of being.

Pindola, who was a historical character, is harder to love. According to the *Buddhist Dictionary of Pali Proper Names* and the *Vinaya* (monastic disciplinary code), Pindola was the son of Royal Chaplain Bharadvaja. He was a Buddhist monk, had a nasty tempera-ment and was a glutton. From these kernels of information, I have imagined him as a second son who, because he was blocked from succeeding to his father's position, chose another route to eminence, one that flaunted everything his father represented. He became a bhikkhu at Ghosita's Park where he pursued his ambition of becom-ing abbot. I have implied that his gluttony was an expression of his frustration.

In the interests of accuracy, ancient Buddhist texts have often been translated into literal, stilted English. This enhances a sense of remoteness that is counter to the spirit of *The Sati Trilogy*. The volumes here present dialogue in modern, colloquial language, for no doubt people then conversed in that way with each other.

Moreover, I have portrayed the Buddha as a human being rather than as a god. The decision carries challenges: In this novel, the Buddha's pivotal conversation with Candana about fear is a case in point. Scriptures teach that the Buddha transcended fear, and his monastic disciples aspired to the same. I assume that supreme enlightenment doesn't incapacitate the amygdala and that, in the face of danger, it and other brain centers trigger appropriate physiologi-cal responses, though possibly in diminished strength. I also assume that a supremely enlightened being expresses fearlessness as non-identification with those physiological responses and, consequently, in actions that aren't driven by them. Of course, not being supremely enlightened, I can't speak from experience, and I don't expect this to be the last word on the subject.

According to a scriptural reference, the Buddha was at Ghosita's Park in the wake of the fire that killed Samavati (that there was a fire appears to be historically accurate). I have made his presence there central to the tale. Otherwise, the monastic dramas portrayed in *The Jealous Heart* are imaginary. I have tried to faithfully portray monastic life in that era.

Early Buddhist beliefs and culture differed significantly from those of our modern world. As an author, not a scholar, I didn't think twice. I largely avoided mention of certain traditional beliefs that are out of line with contemporary thinking, and when it served my purpose, I deviated from the traditional and imposed modern, more secular values on the characters. For example, in that profoundly hierarchical age when bhikkhus and lay followers regarded the Buddha with unquestioning reverence, Sati's initial, rather casual attitude smacks of the democratic. A man ahead of his times, Sati came to venerate the Buddha by way of personal discovery and love. You could say that he made up his own mind. Furthermore, in view of the strict rules governing relations between monastics and laypeople, Asoka probably would not have been allowed to recuperate in the home of a householder. Would he ever have had an awakening experience? And the physician Sirivaddha would likely have been uncomfortable, not elated, when the barrier between him and Candana momentarily dropped.

In the Buddha's day, monks and nuns were understood to be the ones interested in meditation and awakening. Laypeople generally followed the path of faith and accumulating merit in the hope of a better rebirth; theirs was life in "the dusty world," as the Buddha termed it. Historically, this understanding was challenged by the later development of Mahayana Buddhism. Today, it is axiomatic that awakening is the domain of laypeople as well as monastics. Even in the Buddha's time, the two laywomen, Khujjuttara and Samavati, illustrate that layfolk weren't necessarily confined to "lesser" spiritual pursuits.

I hope the good people of *The Jealous Heart,* monastic and lay, who tried to live truly amid dark times will be models for us. Cultural differences notwithstanding, I hope they will be your friends, as they are mine.

A PARTIAL LIST
OF RESOURCES

AuBoyer, Jeannine, *Daily Life in Ancient India from 200 BC to 700 AD*, N.Y.: Macmillan, 1965.

Basham, A.L., *The Wonder That Was India*, N.Y.: Grove/Evergreen, 1959.

Batchelor, Stephen, *Confessions of a Buddhist Atheist*, N.Y.: Spiegel & Grau, 2010.

_____, *Life and Death of Siddhattha Gotama*, eight talks, Spirit Rock Meditation Center, Woodacre CA., October 21 to 28, 2005, available on Dharmaseed.

Buddhist Dictionary of Pali Proper Names, www.palikanon.com, abridged version of G P Malalasekera, *Dictionary of Pali Proper Names*, 2. Vols., first published 1938, reprinted 2004.

Burlingame, Eugene Watson, *Buddhist Legends*, Cambridge MA: Harvard University Press, 1921.

Delabre, Kenneth R., *My Walk on the Parkinson's Path*, Tate Publishing & Enterprises, Mustang, Oklahoma, 2006.

Dhammika, Ven. S., *Middle Land, Middle Way–A Pilgrim's Guide to the Buddha's Path*, Kandy, Sri Lanka: Buddhist Publication Society, 2nd ed., 1999.

Davids, T.W.R., *Buddhist India*, Delhi: Motilal Banarsidass, 1971.

deZoysa, A.P., *Indian Culture in the Days of the Buddha*, Colombo, Sri Lanka: M.D. Gunasena, 1955.

Havemann, Joel, *A Life Shaken; My Encounter with Parkinson's Disease*, Baltimore: John Hopkins University Press, 2002.

Nyanaponika Thera and Hellmuth Hecker, *Great Disciples of the Buddha; Their Lives, Their Works, Their Legacy*, Boston: Wisdom, 1997.

Pali Canon, various scriptures from the *Suttas* (Discourses) and *Vinaya* (Disciplinary Rules).

Schumann, H.W., *The Historical Buddha–The Times, Life and Teachings of the Founder of Buddhism*, trans. by M. O'C Walshe, Delhi: Motilal Banarsidass, 2004.

Wikipedia, the free online encyclopedia, references too numerous to cite.

GLOSSARY

Figures in this glossary are identified as "fictional" when I have created them. Otherwise, they are identified as "historical," even though in some cases they are found in the legend in the *Commentary* to the *Dhammapada* and their historicity is open to question.

Amba (Mango)— A fictional feline. A feral cat who takes up residence at Ghosita's Park.

Ananda, Bhikkhu—Historically, Ananda was one of the Buddha's closest advisors and his cousin. A man with a great heart and a prodigious memory, he was also, according to commentary, extraordinarily good-looking. Reference to his looks appears in this story.

Anjali—A gesture of respect in which hands are lifted to the chest or head with palms joined. Expressed by junior to senior monastics or by laypeople to monastics.

Arahant—One who has reached highest level of spiritual attainment short of Buddhahood. An arahant possesses perfect understanding unblemished by impurities of mind.

Arittha, Bhikkhu—A historical figure. According to the single scriptural reference to him, Arittha was a bhikkhu who had been hunter by trade, thus was a social outcaste by society's standards—though not by the Buddha's. According to the reference, Arittha was castigated by the Buddha for misunderstanding an aspect of the teachings. There is no scriptural reference to his friendship with Sati.

Ariya—The Aryans were a group of related tribes who entered northwest India in the 2nd millennium B.C. and spread across the subcontinent, bringing their religion with them. While discussion of the relations between the Indo-Aryans and the indigenous Dravidian races remains controversial to this day, even during the Buddha's time, the word "ariya," which referred to the Aryan race, carried connotations of superiority. The Buddha radically shifted its meaning by using it in a spiritual context to designate followers who had achieved certain levels of spiritual attainment.

Asoka, Bhikkhu—A fictional figure. A monk in his fifties, who experiences an awakening.

Bakkula—A fictional figure. Bakkula is the youngest son of the family that cares for Venerable Asoka after he sprains his ankle in Saketa. Bakkula decides to become bhikkhu.

Bamboo Wood—A park given to the Buddha for monastic use by King Bimbisara of Magadha. Situated on the outskirts of the capital city of Rajagaha, it was the first and one of the most important of the Buddha's monastic centers.

Bhaddaji, Bhikkhu—A fictional figure. A young, asthmatic bhikkhu at Ghosita's Park whose health challenges drive him to excessive austerity.

Bhagava—A title of reverence by which religious leaders regardless of tradition are commonly addressed. The Buddha's followers often used this title when addressing him.

Bhaggu—The historical name of tribal territory in the kingdom of Vamsa. Its location is unknown today. I have situated it in the wilderness 40 miles northwest of Kosambi. It was also the name of the clan that occupied Bhaggu territory.

Bharadvaja, Unnabha—A historical figure. I found no reference to his first name, so I selected one from the literature of the day. He is characterized as the court brahmin or court chaplain in Kosambi during King Udena's rule. The court chaplain was traditionally the most influential member of a king's government.

Bhikkhu, or monk—One of the terms used to refer to a man who has left family and gone forth into the holy life in the Buddha's order. It is still used today. Bhikkhus were mainly wanderers, settling for only the three-month rains retreat, but even during the Buddha's life, some were becoming more sedentary. They were taking up residence at specific monastic centers like Ghosita's Park. In later times, this more sedentary life-style became characteristic of the order as a whole. Currently, English speakers often use the term "venerable" instead of "bhikkhu."

Bhikkhuni, or nun—A woman who has left family and gone forth into the holy life in the Buddha's order. The order of bhikkhunis was established during the early years of the Buddha's mission, after the order of bhikkhus had been created. In that patriarchal society, it was controversial from the outset, and it died out in the 12th century. In our times, the bhikkhuni order is being revived, again amidst controversy.

Bodhi, Prince—A historical figure, the crown prince, heir to the throne of Vamsa. While texts indicate that Prince Bodhi's mother was Queen Vasuladatta, it suits our story to make him the son of Queen Samavati. Adding to the credibility of this choice is the fact that there is no reference to Vasuladatta's having been a follower of the Buddha and would not likely have named her son "Bodhi," "awakened one."

Brahmin—A member of the priestly class. While in a later era, the brahmin class was viewed as highest in the social structure, during the Buddha's day, both brahmins and warriors vied with each other for that position. In his teaching, the Buddha frequently extracted the word "brahmin" from its social context and conferred on it a spiritual meaning, i.e., one who understands the real nature of things. He referred to himself as becoming a "brahmana" on the night of his awakening.

Buddha—Buddha literally means "awakened one." Siddhattha Gotama was born in the leading family in Sakyia, a republic in the foothills of the Himalayas. He lived in luxury according to the standards of his day, but at age of twenty-nine, he left to begin a spiritual search. After six years of strenuous spiritual practice, he attained full enlightenment. The dates of the Buddha's birth and death are traditionally given as 563 and 483 B.C. More recently, scholars have determined that he lived at a later time. Knowing that his life span was eighty years, they have arbitrarily set his dates

at 490 to 410 B.C.E. Our story uses the more recent dates. In his
time, people used many titles when referring to him, "Bhagava,"
"the Teacher," "the Blessed One," "the Exalted One" and others.

Candana, Bhikkhu—Based on a historical figure identified in the
Vinaya (Disciplinary Rules), Candana (pronounced "Chandana") is
characterized as wise, learned in the Dhamma, intelligent, mod-
est, conscientious and sincere in training—i.e., an ideal monk.
His name isn't given in that text, probably due to the desire of
later monastic editors who wished to protect his identity because
he was at the center of the schism that historically ripped through
the monastic sangha at Ghosita's Park. The story of the schism is
narrated in The Kosambi Intrigue, the first book of The Sati Trilogy.
I selected the name "Candana" because it is euphonious and refers to a deva (minor god) in the Pali canon. It seems appropriate. I have made him a member of the great Bharadvaja clan.
Candana appears in The Jealous Heart as an older, ailing, and still
entirely praiseworthy bhikkhu. The narrative involving Candana
in The Jealous Heart is imaginary.

Citta, Princess—A fictional figure. Vasuladatta's older daughter, age
thirteen at the time of this story.

Cittaka, Bhikkhu—A fictional figure. He is one of the two monks who
accompany the Buddha to Kosambi after the fire.

Class—Society was divided into four classes: the priestly class (brahmins); nobles or warriors (khattiyas); peasants (vessas), a class that
came to include merchants and professional trades like bankers;
and dependent workers and servants (suddas). There were also
the classless or outcastes, who did not have the dignity of class
identification. During the Buddha's era, these classifications
weren't held with the rigidity that developed in later centuries.

Commentary to the Dhammapada—A commentary written in Sri Lanka
around 450 A.D., some eight hundred to nine hundred years after the Buddha's death. It is the source from which the legend
at the heart of this novel is drawn. The author was no doubt a
Buddhist monk. It is not a part of the Pali canon.

Culla Magandiya–A legendary figure, uncle to Queen Magandiya. In the legend, this uncle is known simply as "Culla Magandiya." The term "culla" means "small" or "younger"; hence, he was the younger brother of the queen's father.

Dasama–The king's barber. The figure is fictional, but King Udena must have had a barber, and he likely had the influence described here, for traditionally the royal barber, though from the sudda or lowest of the four classes, was typically the king's confidante.

Dhamma–Teaching. In the society of the Buddha's day, "Dhamma" (or "Dharma" in Sanskrit) referred to the teaching of any teacher. Followers of the Buddha commonly used the word "Dhamma" to refer specifically to the Buddha's teaching. These days it is often referred to as the "Buddhadhamma" (or in Sanskrit, "Buddhadharma").

Dhammika, Bhikkhu–A fictional figure. Dhammika is the monk who helps Asoka walk to Ghosita's Park when he first sprained his ankle.

Dhammapada–A short scripture containing the Buddha's teaching. It is part of the Pali canon.

Dhira– A fictional figure. Candana's wife, long deceased by the time of our story.

Dona–A fictional figure, a brahmin who chats with two companions in the assembly hall at Ghosita's Park after the execution.

Eight-Fold Path–The fourth truth in the Buddha's central teaching of Four Noble Truths. It identifies eight practice elements on the path to spiritual liberation.

Ghat–A landing area on the banks of a river.

Ghee–Clarified butter, used in cooking, medical purposes and lighting.

Ghosita, Anupama–A historical figure. I couldn't find references to his first name, so I assigned him one. He was a banker, the wealthiest man in Vamsa and royal treasurer in King Udena's government. A devout follower of the Buddha, he contributed his beautiful pleasure park for the use of the Buddha and his monks. According to the texts, Ghosita was the beloved stepfather of Queen Samavati.

Ghosita's Park or Ghositarama—The name of the park that Ghosita donated to the Buddha's order. The description in the story is based on historical evidence.

Girimananda, Bhikkhu—A fictional figure. The monk to whom Asoka, when he was laid up in Saketa, entrusted a message asking the Buddha to come to Ghosita's Park.

Going forth—The term used to describe the act of leaving home and entering the homeless life to become a monastic in the Buddha's order.

Gotama—The name of the Buddha's clan, the leading clan in the republic of Sakiya in the foothills of the Himalayas. Sometimes people who weren't followers of the Buddha addressed him as "Master Gotama," a title, which, while not disrespectful, pointedly ignored his status as an awakened one.

Harika, Bhikkhu—A historical figure who triggered the events that led to the monastic schism at Ghosita's Park, which is the subject of *The Kosambi Intrigue*. Though identified in the *Vinaya*, a canonical text, he is not explicitly named, presumably as an act of editorial discretion in order not to blacken the name of one of the brothers. I selected the name "Harika," which I found in an index to canonical texts. Harika's character at the time of the schism, which is portrayed in *The Kosambi Intrigue*, is consistent with that described in the *Vinaya*. I have envisioned him as later developing into a more broad-minded bhikkhu.

Itivuttaka—The word "itivuttaka" translates as, "Thus it was said." According to the scholarly commentary, the name refers to the manner in which Khujjuttara began all the passages when reciting the Buddha's talks in the presence of Samavati and other women in Udena's palace. The *Itivuttaka* is a scripture in the Pali canon.

Jenti—A fictional figure. Chief maid to Queen Magandiya, with a character that is in harmony with that of her mistress.

Jeta's Grove—One of the largest and most important Buddhist monastic centers, located outside of Savatthi, the capital of the kingdom of Kosala, north of the kingdom of Vamsa.

Jinadatta, Princess—A fictional figure. Samavati's younger daughter, age seven at the time of *The Jealous Heart*, she is the only one who survives the fire.

Jivaka—A historical figure. The renown physician to King Bimbisara and later to his son King Ajatasattu of Magadha.

Kammasadhamma—An ancient city near the site of modern Delhi. It was the capital of Kuru country.

Kapilavatthu—The Buddha's birthplace, the capital of the Sakiyan republic, located in the foothills of the Himalayas in present day Nepal.

Kappa, Bhikkhu—A fictional figure, a monk who ordained at the same time as Sati.

Karma—The Pali term is *kamma*, but since the Sanskrit term is familiar in the West, I've used it. Strictly, "karma" refers to volitional action, though it carries the understanding that all actions have consequences. Commonly, it is broadly understood to mean both actions *and* their consequences.

Khujjuttara—A historical figure. The Buddha identified Khujjuttara as the leading female lay disciple among those learned in his Dhamma. The legend on which this book is based portrays her as a slave who was Samavati's devoted servant and who introduced her mistress to the Buddha's teaching. Gifted with a prodigious memory, Khujjuttara attended the Buddha's talks when he visited Kosambi, memorized what she heard and later imparted his words to the women of the harem (who weren't permitted to attend). These words became the scripture known as the *Itivuttaka*. I imagined that she died in the fire along with Samavati.

Kol—A solidified paste made of collyrium and perfumed with sandalwood, used as a beautifier around the eyes and thought to protect against evil spirits.

Kosambi—A major port and rich commercial center at the time of the Buddha. Located on the banks of the Yamuna River not far from that river's confluence with the Ganges, it held a strategic position on the north-south overland trade route and was the capital of the kingdom of Vamsa.

Kukkuta's Park—One of the three Buddhist monastic centers in the Kosambi area. Situated outside the city limits, Kukkuta's Park was donated by one of Ghosita's business associates. It was smaller than Ghosita's Park.

Kumara, Crown Prince—A fictional figure. Since it isn't likely that King Udena didn't have an heir before Prince Bodhi, I've imagined Prince Kumara to have been the sickly son of Queen Vasuladatta. He would have inherited the throne had he lived. In the story, he dies at age twenty.

Lac—A scarlet resin secreted by the female lac bug and commonly used by women as a cosmetic on their hands and feet.

Magadha—Located northeast of Vamsa, Magadha was one of four kingdoms in the Ganges basin during the Buddha's era. During much of the period in which the Buddha taught, Magadha was ruled by King Seniya Bimbisara.

Magandiya, Queen—A historical figure and a central character in the legend, hence in *The Jealous Heart*. Although the *Commentary* identifies Magandiya as the third consort to King Udena, it works better in *The Sati Trilogy* to elevate her to the second spot. She wouldn't have quibbled.

Mendaka, Nanda—A fictional figure. A wealthy citizen of Kosambi whose pleasure park Udena acquires in order to construct a shrine to the memory of Queen Samavati.

Middle Length Discourses of the Buddha—A collection of scriptures in the Pali canon.

Migajala, Bhikkhu—A fictional figure. He formerly lived at Ghosita's Park, but to the relief of many there, he left to become an itinerant bhikkhu.

Migara, Mahanama—A fictional figure. A wealthy layman in Saketa who provides shelter, food and medical treatment for Bhikkhu Asoka when he is injured.

Musila, Bhikkhu—A fictional figure. A friend of Candana's and formerly a resident of Ghosita's Park. At the time of our story he is abbot at Kukkuta's Park.

Mutta—A fictional figure. A maid in Samavati's household who looks after the two young princesses.

Naga—According to folklore, nagas were sacred serpents that frequented landing areas on riverbanks. They were thought to have supernatural powers, and, if properly propitiated, could make women fertile.

Nala—A fictional figure. Candana's older brother.

Nirvana—The Pali term is "*Nibbana*." I have used the Sanskrit in the text because it is well known in English. It refers to the ultimate goal of spiritual practice in Buddhism.

Pali—The language in which the Buddhist scriptures, known as the Pali canon, are written. It is close to, but not the same as, the dialects spoken during the Buddha's day. In the text, I've retained some Pali words for which there isn't a one-word English language equivalent.

Parantapa, King— A historical figure. The father of King Udena. I have imagined him as the creator of the kingdom of Vamsa.

Pavarana—The monastic ceremony concluding the three-month rains retreat.

Pavarikambavanna—Historically, one of the three Buddhist monastic centers in the Kosambi area. Situated outside the city limits, it was donated by one of Ghosita's business associates. It was smaller than Ghosita's Park.

Phagguna, Gopaka—A fictional figure. A wealthy townsman whose pleasure park outside the city limits is the site of the execution of Queen Magandiya and her family.

Pindola, Bhikkhu—A historical figure. Enough is known about him to build a good story. He was the son of Court Chaplain Bharadvaja; he became a monk at Ghosita's Park; he was a glutton and had a nasty temperament. In the story, I have made him Sati's adversary.

Rajadatta, Prince—A fictional figure. Samavati's younger son, age two and a half at the time of this story.

Rajagaha—The capital of the great kingdom of Magadha, far east of Kosambi.

Ratthapala—Fictional. Siha's father.

Saketa—Modern-day Ayodhya, located in northwestern India.

Sakiya—The name of the clan and the land in the foothills of the Himalayas from which the Buddha came. Today, the region is in southern Nepal. During the Buddha's era, Sakiya was a republic governed by the noble Sakiyan clan. It was a vassal state of the kingdom of Kosala to its south.

Sakula—Wife of Royal Treasure Ghosita and stepmother to Samavati. While there must have been such a woman, she is not mentioned in the literature.

Samana—A fictional figure. The woman Sati fell in love with during his first year as a monk.

Samavati, Queen—A historical figure. According to the Buddha, she was foremost in the practice of lovingkindness among his female lay followers. Scripture relates that she died in a fire. The *Commentary* identifies her as daughter of a wealthy merchant who had died, stepdaughter of Royal Treasurer Ghosita and second queen to Udena. In *The Sati Cycle*, I have made her his third queen.

Sangha—Community. In the Buddhist tradition, the word refers to monastic as well as lay followers.

Sangarava—A fictional figure, long since deceased by the time of *The Jealous Heart*. An elderly relative of Candana's who had the shaking palsy (Parkinson's).

Sati, Bhikkhu—A historical figure. Mentioned only once in scriptures, Sati was a monk in the Buddha's order, the son of a fisherman and, at some point, was chastised by the Buddha for misunderstanding the teachings on consciousness. All the rest I have imagined. His misunderstanding is not mentioned in *The Jealous Heart*.

Savatthi—The capital of the great kingdom of Kosala, north of Kosambi.

Siddhattha Gotama—The Buddha's given name, the name by which he was known before he became the Buddha. The Sanskrit version of the name is rendered "Siddhartha Gautama."

Siha—A fictional figure. The wife Sati abandoned when he rejoined the Buddha's order as a bhikkhu.

Simsapa—Trees that are frequently mentioned in the scriptures. No one knows for sure what kind of tree the simsapa was. A good guess, according to Wikipedia, is a rosewood tree, a kind of magnolia. I have described such trees in detail in *The Kosambi Intrigue* and *The Jealous Heart*. They were known to grow in Ghosita's Park during the Buddha's era and presumably flourished in a good part of the Ganges basin. In one of his well-known teachings, said to have occurred in Kosambi, the Buddha, walking in a *simsapa* grove, picked up a handful of leaves and likened them to what he taught (suffering and its end) and then compared the handful to those overhead, which, he said represented all that he did not teach (i.e., the many things unrelated to the ending of suffering).

Sirivaddha—A fictional figure. The generous physician who attended monks at Ghosita's Park.

Sunakkhatta, Bhikkhu—Historically, he was one of the Buddha's attendants before Ananda assumed the role. The dates of his role as attendant aren't known, but I have put him in Kosambi with the Buddha after the fire. Sunakkhatta later disrobed, saying the Buddha had disappointed him by not performing miracles. He denounced the Buddha to the community of bhikkhus in Vesali and followed a series of other teachers. These events aren't part of *The Jealous Heart*.

Takkasila—Historically, the finest center of higher education in the subcontinent. Open to sons of the warrior and brahmin classes, it offered a variety of courses, both theoretical and practical. It was located in what is modern-day Taxila in Pakistan.

Tathagata—A term coined by the Buddha to refer to himself. It means "Thus gone one" or "enlightened one" and points to the fact that, having attained liberation, he is no longer bound by a notion of a self.

Thera ("Elder")—The title of a bhikkhu who has achieved senior status. In our times, the title is conferred after ten years of full ordination, but in the Buddha's time, the situation was probably more fluid. According to one of the Pali scriptures (*Anguttara*) no matter how junior a bhikkhu is, if he demonstrates wisdom, he is entitled to be addressed as a "thera."

Uppalavanna, Princess—A fictional figure. Samavati's older daughter, age nine at the time of the story.

Udayi, Bhikkhu—A fictional figure. One of the seniors at Ghosita's Park.

Uposatha— A traditional observance in the Middle Land, held on new and full moon days. Bhikkhus fasted on those days. Historically, the Buddha introduced the observance at the suggestion of King Bimbisara. It became an occasion for avowal of disciplinary transgressions and purification. Uposatha continues to be observed today by monastics in the Thevadan Buddhist tradition.

Uttara, Bhikkhu—A fictional figure. A senior monk at Ghosita's Park, a bhikkhu who, in the course of *The Sati Trilogy*, grows in wisdom and compassion.

Vamsa—The kingdom ruled by Udena in the southern Ganges basin. Located in the rich triangle of land, known as a "doab," between the Ganges and Yamuna rivers.

Vassa—A three-month monastic retreat, which became customary during the Buddha's day. Held during the rainy season, from mid-June to mid-September, it was a time when the monks gathered to hear the teaching and to get out of the mud and floods that inundated the countryside and made travel nearly impossible.

Vasuladatta, Queen—A historical figure. According to the *Commentary*, Vasuladatta was the first wife of King Udena and daughter of the king of Avanti, to the south of Vamsa. A colorful story is told in the *Commentary* of how Udena wooed her in Avanti and, in the face of opposition from her father, fled with her aboard an elephant to Vamsa. The fact that little else is said about her once she became queen led to my characterizing her as a reserved, quiet woman. In *The Jealous Heart* she evolves into a more nuanced, wiser being.

Vedas—Sacred hymns originating in prehistoric times among the Aryan tribes that moved into the subcontinent. Considered of supernatural origin, the collection of hymns was recited by brahmin priests and became known as Bhraminism or Vedism. Additional vedas evolved over the centuries, ending with the composition of the *Upanishads*, which roughly coincided with the Buddhist era. The vedas form the foundational layer of modern Hinduism.

Vinaya—The monastic rules of conduct of Theravadan monastics. The *Vinaya* is one of the three categories or "baskets" into which the Pali canon is divided. Recited orally during the Buddha's lifetime, it was later written and is the title of the scripture listing the disciplinary rules.

Yakkas—Formless beings popularly believed to live in certain ancient trees and to possess supernatural powers, like making women fertile.

ACKNOWLEDGMENTS

I am grateful to Stephen Batchelor and Leigh Brasington, who generously offered comments, bringing their considerable knowledge of India and Buddhist scriptures to bear on the manuscript. Sara Jenkins and Toinette Lippe were available at many stages during the writing process and unstintingly offered wise comments and publishing advice. I thank Joe Jackson for sharing his firsthand experience about living with Parkinson's. Poppy Furrow supported me throughout during our many walks in the woods and innumerable phone conversations. Sharon Beckman-Brindley, always encouraging, offered helpful (if daunting) marketing suggestions. Mark Tramontin of Sneak Reviews, the last standing video store in Charlottesville, kindly allowed me to buy Indian videos before he opened his prodigious stock for sale to the general public. Denise Gibson of Design Den once again put her sure hand to the book's design and formatting. Finally, I am grateful to the members of the women's group to which I belong and to those in the Insight Meditation Community of Charlottesville who supported and encouraged me in the writing.

ABOUT THE AUTHOR

Photo by Eze Amos.

With *The Kosambi Intrigue,* the first novel in *The Sati Trilogy,* Susan Carol Stone discovered her inner novelist. The second novel is titled *The Jealous Heart* and is likewise based on research and situated in historical and legendary events of the Buddha's day. Susan is also author of *At the Eleventh Hour* (Present Perfect Books 2001), a memoir about caregiving and mindfulness, and co-author of *The American Mosaic* (McGraw-Hill 1995), about workforce diversity. Long engaged in meditative spiritual practices, Susan is ordained as a lay priest in the Zen tradition and has lived in Zen and Theravadan Buddhist monasteries. She teaches Mindfulness-Based Stress Reduction at the University of Virginia, is co-leader of the Insight Meditation Community of Charlottesville, and has taught mindfulness in prisons and at middle school. Susan also has a Ph.D., which has no bearing at all on this novel. She is attempting to encounter her senior years with grace.

Made in the USA
Middletown, DE
18 July 2016